FOR the CAUSE

The Cold War Gets Hot in Korea and Why Young Men Went to War

by

Alfred Wellnitz

ISBN: 978-1-7322171-3-3

Contents

Foreword

The *For the Cause* story has many references to the movements and activities of U.S. Marine units and understanding Marine unit organization will help the reader follow the story. The division is the basic organization for Marine ground operations. The core of a typical Marine infantry division has three infantry regiments that are each further divided into three battalions. Typically, an infantry battalion commands three rifle companies, a weapons company, and one headquarters and support company. Each rifle company is made up of three rifle platoons, a weapons platoon, and a headquarters and support platoon.

Each rifle platoon includes three squads, each with a squad leader in charge of three four-man fire teams. During the Korean War, fire teams included a team leader, a Browning automatic rifle (BAR) man, a BAR man assistant, and a rifleman. A rifleman's full description of his place in a U.S. Marines division might be: First Fire Team, Second Squad, First Platoon, Easy Company, Second Battalion, Second Regiment, First Division.

The Marine division will have what is needed to complete its mission and may include an artillery regiment, engineering and tank battalions, and air support.

Occasionally marines are organized into brigades rather than divisions. A brigade is similar to a division but smaller. For example, the First Provisional Marine Brigade sent to Korea in the early days of the Korean War consisted of the Fifth Marine Regiment—with three battalions of infantry supported by weapons and tank platoons—the Eleventh Marines (Artillery) Regiment and the Marine Air Ground (MAG) 33, with a total of 6,534 men.

Although a Marine infantry division normally has about 20,000 men, when the First Marine Division was deployed in Korea in 1950, it included approximately 25,000 men.

1.
Saturday Night Out

Peter Houser used a scoop shovel to finish cleaning the barn gutter. Peter, called Pete by people who knew him, had been doing most of the cow chores on the Houser farm since he finished eighth grade in the one-room school half a mile down the road. Now nineteen, he had become a strapping, well-muscled, six-foot-tall young man. He pushed the wheelbarrow filled with the steaming sloppy mess out the barn door into the cold February air and dumped the load on the winter's accumulation of frozen manure.

Pausing for a moment, he watched as thirty Holstein cows wandered around the yard or lined up to drink from an insulated water tank prevented from freezing by an electric heater. He had let the cows out of the barn for their daily dose of fresh air and the freedom to move about for a while. The temperature lingered in the single digits so he would be letting them back into the warm barn after an hour or two.

Pete spread fresh straw on the concrete pad where the cows were kept in place by steel stanchions for most of the day during the winter. When he finished, he observed the cleaned barn with satisfaction.

Pete's dad came into the barn through a side door. Emil Houser stood short and sturdy with a square German face perpetually tanned from long days out of doors. He wore his uniform for winter chores, a flannel-lined denim jacket and ear-lapper cap with long johns under his overalls and blue denim shirt, the same kind of overalls and shirt that he wore every day of the year except when going to church.

From late fall to early spring, the Milbank sale barn had a sale every Saturday afternoon. Emil often went to the sale barn on Saturdays to sell or just socialize. He informed Pete he would be going to the sale today with a pickup load of sows. He said. "You can help me load the pickup, and then maybe open up one of those alfalfa stacks. The haymow is getting pretty empty."

Pete had just had his work plan laid out for the day. Since finishing the eighth grade, Pete had been what amounted to a full-time hired man on the Houser farm located in northeastern South Dakota halfway between Milbank and Wilmot, except that he didn't think of himself as a hired man. For one thing, he didn't get paid regularly and he felt he had a vested interest in the farm. It had always been his expectation that he would be running it someday. His sixteen-year-old brother might be assuming the same thing, but Harold was going to high school and had other possibilities.

During the past year or so, Pete had been questioning his future expectations, wondering if they were realistic. His dad had just turned fifty and would be running the show for a long time, maybe longer than Pete would want to work as an unpaid hired man. His dad had lived through some pretty hard times. Pete didn't know all the details, but he knew that the farm they lived on had been homesteaded by his grandfather in the late 1800s. His dad took over the farm in the 1920s and mortgaged the homestead to purchase an additional 160 acres. Shortly after he got the loan to buy the extra land, the economy went south. Insult was added to misery when the worst drought anyone had ever seen kicked in and the only thing that grew were Russian Thistles and dust storms became common. An old German farmer that lived up the road from the Housers said it wouldn't have been so bad if we didn't have the Depression and hard times at the same time. The original homestead and the additional 160 acres were all lost. The local bank that had foreclosed on the farm went bankrupt soon after that, and the title ended up in the hands of a Connecticut insurance company.

Things started to get better in the late thirties, got really good during World War II, and kept going good after the war. In the early forties, Pete's dad bought the farm back from the insurance company that had never wanted to own it in the first place. Since then, he had replaced the horses with tractors and added a silo to the barn. A machine shed had been built for all the new machinery. The house had been remodeled and wired for electricity and plumbed for running water. Things were much better for the Houser family, but Emil still rigorously guarded every penny and every possession.

Knowing all this didn't make it any easier for Pete to ask to use the Studebaker, the first new car the Houser family had ever owned, the car his dad had treated like a crown jewel since he brought it home the previous fall. As much as Pete hated going through the ritual of asking for the car, he had to do it since it would be his turn to drive when he and his friend Chris Engelson and his cousin, Lyle Houser, went for their weekly Saturday-night outing.

"My turn to drive again," he said hesitantly.

"Seems like you just drove," Emil answered. "Be sure you bring it back as clean as you found it."

That afternoon, Pete took the John Deere and a hay rack out to the north eighty where he opened up a stack of alfalfa and wrestled a full rack of hay out of it. He took the load back to the barn and used the haymow fork-and-pulley system to lift the hay into the hayloft. It took four fork loads to get all the hay into the barn. Unloading hay into the loft was really a two-person job. One person could do it, but it required a lot of running back and forth. He hurried to finish so he could get the cows milked for the second time that day. He had to pick up Chris Engelson at eight o'clock. Chris and Pete had been in the same grade in their one-room country school for eight years so knew each other really well.

Pete heard the tires squeak as he backed the Studebaker out of the garage through a light covering of snow a few minutes before eight. By the sound of the tires squeaking, it had to be below zero. The car, kept immaculately clean by Emil, still had a faint new-car smell.

The Engelsons' yard light came on as Pete pulled the Studebaker into the neighbors' driveway and stopped in front of the white two-story frame house. Chris ambled out of the door. A couple of inches taller than Pete, he moved in an easy way that displayed the strength of a young man used to a lot of physical activity. At nineteen, Chris had never had a girlfriend as far as Pete knew, and he wasn't surprised. Chris had a head of unruly red hair above a long face with big ears. Of course, Pete had never had a girlfriend either, but he didn't blame it on his looks. He thought he looked at least average, maybe a little better than average. His face wasn't as square as his dad's or as round as his mom's. Thick blond hair with a heinie cut topped off a head with normal-sized ears. It wasn't that Pete didn't like girls. He spent a large part of his time thinking about them, but not knowing how to act around girls was a problem for him and for Chris, too. Neither of them had gone to high school and neither of them had any sisters. Girls were exotic creatures they didn't know much about.

Chris got into the car and they headed for Milbank to pick up Lyle. "What's the plan for tonight?" Chris asked.

"Probably shoot some pool at Volk's," Pete answered. "What you been doing this week?"

Chris replied, "I joined the Marines."

The unexpected answer left Pete speechless. Finally, he exclaimed, "You what! How come?"

"You want to know the real answer?"

"Why not?"

"I got kicked out."

The answer didn't sound like the Engelsons to Pete. "I don't believe it," he said.

"Maybe not kicked out," Chris replied. "They let me know in a round-about way that I should be looking for a way to make my own way. Guess I couldn't figure it out for myself. I got two younger brothers. All of us boys aren't going to be farmers. I guess I sorta knew that but didn't know what to do about it. I haven't been doing a lot of work around the farm, especially this winter. They don't need me. They don't need me around."

"Why the Marines?"

"It sorta happened. Monday, I took the Milwaukee to Minneapolis. I heard factories are hiring. I wasn't too excited about a factory job, but hafta do something."

"You took off, didn't say anything to anyone?"

"My folks knew."

"You might not have been there when I went to pick you up?"

"I've been kinda screwed up."

"You didn't finish telling me how come the Marines."

"Well, I was walking down Washington Avenue, near the train depot. Not a good street, night or day. A sign in a window read: Be a Man, Join the Army. That sign got me thinking."

They were coming into Milbank. A bright moon made Lake Farley visible on the right side of the road as they entered the town. Lyle lived on the lake side of the tracks in an old two-story that backed up to Whetstone Creek. They could see Lyle looking out of the window when they pulled up.

In their threesome, Lyle was the odd one. He had lived in town all his life and in a different world. He claimed to know all about women, but Pete hadn't seen much evidence for that claim. Lyle was short in stature in comparison to Pete and Chris—less than six feet by quite a bit. He had brown mouse-colored hair and a round face with freckles over the bridge of his nose. As a counterbalance to the sober and steady Pete and Chris, Lyle compensated for his shortness by being boisterous to the point of being obnoxious.

Lyle came trotting out of the house. "Hey, what's the plan?" he said loudly as he got into the back seat.

"Maybe some pool at Volk's," Chris replied.

"That sounds exciting," Lyle replied sarcastically.

"Drink a couple of beers," Chris added.

The Studebaker idled while they discussed the evening's plans.

"Maybe we should do something special," Pete said, "with Chris going into the Marines in a couple of weeks."

Lyle interrupted, "What the hell are you saying? Chris is going where?"

"Marines."

"Why don't I know what's going on?" Lyle asked.

Chris explained, "I didn't know I was going into the Marines last week."

"That don't make a lot of sense," Lyle replied.

Pete prodded Chris, "You still haven't told why you ended up in the Marines."

Chris got back into his story. "Like I was telling you, I saw this sign in the window and started thinking maybe joining the army would be a better deal than working in a factory. I asked a couple of bums sitting on the curb where the army recruiting office was. They were sharing a paper sack with something in it and asked if I could spare a dollar. I gave them a quarter. They didn't have any idea where to find a recruiting office but said to try Hennepin Avenue. They said you could find most anything there."

Lyle faked a yawn. "I got a feeling this is going to be a real long story."

Chris went on. "Well, I'm walking down Hennepin, and those bums were right, you could find just about anything there. Then I saw this sign on the sidewalk, you know, a tent sign, showing a marine in dress uniform holding a sword up in front of him, and I could see myself walking down Main Street in Milbank in one of those uniforms and the girls twisting their necks off looking. So I joined the Marines."

"I'll be damned," Lyle said. "I guess we'll have to do something special."

Silence followed while the three young men considered their options. Finally Lyle came up with a suggestion. "There's a dance at Chautauqua. Maybe we can get Chris screwed. Don't want to go into the Marines a virgin."

Pete had never been to Chautauqua. He knew his folks wouldn't consider it a good place for him to be spending his time, but this would be one of those one-time-only occasions, and he seconded the idea. Chris agreed with the plan although he had never been to Chautauqua either.

Lyle guessed that not much would happen at Chautauqua until ten at least and suggested playing a couple games of Rotation at Volk's would be a good place to start.

Volk's pool hall occupied a storefront in the middle block of the town's three-block main street, a street bookended by the court house at the south end and the Milwaukee mainline tracks at the north end. A bar and a few tables and booths occupied the front half of the long, narrow interior, and three pool tables and a common restroom filled the back half. Being Saturday night, the front half of Volk's was filled with farmers having a beer or two while talking to other farmers about farm machinery, crops, and the weather.

After a couple of beers and two games of Rotation at Volk's, Pete drove the Studebaker the ten miles on Highway 12 to the town of Big Stone and another mile up the Lake Road to Chautauqua Park on the shore of Big Stone Lake, a lake thirty miles long and one mile wide that defined the border between Minnesota and South Dakota along its length. Things were jumping when they arrived, and they had to park on the Lake Road a half block from the dance hall.

"Damn, it's colder than a witch's tit," Lyle exclaimed as they walked from the Studebaker to the dance hall. As they approached, they could hear an old-time German band pounding away. They bought their tickets, and somebody stamped the back of their hands with an ink marker.

The dance hall was a long rectangular building with a serving bar along the west side and long tables with benches that could seat eight or ten people filling three quarters of the space. The band played on a raised platform in front of a polished wood dance floor at the far end of the hall. The bar served only three-two beer but offered mixes for people who brought their own bottles.

Lyle spotted some empty spots at a table near the dance floor and quickly claimed and held them while Pete and Chris made their way across the room. Already seated at the table were three young women and two young men. Lyle signaled a waitress to bring them a pitcher of beer.

Lyle filled his glass and proposed a toast. "To Chris, the best and only damn marine from Wilmot."

They emptied their glasses, and Lyle started to refill them. "No more for me," Pete said. He had already had two beers at Volk's, and he couldn't forget he was driving his dad's nearly new car.

"Hell," Chris said, "you can't get drunk on three-two. You piss it away faster than you can drink it."

Pete wasn't sure Chris's theory held water. None of the three were seasoned beer drinkers.

As though to prove his point, Chris chug-a-lugged his beer and poured another one, then held up the pitcher for a refill.

They began to note their surroundings. The three women scrunched between them and the two young men at the other end of the table didn't seem to be attached to anyone in particular. The band returned from taking a break and started playing a contemporary slow piece to get people on the floor. One of the women was asked to dance and left the table. Then the two men who had been sitting at the other end of the table got up and started dancing with the other two women.

"What're you waiting for?" Pete asked Lyle.

"I wouldn't call them the pick of the crop. What are you two waiting for?"

"Hell, I can't dance," Pete replied. "And if I could I don't know if I would. I'm not sure I'd want to arm wrestle any of them."

Chris had just poured himself another beer. He agreed with Pete. "They're built like work horses."

"Nothing wrong with that," Lyle argued. "They can pitch hay all day and dance all night without working up a sweat."

They continued drinking beer and observing the dancers for a while. Chris spoke up. "Hell, I could do that," referring to people dancing. His voice had a slight slur to it.

The band played a schottische, and most of the amateurs had left the dance floor. That's when Chris persuaded one of the husky women at their table to dance.

Pete and Lyle knew this would be bad. Besides having never danced before, Chris was three sheets to the wind. Besides all that, the music of the schottische prompted a set pattern of steps which would have taxed Chris's abilities if he had been sober. The woman walked away, leaving Chris flat-footed in the middle of the dance floor.

"Did I do good?" Chris asked when he got back to the table.

"You asshole, that pretty much messed up our chances with those women," Lyle replied.

"I did that good?" Chris replied. He hiccupped. He hiccupped again. "I know how to cure that," he said. He filled his glass and drank it down without taking a breath.

Pete suggested that Chris take it easy.

Chris looked puzzled. "Hell, I thought we were goin' to celebrate somethin' tonight."

"We're celebrating Chris going into the Marines," Pete said.

Chris looked surprised. "Chris going to the Marines? Da poor bastard."

For Pete, who remained stone sober, things at Chautauqua were visibly deteriorating. A couple of fights had broken out at the back of the room. A couple at a table across from them looked like they were about to make out. Then he noticed that Chris had disappeared. "Where's Chris?" he asked Lyle.

Lyle looked around. "Hell, he slid under the table."

"We have to get him out of here," Pete said. "I'll get the car and park it by the door."

Pete brought the Studebaker to the entrance, and he and Lyle half dragged and half carried Chris out and dumped him in the back seat.

As they drove away from Chautauqua, Pete wondered out loud. "Now what? We can't take him home looking like this."

"We could set him in a snow bank," Lyle suggested. "That would sober him up pretty fast. What time is it?"

"Little past midnight."

"The Bright Spot is the only place open in Milbank this time of the night. We can get some coffee into him."

They headed for Milbank. About halfway there, Pete heard some coughing and then retching sounds coming from the back seat. Oh, shit, no! Pete thought. "Lyle, what the hell is going on back there?"

"Chris just heaved all over the back seat."

"Jesus Christ!" Pete said. "My dad will kill me, really kill me." He stopped the car and they dragged Chris out of the back seat, but Chris had finished doing whatever he was going to do.

Pete removed the floor coverings and wiped them clean with snow, but the worst of the mess was stuck in the fake mohair seat fabric.

They crammed Chris between them in the front seat and continued towards Milbank. Pete's mind churned, trying to conjure up a solution to the unsolvable problem of the messed-up back seat. They were approaching the town when Chris suddenly wrapped himself around Pete, pinning his arms and completely blocking his view.

"Get off me, you big ass!" he shouted, trying to push Chris off.

He felt the car going off the road, slowly tipping, and finally turning over completely. The sound of grinding metal preceded a complete stop. The three found themselves on the underside of the car's roof. Pete couldn't open his door. Lyle managed to get his open and crawled out. Pete crawled over Chris and then he and Lyle dragged Chris out. Pete could see that the beautiful Studebaker had rolled over on top of a rock pile. The front and back windows were broken out. Pete didn't investigate further. He knew the end had come. The world as he knew it had ended.

Pete asked Chris, "Can you walk?"

"Why walk?" Chris answered. "Damn cold out here."

"That's a good sign," Lyle noted. "He knows it's cold."

"Come on, let's walk," Pete said. "It's less than half a mile."

"Can somebody tell me why we are walking?" Chris asked.

"Cause you barfed all over Pete's new car," Lyle answered, "And then wrecked it."

"Oh," Chris answered.

When the nearly frozen young men arrived at the Bright Spot, a friend of Lyle's greeted them. "You guys look half frozen. Car heater out?"

"Worse," Lyle replied. "Wrecked the car a ways out of town."

"Jeez, anybody hurt? Sheriff know about this?"

As far as Pete was concerned, he would prefer that nobody ever know about it. It's a bad dream that he would wake up from any minute. Unfortunately, Pete knew he was wide awake and still shaking from the below-zero temperature outside. He borrowed the Bright Spot's phone and dialed the county sheriff's number. A sleepy Deputy David Larson answered Pete's call.

"Where did it happen?" Larson asked. "Okay, I'll drive by, take a look at it. I'll meet you at the Bright Spot, write up the report."

The young men took over a booth and had gone through a pot of coffee by the time Deputy Larson showed up. Chris had fallen asleep in a corner of the booth.

"Looks like you did a pretty good job on the Studebaker," Deputy Larson said when he arrived. "Good for scrap and parts." He looked at Pete. "Want to have it towed in?"

The question surprised Pete. Like there was a choice. All the wrecks were towed into the Standard Station. He didn't own the car. Maybe it didn't matter at this point. It had become a piece of junk littering a Highway 12 ditch. Pete reasoned that it would be easier to tell his dad that the car was at the Standard Station than lying on its roof in a rock pile. At least this solved the problem with the mess in the back seat. "Sure, tow it in," he said.

Deputy Larson filled out the accident report. Much of Larson's formerly muscular body had converted to fat since he left the farm to become deputy sheriff five years earlier. As a result, he had bulked up into an even larger presence. The forms he filled out with a stubby pencil seemed miniaturized in comparison to his large fat hand. Pete guessed that filling out accident reports wasn't one of Larson's favorite chores. There were cross-outs and inserted words and the final result was a general mess. Larson pointed to where Pete needed to sign the report.

Pete felt strange signing the form. He had never signed anything important in his life, and signing an accident report that described totaling his dad's car didn't seem like a good way to start. Deputy Larson dropped the three young men off at their homes saying he would take care of getting the car towed in the morning.

2.
A New Direction

At three a.m. Pete crept up the stairs to his bedroom as quietly as possible. He got up at six a.m. as usual to feed and milk the cows. Pete had just about finished milking when Emil came in the side door of the barn.

"Where's the car?" he asked.

The moment had arrived. The world as Pete knew it would end. "The car is at the Van Dorn Standard Station. I wrecked the car last night," Pete said. "Totaled it."

Emil, whose face had turned red and looked like it could explode, said, "Shit." He repeated himself. "Shit. You're a big help. Try and get ahead and you bust something. Always busting things."

Pete listened. There was some truth in what his dad said. Things did seem to break down around where he was working. Last summer he was pulling a load of grain with the tractor, and somehow it came unhitched, went in the ditch, and tipped over; a big mess. A week later he backed the pickup into the granary door. Took two days to fix the granary door, and the pickup bumper is still hanging. Then the worst—early this winter he forgot to drain the water out of the radiator after using the John Deere tractor. It froze up and busted the block.

Pete took a deep breath. "You won't have to worry about that anymore. Chris and I are joining the Marines. Be leaving soon." Pete watched as the redness and angry look leaked from his dad's face.

When Pete had finally gotten to bed earlier that morning, he lay awake worrying about what had happened and what would happen. He couldn't imagine any good scenarios that would get him out of the mess he found himself in. It got him to thinking about another problem he had become aware of recently, the same problem Chris had. Pete had come to realize that his dream of someday farming the home place might never happen. He wasn't any closer to being a farmer than he had been five years ago when he finished the eighth grade, and he likely wouldn't be any closer five years from now.

Then a solution suddenly occurred to him. He would join the Marines like Chris had done. It would diminish the current car wreck crisis by merging it with another attention-getting situation and at the same time get him out of the going-nowhere rut he was in. After resolving the matter in his mind, he fell into a deep sleep until the alarm went off a short time later.

Finally Emil responded to Pete's revelations. "How are you going to pay for it?" he asked.

Pete hadn't thought about that part of the problem. His mind had focused on the punishment part. He didn't really have an income. He got spending money when he needed it. He got a litter of pigs to call his own and got the money for the sale of the pigs when they went to market. As a result, he had a little more than two hundred dollars in a savings account.

"What's it going to cost?" Pete asked in turn.

"There's the two-hundred-dollar deductible and then the new license, probably some things I don't know about."

"There's about that much in my savings account," Pete replied. "You can have whatever's in there."

That finished, Emil asked, "When are you leaving?"

Pete really didn't know how soon it would be, or if he would even get into the Marines, but answered, "Couple of weeks."

Emil turned on his heel and walked out of the barn. After finishing the cow chores, Pete went back to the white two-story farmhouse for the breakfast his mother would be preparing. Emil came into the house soon after. They both sat down at the breakfast table and poured themselves a cup of coffee from the steaming pot sitting in the middle of the table. Neither one said anything to the other. Florence, Pete's mom, set large plates with two eggs over easy and three strips of bacon in front of both Emil and Pete and put a large plate of toast in the middle of the table.

Pete's mom, despite eating like a man, remained skinny as a rail, probably because she acted like an intense perpetual-motion machine. She cleaned incessantly, cooked big meals as a matter of course, taught Sunday school, was a 4-H club leader, and volunteered for every opportunity that came along.

Harold came to the table dressed for church. Although Harold worked in the fields during the summer, he'd been exempted from normal chores the rest of the year when he was busy with school activities and basketball.

Florence put a box of Kellogg's Corn Flakes and a pitcher of milk on the table for Harold and brought a plate with two eggs and bacon for herself and sat down. All the family members automatically bowed their heads as Florence said an extemporaneous breakfast prayer.

Silence prevailed as all the family members worked on their breakfasts. Emil finally broke the silence. "Pete has some news for us this morning."

Florence and Harold looked up expectantly.

"He wrecked the car last night."

"What!" Florence exclaimed. "How will we get to church?" Florence never missed attending the Mount Hope Lutheran church in Wilmot, a town with a one-block-long main street, two gas stations, and three Lutheran churches. If they gave out gold stars for church attendance, she would have a chestful.

"Never thought about that," Emil replied.

Pete volunteered a solution. "I'll stay home. The rest of you can fit into the pickup."

Emil gave a grunt. "You're the one that really needs to go to church."

Florence, apparently having given the wrecked car information more thought, asked, "Was anyone hurt? How did it happen?"

Pete had been hoping that the how-it-happened question wouldn't come up. "Nobody was hurt," he said. "We were driving back from Big Stone."

"What were you doing in Big Stone?" Emil wanted to know.

"We spent a little time at Chautauqua."

Florence sniffed. "That den of iniquity."

Pete ignored his mother's comment. "We were all riding in the front seat and Chris was in the middle. I guess he fell asleep. Suddenly he wakes up and crawls on top of me. I couldn't see, couldn't get my foot on the brake. We went into the ditch, rolled over on a rock pile."

"Omph," Emil said, adding, "Pete has more news. He's joining the Marines."

"Joining the Marines!" Florence exclaimed. "You don't have to do that. I'm sure whatever happened wasn't your fault." One thing that Florence knew for sure, despite evidence to the contrary—her boys could do no wrong.

"I want to join the Marines," Pete replied. He could have added for a lot of reasons, but didn't. No need to make things complicated for his mother.

Harold supported Pete's decision. "I wish I could join the Marines,"

Florence agreed reluctantly that the pickup would be used to get to the Mount Hope Lutheran church in Wilmot and that Pete would have to miss church in order to eliminate the need for anyone to sit in someone's lap. It would be one of the few times Pete had not attended church since he could remember. If you were a Houser, going to church on Sunday is something you did, like breathing. You didn't spend a lot of time thinking about it or deciding if you would or wouldn't go to church. However, now that he didn't have to go to church, he felt a kind of relief, plus this gave him a chance to do something he had to do soon if he wanted to go into the Marines with Chris. He had to talk to Chris.

If he cut across the fields it would only be three-quarters of a mile to the Engelson farm. The Engelsons weren't church people so they would be home on Sunday morning. It would be cold—the thermometer still showed five below zero—so Pete pulled on an extra pair of pants, put a sheepskin over his denim jacket, a heavy stocking cap on his head, and pigskin mittens with wool liners on his hands. He had double socks on his feet and pulled four-buckle overshoes over his lace-up shoes. Then he took the .22 rifle off its rack in the cellar stairs. He didn't go many places around the farm without his .22 just in case there would be something to shoot.

Chris's mother, Carol Engelson, a farm housewife overweight from testing too much of her own cooking, met Pete at the door and said Chris was still in his bedroom. "Must have caught the flu or something," she said. "Go on up, you know where he sleeps. I'm sure he's awake."

The Engelsons lived in a typical farmhouse where all the kids slept upstairs in two bedrooms. If there had been girls, they would have slept in one room and the boys in another. As it was, Chris had one room to himself and his two younger brothers slept in the other room. Pete went up the steep stairs and knocked on Chris's bedroom door.

"Yeah," a voice said.

"It's Pete."

"I'm sure I will live," the voice replied.

Pete opened the door and went in. Chris was still in bed holding his head.

Chris groaned, "You can't get drunk on three-two, but you sure can get one hell of a hangover. What happened last night?"

"We wrecked dad's new Studebaker among other things."

"I remember something about that. Does he know?"

"Well, when he couldn't find the car, he got curious. Yup, he has the whole story. Well, maybe not all of it, but the important stuff."

"So, I bet your dad blew a gasket."

"Just about, but when I told him I was joining the Marines it sorta took the wind out of his sails."

"What the hell are you saying!?" Chris blurted. "I'm the one joining the Marines, remember. I think that is what we were celebrating last night. That's why I have this big head."

"Last night after I got to bed," Pete answered, "I thought about all the trouble I was going to be in and some other things too. Suddenly it occurred to me that a way to solve a bunch of my problems would be to join the Marines. Think I could get in with you, be together?"

"Well, that would be pretty damn neat," Chris replied. "I have to be back in Minneapolis March 13 when they say a group of us will be going to San Diego for boot camp. I bet you could get into the same bunch if you hustle down to Minneapolis. You'll have to pass a physical, and be sure to take a certified birth certificate. I didn't have one so had to mail it to them. That's all you'll need."

Pass a physical. The words reminded Pete that joining the Marines involved more than signing some papers. What if he didn't pass the physical? He didn't want to even think about the possibility. He wasn't aware of anything being wrong with his health. He had had all the young-kid stuff that everyone has—the chicken pox, measles, and whooping cough. Someone came around and vaccinated everybody in the school for small pox. He'd never seen a doctor as far as he knew. He figured he was healthy, but the uncertainty bothered him.

"What's this physical, what do they do?"

"They have you strip down naked, weigh, measure you, look in your mouth. They have this thing doctors always have hanging around the neck, they put it in their ears and probe around your back and front and have you breathe in and out and hold your breath. Then they push a finger up by your balls and have you cough. They check your eyes to see how small a number or letter you can read. That's about it."

After visiting with Chris, Pete walked a couple of sloughs to see if he could scare up a jackrabbit or two on his way home. Pete had gotten pretty good at picking off rabbits on the run with his .22, but he could only get a dollar for a rabbit carcass from a fur dealer in Ortinville, so he hunted rabbits more for sport than money.

The family had returned from church by the time Pete got home, and his father and mother were seated at the kitchen table drinking coffee. His mom looked a little agitated. His dad, on the other hand, looked sterner than usual and asked where Pete had been.

"Visiting Chris," Pete answered. "Talked about the Marines, other things."

Pete's mom and dad looked at each other. His dad cleared his throat. "Mom and I've been talking," he said. "We been talking about this Marine idea you have. I've been thinking too, thinking for a while about buying some more land. The Johnson farm has been for sale since last fall. I'm thinking about making an offer. It bounds the east pasture. The buildings are falling down, but buildings can be fixed up."

Pete was taken aback by what his dad had revealed. He had no clue that his dad had any such thoughts. However, it didn't surprise him. The family had never communicated much beyond what was needed to get a day's work done. Thoughts were not often revealed. Pete did appreciate that his dad was ready to let the previous night's activities go by the wayside.

Pete's father continued, "It would be a way for you to get started on your own. Use my machinery until you could afford your own. You could work the Johnson land on shares and help out here for use of the machinery."

The words solved one of the problems that had been bothering Pete for much of the past year: a way to get unstuck from his current situation and to get started towards becoming a real farmer.

Pete's dad finished what he had to say and then asked what Pete thought of the idea. A year ago, Pete would have jumped at the chance his dad offered. But the past day had opened up new boundaries in his mind, and he felt a freedom he had never felt before. The prospect of seeing and experiencing the world beyond Wilmot and Milbank excited him, and the dream of becoming a farmer faded as these new thoughts took shape. Pete had the answer to his dad's question but didn't know how to say it. He had reached a fork in the road and his young mind knew which way it wanted to go. One of the forks led down a path which Pete knew well and had hoped to follow. The other path, only recently revealed to Pete, veered into unknown but tempting territory. Pete wanted to do what any young man would do under the same circumstances: go the illogical route, down the path of the unknown to see what he would find. His dad had made a magnanimous offer, and Pete had to turn it down.

The kitchen became quiet while Pete tried to conjure up the answer to his dad's offer. How could he tell them that he had suddenly become hell bent to explore the world and that was more important than pursuing his young lives goal of becoming a farmer?

Finally, Pete began mouthing words that mixed his thoughts with what his mom and dad would expect him to say. "I think it would be good for everyone if I got away for a while. Chris wants me to go into the Marines with him, and I've decided to do that. Chris has signed up for three years and I'm going to do the same."

Florence's face sagged after Pete spoke. A look of disbelief showed on Emil's face.

After the impromptu kitchen meeting, there could be no turning back for Pete. Pete told his folks he would have to go to Minneapolis to enlist and take a physical, and Florence drove him to the Milwaukee train depot in Milbank to catch the train on Sunday evening the twenty-sixth of February. He told his mom he would return Tuesday on the noon train from Minneapolis. He didn't know exactly how long he would need to be in Minneapolis, but according to Chris, one day should be enough time to enlist and get his physical.

Pete had no trouble finding the Marine Corps recruiting office. The people there seemed genuinely happy to see him and got him signed up in no time. The physical went fine, and he was given instructions to be back in Minneapolis on March 13. He would be in the same contingent as Chris going to the San Diego Marine Corps training center.

3.
Turning the Page

Chris and Pete caught the evening train out of Milbank bound for Minneapolis on Sunday the twelfth of March, 1950. Pete's mother, Florence, drove them to the Milwaukee Depot in the pickup truck as the Houser family car still hadn't been replaced. Florence was the only one to see them off since it was chore time and the men were busy milking the cows and feeding the livestock and Pete's younger brother, Harold, had basketball practice. The Houser family hadn't done anything special because of Pete's impending departure. The family had been busy as always with farm-related things, particularly now that Emil had the cow chores added to his schedule.

There wasn't much conversation while they drove into Milbank, and Pete found himself thinking about his future. His past, rooted in the scenery he viewed through the pickup windows, would be left behind for a future different than he had anticipated only a few short weeks ago. That he would be seeing things he had only read or heard about excited Pete. He would be seeing mountains for the first time, an ocean, and California where all the movie stars lived. Becoming a marine didn't excite him as much as it raised questions in his mind. Pete didn't have a good handle on what the Marines would be like or what they did. He had decided to join the Marines because one, his friend Chris had joined the Marines, and two, joining the Marines provided an alternative to his unlikely future as a farmer, and three, joining the Marines provided a way to escape the consequences of his recent bad luck in totaling the nearly new family car. His dad's offer to help start up farming put a question mark on reason number two, but the Marine Corps idea had opened a door and Pete wanted to go through it.

Florence stopped the pickup in front of the small one-story Milwaukee train depot and left the engine running as Chris and Pete got out. Pete turned to wave good-bye to his mother. She waved back, but then got out of the car, trotted over to where Pete stood, and hugged him. There were tears in her eyes. "Be careful and be sure to go to church," she said.

Pete was embarrassed. The Housers never hugged in public, or in private for that matter, but the warmth of his mom's hug felt good. Whatever the circumstances, Pete never had to question his mom's affection.

Florence turned to go back to the pickup. Her final words had been, "Be good."

Chris and Pete carried no luggage. Pete had a half-dozen pairs of socks and underwear, a tooth brush, and a razor in a paper bag. A ten-dollar bill in his coat pocket would pay for lodging in the Y that night and breakfast the following morning.

The next day, Chris and Pete joined eight other young men at the same U.S. Marine Corps recruiting station where Chris and Pete had previously signed up and been given physicals. All the members of the group were put into a room not much bigger than it needed to be. While they waited for something to happen, they started to get acquainted. Two members of the group were from Minneapolis, and the others were from farms or small towns in Minnesota and the Dakotas. Pete thought the two from Minneapolis seemed a little cocky and acted a little superior to the rest of the group. Maybe they were.

After a short time, two marines entered the room. Chris whispered to Pete that one of them was an officer. Pete didn't know which one. Both had green uniforms. One had stripes on his sleeves and the other one had small silver bars on his shoulders. The one with the silver bars said something about swearing in, and they all raised their right hands and swore to something. The marine without the stripes then introduced the marine with the stripes as Sergeant Jones, a seven-year veteran and survivor of the invasion of Okinawa who would be in charge of the group until they got to the U.S. Marine Corps training center in San Diego. "You're lucky," the man said. "Most recruits are on their own until they get to San Diego."

After the marine with silver bars left the room, Sergeant Jones addressed the group. "Okay, listen up, recruits. Like Lieutenant Young said, you're lucky. You get an escort. I'm transferring to San Diego so get the privilege to babysit you shitheads. We'll be taking a Milwaukee coach to Chicago this afternoon where we transfer to the Santa Fe that takes us to San Diego. We'll be in Pullman cars on the Santa Fe, spend tonight, tomorrow, and tomorrow night on the train, get into San Diego Thursday evening. On the train we stay together as a group at all times. We stay in the car we are riding in except when we go to the dining car to eat. I don't want any recruits wandering around loose on the train."

The sergeant had a taut look on his face and stood ramrod straight. He spoke with a commanding voice in a drawly sort of way. Pete guessed because of the drawl that the sergeant had come from somewhere south of the Upper Midwest. The sergeant wasn't a big man—medium height, medium build—but to Pete, he seemed like a man with a lot of authority and a big presence.

Sergeant Jones reminded the recruits of their status. "You guys are in the Marines now but you're not marines by a long shot. You are the lowest thing that crawls until you finish basic training. After you finish basic, if you finish basic, then you will be a marine and a changed person. You will be changed from a dumb kid from the country into a marine. When we get to San Diego, I'll turn you over to drill instructors whose job it is make you into marines. During the process they will be making your lives miserable for three months. They're good at what they do."

Pete didn't know exactly what he had signed up for, but being made miserable for three months hadn't been among the things he thought it might be. At least he now had a clue about what the immediate future might hold, and it left him feeling apprehensive. Maybe he should have put more thought into the idea his dad had proposed before joining the Marines.

Sergeant Jones wrapped up his introduction to the Marine Corps with some foreign sounding word, He then added he would lead the group on the short walk to the Milwaukee train depot. "Get whatever you are taking with you and be ready to go in five minutes."

Pete asked Chris what that foreign word Sergeant Jones used was. One of the Minneapolis enlistees volunteered, "It's Semper Fi, word marines are always saying. It means 'always faithful' or something like that." Pete was beginning to wonder if the marine corps was some short of religion.

Five minutes later a compact group of anxious-looking young men were following Sergeant Jones at a fast pace down Hennepin Avenue. One recruit momentarily broke from the group to admire a drawing of a voluptuous female in a strip joint window. Sergeant Jones yelled, "Hey shithead, get your ass back here with the rest of the group!"

The group bunched together more tightly and soon reached Washington Avenue and the Milwaukee Depot where they boarded a train bound for Chicago.

The train ride ended at the Chicago Union Station in the early evening. The group of young marine recruits and Sergeant Jones transferred to the Dearborn Station by bus in order to catch the Santa Fe train that would take them to San Diego.

It had already turned dark by the time they were on the bus and Pete could see little except the lights of many very tall buildings which outlined the immensity of downtown Chicago.

The flickering lights also impressed Chris. "Damn, look at the size of those buildings," he said. "Makes Minneapolis look like a hick town, not to mention Milbank."

Pete didn't reply. His thoughts had returned to when his mother hugged him at the train station. He already missed his mom.

On the Santa Fe train, the marine recruits were assigned to a car that appeared to be only half filled. Bench seats faced each other with a small table between them.

"Give you room to spread out a little. They'll soon be converting to Pullman beds," the sergeant said. "You guys hungry?"

The question reminded Pete he had not eaten since breakfast, and he and the rest of the recruits responded with a loud "Yeah!" The sergeant said the dining car wouldn't be open tonight but he would see what he could do. He took off and soon returned with a Negro carrying an armful of boxes that each contained a beef sandwich and an apple.

The sergeant joined Chris and Pete in their booth to eat his sandwich. Sergeant Jones asked if Pete and Chris were farm boys. After they admitted that they were, Sergeant Jones said farm boys make the best marines. "They're physical, not afraid to work hard, and are used to using guns. Big strapping farm boys like you won't have any trouble becoming marines. Biggest problem for guys like you will be the beach, that's where you get into trouble."

"Beach?" Chris questioned. "Whatta ya mean, beach?"

Sergeant Jones explained. "In the navy, the beach means being off the ship or base and where there's booze and women and sharpies looking for innocent young marines. You guys virgins? Pete and Chris looked at each other. Neither one answered the question. Sergeant Jones continued without waiting for an answer. "It's nothing to be ashamed of. A lot of farm boys just don't have many opportunities. Don't worry, you won't be virgins for long."

Pete hadn't been worried about the problem before Sergeant Jones mentioned it and thought the question sort of strange.

The sergeant fished a flask out of his pocket and took a drag. "Want something to wash your sandwich down?" he asked.

Pete took a taste that stung his throat but mellowed out as it warmed his stomach. After finishing his sandwich, Sergeant Jones said he would be taking off for a while but that the recruits were to stay put. "They will be making up the beds soon and you guys can get some sleep. We'll eat breakfast in the dining car at 0700 so be ready to go."

One of the Minneapolis recruits started a poker game. The other Minneapolis recruit and two from southern Minnesota got into the game. Pete looked on but had never played a game for money—his mom wouldn't like to see him play a game for money. The people around Milbank and Wilmot played pinochle and whist mostly. Pete didn't know anyone in his neighborhood that played poker or any other game for money.

At ten p.m. a porter made up the Pullman beds and turned off all but the night lights. Chris had the lower bunk and Pete would be above him. Pete got into his bunk and his thoughts turned to all the things that had happened that day, He was in a different world than he had been the day before and wasn't sure what kind of world it was. All that had been familiar had been left behind, being replaced by things unfamiliar to him. It was frightening and exciting all at the same time. His family and his South Dakota home filled his thoughts as the train moving down the track carried him further from them.

Pete had adapted to the swaying motion of the train, but he hadn't lost his wonder at the sounds the train made as it rushed through the night— the air-horn announcing the train's approach to important intersections, the rumbling and clicking sounds that accompanied tons of railroad cars moving rapidly over steel tracks. They were powerful yet soothing sounds.

Sometime during the night, he heard Sergeant Jones come back and was saying something to Chris. He was talking low and Pete couldn't make out what he was saying.

In the morning, Sergeant Jones made sure his recruits were ready to go to the dining car at 0700. He wore a freshly pressed uniform with a sharp crease. By the looks of his puffy, red rimmed eyes he must have had a big night. Otherwise he didn't show signs of wear and tear from his previous night's activities.

It seemed to Pete that Negroes ran the train. The porters were all Negroes, as were all the cooks and waiters in the dining car. Pete had seen a few Negroes before, in Minneapolis during the short time he had been there, and he could remember seeing one in Milbank when a young boy. The Negro he saw in Milbank looked old. He had grey hair and jet-black skin and was thin as a rail. Pete couldn't figure out why the man had black skin. "Because he's a Negro," his mom said. The reply had not really answered Pete's question but he had never forgotten seeing the strange-looking man.

The recruits occupied three tables in the dining car, and the sergeant joined Pete and Chris at one of them. The dining car provided menus, but the recruits would all be eating the same pre-ordered meal. Water and a coffee pot sat on each table. The recruits weren't allowed to order liquor, but the sergeant could and did. He ordered some kind of orange juice and gin drink. He tipped the drink up and drank it down without catching a breath.

"This is the working man's diner," the sergeant said. "You should see the diner on the all-Pullman Santa Fe that the rich and famous ride. I rode it once, that's the way to travel." Pete had thought the dining car they were in pretty fancy until Sergeant Jones put it down. It had white table cloths and fancy dishes and fancy-dressed Negroes waiting on the tables.

Sergeant Jones continued, "But we are lucky to be on a Pullman train at all. We sometimes send the recruits on a milk run, no Pullman cars and that stop at all these little towns we are whizzing through. That is really the pits.

Most of the rest of the day Pete and Chris watched large swatches of the country pass outside the windows of the train. In the morning they were in the high plains where they rolled through depressing small towns that hadn't fully recovered from the Dust Bowl days. By noon they were into the mountains Pete had anticipated seeing. He found the scenery awesome, but as in the high plains, found that the trash and dilapidated buildings along the rail route detracted from the beauty of the scenery. The mountains in Pete's imagination were based on pictures intended to empathize the beauty and majesty of mountain scenery. Pete wondered why people couldn't complement the beauty of where they lived instead of putting warts on it? He thought about Milbank and wondered what people saw when they traveled the Milwaukee Line through his home town. Maybe it looked pretty cruddy to them. The people who lived in Milbank were used to the way it looked. Pete asked Chris what he thought of the scenery, the mountains.

"Real pretty," Chris answered. "But whatta you do with them? You can't plow mountains or plant stuff on them. By the looks of these towns, it's a tough place to live."

Pete laughed. "You're a real flat lander."

"First mountains you ever saw and you are calling me a flat-lander. If you're so smart, tell me how you make a living off a mountain."

Pete thought for a while, then replied, "Don't know, but I'd build a nice-looking house, maybe like a Swiss chalet, and I'd keep it fixed up and the trash picked up."

"You'd stand out like a naked woman on Main Street," Chris said, then changed the subject. "Whatta ya think of Sergeant Jones?"

"Kind of scared me at first, but seems friendly enough."

"Too friendly at times," Chris answered. I think he was propositioning me last night when he came from where ever he was and smelled like an empty whiskey bottle. Pete was puzzled, "What do you mean propositioned you?"

"I think he is queer," Chris replied.

"Queer, what's that?" Pete asked.

"Don't you know? I have an uncle, was in the army World War II, told me about them. It's men that like men."

Pete thought about that for a while. "Seems weird," he said.

"It is; can't believe you never heard about it.

Peter tried to get his mind around the idea but it was difficult and went back to watching the scenery.

The next morning the sergeant again led his recruits to breakfast at 0700. When the group reached the dining car, they found it filled. They would have to wait for open tables.

Sergeant Jones erupted. He demanded to see the head waiter. A portly Negro soon appeared. Sergeant Jones tore into him in a loud commanding voice. "Nigger, we're scheduled to eat at 0700, and we are here. Where in hell are our tables? Can't you manage your goddam diner?"

The head waiter, who stood about a head taller than the sergeant, looked the angry man in the eye. "Suh," he replied, "we're runnin' fifteen minutes behind. There'll be a little wait."

"A little wait, a little wait," the sergeant repeated. "Don't you know your job, nigger? When you have a group of eleven scheduled at 0700, you better damn well have tables ready."

The head waiter appeared to be attempting to remain calm, but his frustration showed. "Sorry, suh, but you gonna hafta wait 'bout fifteen minutes."

The sergeant got on his toes and stuck a finger into the chest of the head waiter. He was shouting now. "Nigger, you tellin' a marine sergeant what to do? You don't tell a marine sergeant to do anything. Anything, hear me!"

Pete felt very uncomfortable watching the conflict. Other people in the car had turned to see what was going on. He didn't understand why the sergeant made such a big deal over a few minutes of a day when they didn't have anything to do but watch the scenery.

A new authoritative voice interrupted the confrontation. "Sergeant," the voice said, "If you want to be a passenger on this train, you will act in a civil manner."

The sergeant turned and saw the train conductor standing behind him. The train conductor was a big man and white. The sergeant absorbed what the conductor had said. He turned again to face the head waiter. "See that my men get seated," he said, then turned and left the car.

By noon the train had cleared the mountains and proceeded through a valley filled with irrigated fields, finally arrived in Los Angeles where the recruits changed trains and continued on to San Diego. In a few places along the route to San Diego, Pete and Chris caught glimpses of the Pacific Ocean, the first ocean either of them had seen.

The Yellow Foot Prints

DI (Drill Instructor) and recruit conversing

These images are in the public domain.

4.
Boot Camp

At San Diego, Sergeant Jones led his charges off the train and onto a green bus that waited to take them to the nearby U.S. Marine Corps Recruit Depot where they would be trained as marines. The bus, already half filled with recruits from other areas, departed from the rail station as soon as the Minneapolis contingent found seats.

When they arrived at the training depot, a drill instructor with a wide-brimmed hat stepped onto the bus and started shouting. "**Listen up, recruits! You will get off this bus and plant your feet in the yellow footprints! STAND UP! MOVE!**"

Pete thought, what yellow footprints? You don't need to shout, every-body can hear you. People around Milbank don't shout; they don't even talk loud.

Chris must have been thinking the same thing. "What's he yelling about? Yellow foot prints?"

"**Shut up, shitheads!**" the drill instructor commanded. "I talk, you listen!"

Pete and Chris struggled off the bus with the rest of the recruits. As soon as they got off the bus, they saw outlines of yellow footprints painted on the blacktop right outside the bus. They each quickly picked a pair to stand on.

The drill instructor continued shouting. "**Recruits, stand at attention! Stand straight and tall, chest out, belly in, arms at your side, head up, look straight ahead**. Hold that position until I give the at-ease command!"

After getting the recruits to take the attention position, the drill instructor became silent for a long time, maybe twenty minutes, maybe half an hour. Pete didn't dare look at his watch. Finally, the drill instructor began shouting again. "**You are now aboard Marine Corps Recruit Depot San Diego California, and you have taken the first step towards becoming a member of the world's greatest fighting force, the United States Marine Corps!**"

This was followed by another long pause before the drill instructor resumed shouting. "**Listen up, recruits! During basic training you will never ever say 'I' or 'me!' It will always be 'this recruit!' When told to do something you say, 'Yes, sir!' Understand**?"

The recruits sensed they were to respond, and an uncoordinated "Yes, sir!" emerged from the group standing in the yellow footprints.

"**Can't hear you**!" shouted the drill instructor.

This resulted in a louder, better coordinated "Yes, sir!"

"**Louder**!" the drill instructor shouted.

The recruits got into it and shouted "**Yes, sir!**" as loudly as they were able. Pete joined in. The shouting relieved some of the long-term standing-at-attention agony. In a way, shouting with abandon felt exhilarating— letting go with no reservations, free of his deep-rooted Lutheran restraint.

The drill instructor went into the Uniform Code of Military Justice, which to Pete sounded like rules for service people heaped on the rules that applied to everyone else. The drill instructor droned on while the new recruits continued to stand at attention. Pete would have given a great deal to momentarily squat, stretch, or move some part of his body. Pete's legs ached, his arms were numb, and he needed to go to the bathroom. The drill instructor moved on and got into Marine traditions and what it meant to be a marine. Pete sensed the end of the ordeal when the drill instructor started shouting words about the silver doors.

"When dismissed," the DI shouted, "**You recruits will enter the silver doors to your right! You will pass through those doors one time only! When you pass through those doors, you are leaving your past behind and it's where becoming a marine begins**! Recruits, at ease! Dismissed!"

The greatly relieved recruits moved quickly through the silver doors into what appeared to be a large warehouse where mayhem reigned. Marines stood on long counters shouting directions to the recruits who shouted "Yes, sir!" at the top of their lungs while half understanding what they were supposed to do. Behind the counters were large bins from which other marines were handing out uniforms, bedding, and other essentials to the recruits. Somehow Pete and Chris ended up loaded down with what they were supposed to receive and followed the crowd to the receiving barracks that would be their first basic training home. The barracks, a two-story building with a light-yellow stucco exterior, sat at the end of a long row of identical buildings. Pete, who had had the luxury of a separate bedroom in his South Dakota home, felt some anxiety when he saw that inside the barracks was a large open space that contained thirty double-decker bunks.

Once in the barracks, the recruits were ordered to strip off their clothes and throw everything into boxes which would be mailed back to a home address. They then showered and dressed in the clothes they had been issued.

A drill instructor explained barracks etiquette in a loud, commanding voice. "Shitheads, you are in the receiving barracks, and it will be your home for the next five days. Your bed will be properly made when not being used. You will not use your bed for anything other than sleeping. You will not lean on it or sit on it. All gear will be properly stored at all times. The area around your bunk will be policed by you."

The recruits were taught how to properly store their gear and how to make a bed. Pete felt a measure of accomplishment when he, after about a half dozen tries, made his bed with a sheet so taut that an inspecting drill instructor's quarter bounced when thrown on it. Chris had a harder time and worked on his bunk for an hour. Things finally settled down and lights were turned off at 2200.

After the lights were out, Pete lay on his bunk in the dark wondering what in hell he had gotten himself into. He wasn't the only one. He could hear the sniffling of grown young men crying in the dark. He understood. He missed his mother, his bed, everything he had experienced up to this point in his life.

At 0500 the next morning, a drill instructor turned on the lights and started banging on a garbage can. "**Reveille**!" he yelled. "**Up and at em, both feet on the floor**!" The drill instructor walked through the barracks hitting bunks with a large club. One recruit didn't respond fast enough and he, his mattress, and pillow hit the deck all at the same time. During the next two days, the recruits got their heads shaved and were probed, tested, and measured. A bed-wetter was identified and eliminated. In between all these activities, the recruits became acquainted with close order drill. Pete quickly learned that precision close order drill does not just happen, at least not with a company of new recruits who come with a wide range of capabilities and backgrounds. It happens in a Marine company only because yelling, sweating, hitting, swearing drill instructors make it happen.

"What do you think makes these DI's tick? Pete asked Chris. "They've all got the same bad-ass attitude and personality, like peas in a pod."

"Yeah," Chris replied, "If you've seen one you've seen em all. They must stamp them out somewhere. Maybe that's what it takes to turn rubbish into marines."

Pete agreed. "DI's have one tough job."

Pete soon learned that every hour of every day would be scheduled, including church on Sunday. Going to church wasn't a requirement, but for Pete going to church on Sunday was something a Houser did. So, on the first Sunday in boot camp, Pete planned to attend church and persuaded Chris to join him. Chris's family weren't church people, but he considered the choice between going to church and policing the barracks an easy one.

Pete was disappointed to learn there wouldn't be a Lutheran service, just one for Protestants and one for Catholics. He also found the order of service wasn't anything like he knew in his home town Wilmot Lutheran church. The minister, some kind of Baptist, didn't impress Pete, but he recognized some of the hymns, and the rendition of the Marine hymn at the conclusion of the service gave him a lift.

Early the following week, Pete and Chris were moved into a similar but different barracks. There they became part of Company Thirty-Three and were introduced to the drill instructors that would be working with them during basic training.

The recruits learned that the day could start anytime between 0300 and 0600 in the morning and would run at a fast pace until 2000 in the evening. Between 2000 and 2200, they were confined to the barracks but free to do whatever they had to do to get ready for the next day. That was unless a drill instructor got a wild hair up his ass and decided to harass the recruits during the unscheduled time. They devoted the free time to cleaning gear, washing clothes, shining shoes, and writing letters home.

The second night they were in the Company Thirty-Three barracks, Chris gathered up his dirty clothes and took them to an area outside the barracks where he could wash them by hand and hang them on lines to dry. Pete, who had never been separated from his family and missed them terribly at times, decided to write a letter home. He found paper and a pen and sat down at one of the two tables near the center of the barracks to do his writing. He found a spot next to Sam, one of a half dozen Negroes in the company. Sam made up for his small size with a solid, conditioned body and a quickness that enabled him to hold his own physically with any recruit in the company.

Two more recruits were writing letters at Pete's table, and a group of three white recruits sat at a second table nearby, polishing their shoes and bullshitting. A buddy of Sam's came up and asked what Sam was doing.

"Writin' a letter to my girlfriend," Sam replied.

One of the recruits at the other table heard Sam and commented loudly, "Didn't know niggers could write." The commenting recruit smiled as he spoke, and the other shoe-shining recruits laughed.

Sam grabbed an ink bottle sitting on the table and hurled it at the shoe polishers. The bottle shattered when it hit their table, and ink splashed onto the table and all three of the recruits sitting there. The affected recruits jumped up, overturned their table, and started going for Sam. Other recruits grabbed hold of the potential combatants and cooled them down.

A cleanup got underway, but the ink stains on the tabletop couldn't be completely removed, and the stains splattered on the clothes couldn't be washed away.

The fracas shook Pete up but, still anxious to communicate with his family, he got back to working on his letter after the mess had been cleaned up as best it could be and things had calmed down. He had never written a letter before and found it rough going. He discarded a couple of attempts and ended up with:

Dear Folks

Hope everything is going good at home. We been here at the marine boot camp just over a week and things are pretty hectic. A lot of yelling and confusion. Busy from revelry to 2000, that's 8 at night. So far lots of testing. Did pretty good in the running and strength tests. Chris and me are in the same company and have bunks close together. Saw mountains, desert and the Pacific Ocean on the trip here. Miss you all and would like to know what is happening back home. Send letters to this letter's return address.

Pete

The next morning the ink bottle incident became known to the reveille DI. "What the hell has been going on here?" he demanded when he saw the ink stains on the table.

Nobody said anything. The drill instructor grabbed a skinny recruit with bad acne two bunks away from where Pete stood at attention. "What the fuck happened here last night?" He shook the recruit viciously. Whether mute from fear or stubbornness, the recruit said nothing.

The drill instructor ordered the men to fall out and assemble in company formation in front of the barracks in five minutes dressed in the uniform of the day and with their rifles. A second drill instructor joined the reveille DI. He shouted, "Company Thirty-Three, for breakfast this morning you will form in a single file, rifles above your heads, and run around the parade grounds six times." Using extemporaneous commands, the drill instructor started the company on its run.

After a couple of loops Pete's arms were hurting, but eventually they became so numb he couldn't feel them. While running on the far side of the parade grounds where there were no drill instructors to observe them, Chris complained to Pete between pants that he didn't mind running but he didn't like missing breakfast.

Pete had seen the menu posted, and gasped, "Its shit on a shingle."

Chris laughed, replied, "Scratch my last remark."

The skinny recruit who had been shaken by the drill instructor at reveille stopped to heave his guts near the finish of the run and got a kick in the ass as a reward. After the run was completed, the top drill instructor addressed the company.

"Listen up, recruits," the DI yelled. "What one or two of you scumbags did affected the whole company in a bad way. It's the same in combat, a dumb move by one or two can affect the whole company in a bad way. Let this be a lesson to all of you."

The top drill instructor then introduced a marine officer with gold bars. The officer read a portion of the executive order that had integrated the United States military in 1947.

Oh, oh, Pete thought. They know what happened.

After reading the executive order, the officer addressed the company directly. "There will be no racial intolerance in the United States Marine Corps. You are all members of an organization that is dependent on each other to survive and to succeed. You are United States marines. You are not white, brown, black, red, or yellow marines. There are only green marines. When in combat you depend upon and must trust the team you are a part of. Marines will be color blind. It's the only way the Marine Corps can

43

succeed in combat and it's the law.

"Marines breaking this law can be court marshaled, dishonorably discharged, and serve time in the brig. The incident that occurred last night will not be referred to the Marine Corps justice system. Just don't let anything like this happen in the future. You are now informed and will be held accountable."

The three months of recruit training went quickly. Being farm boys used to working hard out of doors, Pete and Chris had little trouble with the physical part of Marine training.

Pete, who could pick off a running rabbit or a pheasant on the wing with a .22, and Chris, who also did a lot of hunting, impatiently anticipated the two-week marksmanship training. It took Pete and Chris a little while to become accustomed to firing the heavy high-caliber M1 Garand, but they both qualified quickly as marksmen and went on to qualify as experts.

However, being familiar with firearms didn't keep Pete from getting into trouble about firearm nomenclature. In South Dakota, rifles, shotguns, and pistols are all guns. Not in the Marines. A drill instructor heard Pete asking Chris to hand him his gun. Pete knew the price as soon as he realized what he had said. He had to stand on a table and point at his M1 and a part of his anatomy for an hour while repeating, "This is my rifle, this is my gun. This is for firing, this is for fun."

Weapons and physical training dominated recruit training, but there were also lectures and training that covered mundane subjects such as field sanitation, venereal diseases, and even more mundane subjects like Marine Corps organization.

Close order drill seemed to be the thing that most often set the drill instructors off. A common reaction to a drill infraction was for the drill instructor to pull off the recruit's cloth cap and slap him about the head with it until the DI got tired of doing it. Once, a poor kid from Kentucky had a momentary lapse of attention when the to-the-rear-march command was given, and he kept going and knocked down several people who had been marching in front of him. The drill instructor went berserk. He brought the platoon to a halt, grabbed the kid, and punched him in the belly. The kid went down and didn't get up. The drill instructor ignored the recruit and continued drilling the rest of the company. Eventually an ambulance came along and carried the recruit away.

Pete noted that Chris, never missed a beat in close order drill. Apparently, his focus was pretty good.

Pete understood the need for physical conditioning and marksmanship, but the value of some of the other activities wasn't so obvious. Close order drill stood at the top of the list. One night while they were relaxing, he and Chris talked about why they had to practice close order drill and give an automatic "yes, sir" to any dumb drill instructor command.

"What's the point?" Pete asked. "We aren't going to be doing any close order drill on a battlefield. That went out about the time of the Civil War."

Chris guessed it conditioned a person to respond to any dumb command without thinking. "You know, it's ours to do or die, not to wonder why. The whole chain of command depends on it. Some general comes up with an idea, you know, like to charge that fortified hill with bayonets. The order goes down the chain. Nobody in the chain is going to say, 'now wait a minute, that's a dumb idea.' They are just going to implement the command. Some dumb grunt like you or me will go charging up the hill with a bayonet. That's what close order drill is for."

Basic training ended with an inspection and parade on June 17, 1950. Despite all the trials and tribulations of close order drill, when Company Thirty-Three marched in the commencement parade they were like a well-oiled machine. Every boot hit the ground at the same instant with a loud thump. A marine officer gave a short speech, telling the new marines that during the past three months they had been transformed from what they had been into the world's best fighting men. They had been changed and would never go back to what they had been regardless of what the future might bring. The officer concluded his speech by congratulating the new marines for successfully completing basic training and wished them success in their marine careers.

Pete listened to the words and realized they applied to him and Chris. They had been changed from farm boys into marines. He didn't feel different but knew he had become someone other than who he had been three months earlier.

The day before they finished basic training, Pete and Chris found out about the next chapter in their marine careers. They would both be granted a twenty-day furlough starting June 19. After the furlough, Chris would report to Camp Pendleton and the First Marine Division and Pete would return to San Diego and wait for transport to the Philippines where he would join a marine contingent stationed at the Sangley Point Naval Air Station. Chris and Pete's paths were about to diverge.

5.
First Liberty

On Sunday Pete and Chris were given liberty passes that started at 0800 and ended at midnight. It would be their first opportunity to leave the Marine Corps Recruit Depot since they arrived for training in March.

Soon after 0800 on Sunday morning, Pete and Chris stood outside the marine base gate waiting for a city bus. Pete had a plan. He had used the San Diego yellow pages to find a Lutheran church and learn the times of Sunday morning services. He then used a city map to locate the church and found it to be only a few blocks off the main bus route to downtown. He could easily make the 0900 service by catching a downtown bus and walking a few blocks.

Chris thought it a waste of precious time but didn't want to go into town alone, so he agreed to accompany Pete, who thirsted for a real Lutheran church service.

The sign in front of the church announced the time services were held as well as its affiliation with the Missouri Synod, the same synod as the Wilmot church Pete's family attended. The church had a faded yellow stucco exterior, different from what Pete thought a Lutheran church should look like, but inside, the altar, pulpit, and song board were familiar. So were the hymnals and the somber hymns song by untrained voices.

After the service, they walked back to the main bus line and took the bus to downtown San Diego. They found the city center overrun by service people, many of them fresh out of the navy or marine training centers. The pair walked around downtown San Diego for a while, enjoying the warm sunshine and the freedom of being outside the marine base. The walking around began to get old, and they considered what else they could do. They were underage and couldn't go into a bar and weren't familiar with the city or things to do besides walking around.

They took a break and sat on a bench in a small park in the middle of the city and watched other sailors and marines walking around looking for something to do. Pete studied the palm trees in the park, wondering what they were good for. They made very little shade and wouldn't block any wind. It seemed like God may have goofed on that one.

Two other marines from Company Thirty-Three, Sam Jenkins, the Negro ink-bottle thrower, and Tony Gutierrez, a Texas Mexican, wandered by. They were an unlikely pair. Sam, small in size and full of bouncy energy contrasted with Tony, the stoic Mexican. Birds of a feather generally flock together and, from what Pete had seen, so did off-duty marines. These two misfits were apparently an exception to the rule. From what Pete had observed in boot camp, both Sam and Tony had their heads screwed on right. Tony's appearance matched Pete's expectations of a Mexican. He had a strong square face, deep brown eyes, thick, coarse black hair, and a muscular, compact body.

Sam and Tony stopped to talk. "Whatcha doing?" Sam asked.

"We got tired of walking so we're sitting," Chris replied. "What're you recruits doing?"

"Ain't recruits no more," Sam said. "Remember, we's motherfucking marines now. Do ya see the difference?"

"Nope," Chris answered. "So, what're you motherfucking marines doin'?"

"Walkin' around," Sam said. "Got any better ideas?"

None of the four marines knew the city, and none had any suggestions until Sam mentioned Tijuana.

Pete remembered all the horror stories about Tijuana circulating in boot camp. He repeated one of them. "They'll throw you in jail down there and you'll disappear, never to be heard from again."

"Most of those stories are exaggerations," Tony stated, speaking as an authority that had lived on both sides of the border. "You can get into trouble anywhere if you work at it."

"I never been in a foreign country," Sam confessed. "Walkin' round Tijuana sounds more cool than walkin' round San Diego."

Chris agreed. "I've seen about as much of this town as I want to see for today."

Curiosity about the unknown with a little potential excitement thrown in also affected Pete's thinking, and he also favored the idea.

"Okay, how do we get there?" Sam asked.

Tony pointed to a busy bus stop on the other side of the park. "Probably right there."

They found out that Tony had it right and caught an express bus to the border from the park bus stop. The bus was already half filled with service people, some in uniform and some in civilian dress, and two elderly couples. At the border, the four new marines walked past a bored border guard into Mexico in the middle of the afternoon. They learned that it would take half an hour to walk downtown, or they could rent a taxi for a dollar. They decided to take a taxi and save the walking for when they got downtown. They piled into a well-used prewar Chevrolet now serving as a taxi and were soon bouncing over a very poorly maintained road into the city of Tijuana.

Pete became aware of an abrupt change. Everything appeared grey. There were no lawns and few trees. Buildings needed paint and repair as did the road the taxi took into town. The abrupt contrast puzzled Pete. One side of the border is lush and green, and the other side, grey and desolate. How could things change so abruptly and so completely?

Pete's thoughts were interrupted when Chris exclaimed, "Hey, bullfights!" and pointed to a sign in English and Spanish that read "Bullfight Arena." It looked like there would be bullfights that afternoon.

Tony spoke to the taxi driver in Spanish and then translated. "The taxi driver said admission is five dollars for cheap seats and the fights are half over."

Sam wasn't disappointed. "Five dollars to see bulls gettin' killed? No way."

The idea kind of intrigued Pete who had found himself relishing seeing and experiencing new things, even the bizarre and unpleasant, but he didn't voice his thoughts. Besides, five dollars would put a good-sized hole in the money in his pocket.

The taxi dropped them off in the middle of the Tijuana business district and the four marines found themselves attracting a crowd of young boys that wanted to shine their shoes, sell them some trinkets, or just wanted the marines to give them money so their mother could buy food. They escaped into a tavern where they discovered their age presented no barrier to buying a beer. They arranged themselves at a long bar and sipped their beer and noted their surroundings. Two local-looking men sat at the far end of the bar and two or three young women sat in the shadows in the back of the room.

Sam noted, "Not much going on here."

Tony observed that if it's like Laredo, and it looks like it is, things can change fast, and they usually do.

Pete noticed that a couple of the women who had been sitting in the shadows were coming towards them. They were young and attractive in a foreign sort of way, with straight, dark hair pulled back and skin a summer-tan color. One of the women appeared shapely in a tight dress. With the other it was hard to tell because she wore a loose-fitting dress. They both seemed pretty exotic looking to Pete, he being used to white, blondish women.

The women came straight towards the marines. "Buy drink?" the woman in the loose-fitting dress asked as she slid onto a stool beside Chris.

The shapely one moved up to the bar between Pete and Sam. "What you marines looking for?" she asked.

Pete felt a hand groping his crotch. "What the hell!" he exclaimed and pulled the hand away. The shapely one laughed. "Hey, we have a virgin," she said loudly. The remark got a laugh out of the other woman and the bartender. Pete didn't laugh and neither did Chris who appeared to have his hands full with the woman sitting next to him.

The shapely one turned her attention to Sam, who seemed more receptive to her presence. Things moved pretty fast, and soon Chris and Sam were being led somewhere outside of the tavern.

Pete had no experience with these kinds of things, but one thing he knew for sure: his mother wouldn't approve. Tony consoled Pete, "You're better off spending your money on beer."

Pete, curious, asked what Tony thought it cost.

"I'd guess five dollars," he replied.

They started talking about other things. Pete asked where Tony had been assigned.

"Sangley Point in the Philippines," Tony replied.

"Well, I'll be damned," Pete responded. "That's where I'm going."

Chris and Sam returned, appearing subdued and ready to move on. They went back out in the street which had begun to fill with more servicemen and tourists. As evening set in, some of the night spots started warming up, advertising erotic dancers and other sensual delights.

The four marines ventured into one promoting "topless and more" dancers. They discovered that "topless" also applied to the women waiting on tables. Pete was certain his mother wouldn't put her stamp of approval on the place, and it took him a while to adjust. He had never really seen fully exposed breasts before, not even his mother's.

"Jeez, look at those knockers," Sam said when a well-endowed waitress approached their table.

Chris observed, "After you've seen a couple it starts to get boring."

"Speak for yourself," Sam replied.

Later a topless and almost bottomless dancer performed on a small stage. She had ponderous breasts and could get them churning in either the clockwise or counterclockwise direction.

Pete admitted he was impressed by the dancer's capabilities.

Sam said that if she could get one going clockwise and the other counterclockwise at the same time, he'd be impressed.

They visited another night club after which they did a quick audit of their remaining funds and determined they needed most of what remained to cover their taxi and bus expenses to return to San Diego. On the bus back to San Diego, Pete asked Chris how it was. Chris didn't answer right away. Finally, he said, "You know what?"

"Haven't a clue," Pete answered.

"She's three months pregnant."

"What! How do you know?"

"She told me. So whata you think of that? For some reason, at that point, I lost all interest in what was going on.

Pete couldn't stifle a laugh. "That is about the funniest, dumbest thing I have ever heard. Almost lost your virginity to a pregnant Tijuana whore. You should've asked for a refund."

I did, didn't work.

6.
First Furlough

Chris and Pete took the Greyhound bus, the most reasonably priced means of travel, back to South Dakota for their twenty-day leave. The round trip would eat up five days' travel time, but the train wouldn't do much better.

Chris's vision of walking down Milbank's main street in a full marine dress uniform and all the pretty girls twisting their necks off looking never happened. Part of the reason was that Pete, raised as a modest Lutheran and averse to standing out in a crowd, couldn't bring himself to wear the midnight-blue coat with the standing collar and white belt when they went into town.

"I'd look like a damn peacock," he said, so they wore the more modest khaki shirt-and-tie version of the dress uniform.

The Houser family had gotten a new replacement for the Studebaker that Pete had totaled, and he was surprised that his dad let him use it, especially on a Saturday night with the friends who had been involved in totaling the original car.

Pete and Chris were wearing their uniforms when they picked up Lyle in the really new-smelling Studebaker.

Lyle took one look at the two marines and said, "Wow, should I salute you or something?"

"Yeah," Chris replied. "And whenever I tell you something, you say 'yes, sir' as loud as you can."

Lyle asked, "Remember the last Saturday night we did this?"

Chris volunteered that he didn't remember a thing.

Pete said it would be best if nobody remembered it.

"Well, sounds like we all agree on that," Lyle replied. "A lot of water has gone over the dam since. So, what's it like to be a marine?" he asked.

Chris answered, "If you really want to know, you join up and stand in the yellow foot prints and walk through the silver doors."

"Yeah," Pete agreed. "You really won't understand from us telling it. You hafta live it."

Lyle didn't want to know the answer that bad and went back to the night's plans. "You know what? Maybe we should go back to Chautauqua to commemorate our last Saturday night out."

Pete said going back to Chautauqua would be a really bad idea.

Chris disagreed, saying they would do it right this time. "For one thing, I know you can get stinking, throwing-up drunk on three-two beer. Won't do that again."

Lyle laughed. "Most people know the answer to that one without getting stinko." After more discussion, Pete reluctantly accepted the majority decision to re-enact their previous Saturday night out, but with a happier ending.

They started out with a beer and some eight ball at Volk's pool hall. While they were there, a young-looking farmer came up to their table and said he had been a marine, fought at Okinawa. "Got a Purple Heart. Real lucky to get out of there alive." The revelation transformed the man in Pete's eyes. For the first time, he felt the brotherhood that existed between marines and former marines. They shared a unique experience that set them apart from other men, and he and Chris were now part of that fraternity.

After completing two games of eight ball, the trio headed for Chautauqua. They rolled the windows down to enjoy the balmy early summer evening, a stark contrast to their previous frigid Chautauqua experience. At Chautauqua they found room at the table where they had sat the last time they were there. And like the last time, there were three young women at the other end of the table who looked as if they might have spent the day making hay. An old-time band cranking out polkas, waltzes, and an occasional contemporary tune rounded out the picture.

Chris, sipping his beer rather than gulping it, noted that other than the weather, little had changed. Lyle, noticing the ladies at the end of the table throwing glances in their direction, disagreed. "Those gals down at end of the table are giving you the come-here instead of the get-lost look."

Before the evening ended, the young ladies had moved down to their end of the table, which resulted in some lively conversation and some brave attempts at dancing by Pete and Chris. As the party ended, there were promises to stay in touch, and names and addresses were exchanged. As planned, the replayed Chautauqua episode ended in a positive way.

Pete turned on the radio as they drove back to Milbank, and the song "Harbor Lights" emanated from the speaker. A voice interrupted the music and announced, "WCCO radio is interrupting this program to bring you breaking news. An Associated Press report confirms that at dawn, Sunday the twenty-fifth of June, elements of the North Korean Army crossed the border into South Korea, and it appears that a full-scale invasion of the south by the north is occurring. Stay tuned for further developments." WCCO switched back to normal programming, and the sounds of "Mona Lisa" drifted into the Studebaker.

"What the fuck?" Chris exclaimed. "Where is Korea?"

Pete had a pretty good idea where things were located in the Orient. "Hangs off Northern China," he replied with an air of certainty.

"Okay," Chris said. "I remember now. It hangs off China like somebody's dick."

Lyle knew Pete would be going to the Philippines, asked, "Pete, anywhere near where you're going?"

"Closer than South Dakota, but not real close," Pete replied.

"You think we'll get involved?" Chris asked in a way that sounded like he knew the answer.

Lyle didn't think so. "Can't be very important if I never heard of the place."

"Because you don't know shit about Korea doesn't mean it isn't important," Chris declared.

Pete followed current events closely, like other people followed sports. "It isn't about Korea," Pete said. "It's about communism. North Korea is communist and South Korea isn't. That's why it's important."

"Don't like what I'm hearing," Chris said. "This isn't in the plan."

"What plan?" Pete asked.

"Our marine enlistment plans. It's about seeing the world and meeting some wild women, nothing about war."

"Never told me about any plan," Pete said.

"Not on paper," Chris replied. "But that's what I've been thinking. No war in the plan."

Lyle chimed in, "Sounds like you need to update your plan."

"Don't get too smug, Lyle," Pete said. "They could be cranking up the draft again."

"You think so?" Lyle asked. "They wouldn't."

"You can beat that. Join the marines," Chris suggested.

"That sounds like shooting yourself in the head to save your foot," Lyle replied. "No thanks."

After the chatter died down, Pete worked the unexpected news over in his mind. Things out of his and Chris's control were happening that could affect their lives in a bad way. This wouldn't be something he and Chris would read about, it would be happening to them.

The next day, Sunday, June 25, the Houser family went to church. His mother insisted Pete wear his uniform. "You look so good when you wear it," she said.

Pete had not said anything about the news he heard the night before, and since his folks hadn't mentioned Korea, he assumed they hadn't heard anything. They were walking from their parked car to the church when

Ralph Shuman, a neighbor that lived south of their place, asked them what they thought about the Korean news.

"What news?" Pete's dad asked.

Shuman replied, "Something about the north invading the south. It's all over the news."

They listened to the car radio while driving home after church. Korea dominated the news.

There were emergency meetings in Washington, and the United Nations would meet on Monday to discuss the crisis.

"What's this all about?" Pete's mother wanted to know.

"Just hope we don't get involved," Pete's dad declared. "Let em fight. Who cares?"

From what Pete heard on the radio, it seemed clear that the United States would become involved. It wasn't being described as a war between two parts of a small divided country; rather it was part of a bigger picture, a part of the Red Tide, the communist threat to the free world.

Pete's mother didn't seem concerned about the big picture. She was concerned about how it would affect her boy. "Will you have to go to Korea?" she asked Pete.

"I have orders to go to the Philippines," Pete replied. "A long way from Korea." He didn't mention his thoughts about the possibility of current events changing those orders.

Pete and Chris got together Sunday afternoon. Korea dominated their thoughts. By this time, they had little doubt that Korea would involve Marine Corps participation.

"Marines will lead the charge," Chris mused. "Guess it's what we trained for. War and killing people. Boot camp wasn't a waste of time after all, except if you get assigned to Sangley Point."

"Somebody has to do it," Pete replied.

Chris laughed. "Sure, somebody has to be sure the sailors get to bed on time. It's the luck of the draw, and what the hell, who knows what the First Marine Division is going to do. Anyway, what are you going to be doing for the next week and a half we still have at home?"

"I'm thinking of helping the folks stack some alfalfa, maybe get reacquainted with our milk herd. See if they still remember me. Maybe have a beer or two once in a while. Shoot some pool at Volk's."

"Me, too," Chris replied. He mused, "I guess we haven't completely cut the cord. Last week I spent a day cultivating corn for my folks. The sun was shining, it had rained the day before and the ground had that new rain smell to it, and I thought, I'm really gonna miss this."

On June 29, President Harry S. Truman ordered a naval blockade of the Korean coast and authorized General Douglas A. MacArthur to send U.S. ground troops into Korea. On July 2, General MacArthur requested of the Joint Chiefs of Staff that a Marine regimental combat team be deployed to the Far East.

These events answered any questions in Chris and Pete's minds with regards to how the United States would respond to the invasion of South Korea.

Early on Thursday morning, July 6, Pete, Chris and their families waited outside of the drug store where the Greyhound bus would stop to pick up passengers. When they left to go to boot camp, only Pete's mother had been there to send them off. This time, current events drew everyone in their immediate families to the departure. Although not discussed openly, the possibility of these young men going halfway around the world to unknown dangers weighed heavily on these families. Pete's mother, who had become emotional when they were leaving for boot camp, hugged Pete long and warmly but remained stoic during the sendoff, as if to demonstrate strength during a crisis. Even Pete's dad moved outside his comfort zone and gave Pete a warm hug.

As the bus pulled away from its Milbank stop, Pete wondered when he would be returning. He would be traveling across a broad ocean to a foreign place, not one completely unfamiliar since he had read many stories about the battles being fought in the Philippines during the war. He looked forward to seeing some of those places.

As the bus neared the Pendleton Marine Base where Chris would be getting off, it occurred to Pete that he and Chris would be separated by distance and circumstances for the first time since he could remember. They played together at each other's farmsteads, attended the same one-room school, and had remained close friends ever since.

Pete looked at Chris, who was intently studying the hills where Pendleton was located. Pete got his attention. "We've got to stay in touch," he said. "Do you think I can use the First Marine Division at Pendleton as your address?"

Chris didn't know but guessed they could get the addresses through their families if necessary. "We'll stay in touch, one way or other. You're not going to get rid me just because we are a few hundred or thousands of miles apart."

Pete helped Chris retrieve his duffle bag from the overhead rack when the bus stopped at Camp Pendleton. They shook hands, looked each other in the eye, and uncharacteristically embraced. Pete watched as Chris exited the bus, slung his bag on his shoulder, stopped, waved, then turned and walked towards the Pendleton main gate. Pete kept his eyes on Chris as the bus pulled away and could feel a tear streaming down his cheek.

Pete continued on to the city of San Diego where he would wait to catch a navy logistics flight to Sangley Point Naval Air Station in the Philippines.

U.S. Navy Air Station Sangley Point Philippines

This image is in the public domain.

7.
The New Reality

When Pete got to San Diego, he checked into Marine Transient Billeting and found Tony Gutierrez from Company Thirty-Three already there. After a two-day wait they were both assigned to the same plane going to the Philippines. Accompanying them to Sangley would be a marine sergeant who had been on an emergency leave to attend his father's funeral.

Pete had never been in a plane before and felt some anxiety when he went up the steps to enter the large four-engine cargo plane. About half of the plane was filled with cargo, and the other half set up with temporary seating for the passengers. A female airman showed Pete and the other marines where they should sit. Pete sat between the sergeant and Tony.

As the plane taxied to the runway, the sergeant introduced himself as Sergeant Kolowski and asked where Pete and Tony were headed. When they replied they were being assigned to the Sangley Point Security detachment, Sergeant Kolowski told them that is where he was going and said they were lucky. "Some of the best duty in the Marines."

The four engines roared, and the lumbering cargo plane gained speed and lifted off. Pete felt nervous as the plane became airborne but also excited. He was headed for the other side of the globe and he would be seeing another part of the world he had only read about. As the plane gained altitude, the sergeant continued his description of Sangley Point.

"There's an enlisted men's club you wouldn't believe. Cold mugs of San Michael, ten cents. Mixed drinks, fifteen cents. Dance nights with big bands from Manila. Got me a woman in Cavite, the town right outside the base."

Pete and Tony were taking in all the details as the sergeant spoke. From what the sergeant was saying, Pete concluded that Sangley wouldn't be a hardship post. At the same time, the sergeant wasn't mentioning anything about what marines did at the air station besides go to the enlisted men's club and activities like having a woman in Cavite.

Tony asked the sergeant what he thought about Korea.

"The Korea thing don't sound good," the sergeant replied. "Just signed up for another four years, don't need any more of that shit. I saw a lot of war during the big one, thought we'd settled that crap for a while. Enjoy the Philippines, eat, drink, and make Mary and all the other broads you can. You'll never know what might happen tomorrow."

By the time they reached Hawaii, Pete felt like a veteran flyer and marveled at how long distances could be traveled in such a short time. Hawaii, which in Pete's mind seemed like a remote place in the middle of the Pacific, took only eight hours. After an eight-hour layover in Hawaii the marines caught another plane and it flew to Johnson Island, Guam and finally the Philippines in another fourteen hours.

Pete knew from seeing the size of the Pacific Ocean on maps and globes that it would be big, but experiencing its size by flying over it for hours and hours gave him a better sense of its immensity. Pete had moved to a window seat on the last leg of the flight, and as the plane descended in its approach to Sangley Point, Manila and Manila Bay became visible. The sight caused Pete to feel chills as he remembered his history. Admiral Dewey destroyed the Spanish Fleet in this bay. During World War II, the battle for Manila had been fought here. Out in the distance, he could see the entrance to Manila Bay where he knew Corregidor would be, and to the north of it would be the Bataan Peninsula. He remembered reading about the battles there in magazines and newspapers and hearing about them on the radio during the war. Those things happened in places he could now see through the plane window.

When they deplaned at Sangley Point, Pete felt the reality of being in the tropics. "Wow!" he exclaimed. "It's hot here."

The sergeant assured him, "You'll get used to it in a few days. Your blood thins out, it'll feel like normal."

Tony agreed. "Feels like I'm back home in Texas. You northerners just don't know good weather when you find it."

A waiting Jeep took the marines to a large stucco administration building set among large trees on a large manicured lawn. They checked in and picked up identification cards and passes good for that night.

The corporal who checked them in warned them, "Keep track of the time. Midnight curfew."

The Jeep then took them to a clutch of Quonset huts near the tip of the peninsula on which the Sangley Point naval base was located. The short Jeep ride revealed a compact base with an aircraft runway along one side that took up a good-sized portion of the space. Navy patrol planes sat parked on the edge of the runway. The base appeared neat and well maintained.

During the ride, Sergeant Kolowski said he would be going into Cavite to see his woman and asked if Pete and Tony wanted a tour of the town.

Tony and Pete looked at each other. "Sure, why not?" Tony answered.

"Good," Kolowski replied. "I'll stop by your hut after I shower and change."

When they got to the Quonsets, the sergeant pointed to a hut. "You'll be in number twenty-one. I'm in twenty-three."

He then pointed to a smaller Quonset. "That's the head shed. Everything nice and handy."

Pete and Tony grabbed their gear and went into hut number twenty-one where they were greeted by a group of marines playing poker.

"Moving in?" one of the marines asked.

"That's what we been told," Pete replied.

"There's a couple of empty bunks by the back entrance," the marine said. "You can grab them."

Pete claimed the upper bunk and Tony the lower. They had showered and were digging out a change of clothes when Sergeant Kolowski stopped at the hut. The sergeant wore a short-sleeved flowered shirt untucked over white slacks.

Pete had noticed other men in civvies wandering around the area and wondered what the rules were.

"Just like the states, off duty wear what you want as long as it's decent." Sergeant Kolowski explained. The natives can spot a serviceman a no matter what you wear. We'll stop at the enlisted men's club. Convert some dollars for pesos. You can use dollars anywhere but you aren't supposed to. Sergeant Kolowski had described the enlisted men's club in glowing terms, and a cursory look seemed to back up his description. Large, clean, and crowded was their first impression.

When they got off the bus at the Sangley Point main gate, marine guards checked their passes and greeted Sergeant Kolowski by name. The three marines then piled into the back of a Jeepney.

"Margareta's," the sergeant told the Jeepney driver. The driver headed away from the base down a poorly maintained paved two-lane road. They saw a mix of residences, mostly small shacks with thatched grass roofs on stilts, and small businesses—stores, Chinese take-outs, and bars—along both sides of the road.

They hadn't gone too far when Pete spotted a toddler squatting in the yard of one of the thatched-roof shacks.

"Hey," Pete called out, "that little kid is shitting right in front of that shack." Pete had noticed a pervasive odor when they got outside of the base. He asked, "Is that why this place smells?"

"The whole Orient smells that way," the sergeant answered. "You got a billion people shitting wherever, it's going to smell. You'll get used to it and think it's normal. When you get back to the states, you'll wonder why things smell so weird—fresh and clean."

The Jeepney stopped to pick up two more passengers who spoke to the driver in a language foreign to Pete. A little while later they picked up another passenger. It had become crowded in the back of the Jeepney.

"All these people going to the same place? "Tony asked.

"Nope, all going to different places. The driver figures out his route depending on where everyone is going. You can go on some pretty long rides sometimes. The place we are going is on this road up ahead a little way. We'll be the first ones off."

Margareta's occupied a modest cinder-block building that had recently been brightened up with a coat of white paint. The inside featured a lot of vinyl, with orange tabletops, yellow-painted walls, a tile floor, and bright lighting. It reminded Pete of a California Denny's.

"Good place to buy a beer," the sergeant said. "They keep the mugs in a freezer, fill them with San Michaels. Order another beer, and you get another frosty mug. Forty centavos, twenty cents."

The three marines claimed a booth, and a curvaceous waitress with a pretty face came to serve them.

The sergeant introduced Tony and Pete to the waitress. "Just arrived," he said. "Bring us three frosties."

After the waitress went to fill the order, the sergeant asked, "Whatta ya think of that?"

"You mean the waitress?" Pete asked. "Nice looking."

"Cost you ten pesos."

"You mean. . .?" Pete left the sentence hanging.

"Way to make a living," the sergeant replied. "Best business in town."

Pete realized his thinking would need some adjusting to fit into a world where the norm seemed radically different from what he had been used to. Two of his mother's final instructions, 'Be careful' and 'Go to church,' left room for adjustment, but her last instruction, 'Be good,' seemed more problematic. Pete suspected that being good in Milbank was a lot different than being good in Cavite. Which applied here? He imagined that his mother intended the Milbank definition to apply in all cases.

The waitress returned with three frosty mugs filled with San Michael tap beer. She looked towards Pete and Tony and asked, "How you like Philippines?"

Pete didn't give the question much thought and replied, "It stinks."

The waitress said what sounded like some nasty words in a foreign language and stomped off.

The reaction surprised Pete. "What did she say?" he asked.

The sergeant answered. "You insulted her and her country. I'm impressed, takes real talent to insult a whore."

Pete felt embarrassed and realized he had been rude. To insult someone's country is like insulting someone's mother. No matter how humble, home and country can't be replaced.

The three marines sipped their beer and started to talk shop. Tony wanted to know what the marines did at Sangley Point.

"There's ninety enlisted men and seven officers, give or take one or two at any one time," the sergeant replied. "We man the main gate, guard the base perimeter, raise and lower the flag, and stand inspection about once a month."

Pete said that sounded like pretty easy duty.

The sergeant agreed. "Don't need ninety marines for those things, half that many could handle a base like this. Did I mention the Huks? Ever hear about them?"

Pete and Tony shook their heads. Neither had ever heard about Huks.

"That's what they call the Philippine communists. Huks. They have some fancy name nobody can pronounce so everybody calls them Huks. The Philippine government and the Huks are fighting a war nobody knows or cares much about. The Russians equip and finance the Huks, so they have the resources to do bad things."

Tony said it sounded like a good reason to have a few extra marines around.

The sergeant agreed. "We got weapons, things you wouldn't need for ordinary base security. Recoilless 75s, mortars, 50-caliber machine guns.

We could make things interesting for anyone doing bad things."

"How real do you think it is, the Huks doing bad things?" Pete asked.

"Don't know," the sergeant answered. "They're all over the island. They've probable got easier pickings outside Sangley Point. Best not to be on the roads outside the cities at night."

The sergeant looked at his watch. "'Bout time for my woman to get off work at the Kitty Kat. We'll catch a Jeepney, and I'll let you guys do some exploring on your own."

"Got any recommendations?" Tony asked.

"You could spend time at the Kitty Kat. Don't go to the Palace. The women got clap and what have you in that place."

After they arrived at the Kitty Kat, the sergeant introduced Pete and Tony to his friend Marinda, a tiny woman with surprisingly full female features and a face brightened with a liberal use of cosmetics.

The Kitty Kat bar and restaurant was a large two-story stucco building in the middle of downtown Cavite, strategically located at the intersection of the road from Sangley Point and a road leading to the highway to Manila. The first level was divided into two parts, a dimly lit bar with bar stools and small tables on one side and a dining area with tables and booths along the other wall. Pete and Tony took a table in the bar area and ordered beer. Shortly after the beer was served, two women approached their table. One, the more diminutive of the two, looked like many of the native women Pete and Tony had seen that evening. She was fine featured with olive skin and straight dark hair. The second woman didn't fit the pattern, being larger and better endowed than the average Filipina woman, with lighter skin and hair that seemed to have some natural curl. Her facial features were pronounced, with a nose big enough to be American. Pete thought she could have passed with little notice in Milbank. The smaller woman asked, "Would marines want company?"

Pete looked at Tony, who shrugged and said, "Why not?"

The women introduced themselves. The smaller one was Fannie, and the other, Maria.

The women got the conversation going by asking questions. Where were the marines from? How long had they been in the Philippines?

After Tony revealed himself as Tex-Mex, Maria said, "So you have a Spanish family name. What is it?"

"Gutierrez."

"Mine is Mendez," Maria replied. "Habla usted español?"

"Of course," Tony replied.

After talking briefly in Spanish to Tony, Maria switched back to English and brought Fannie and Pete into the conversation.

Their waitress came around to see if they needed refills. Pete, finding the talk interesting and feeling more than ordinarily generous, ordered drinks for the women and more beer for Tony and himself.

Maria explained what the Spanish conversation had been about. She said that a large, close-knit, Spanish-speaking mestizo community lived in the Manila area. She told Tony that she could introduce him to people in the community if he was interested.

Tony added, "I asked Maria if I could bring a dumb German along and she said, 'Sure, Pedro would be welcome.'"

Pete didn't understand everything he heard, like the word mestizo. "What's mestizo?" he asked.

"The Spanish thought they owned the Philippines for over three hundred years," Maria answered, "They sent men to back up their claim, soldiers and priests, no women. Guess what happened? Mixed-breed babies. Mestizos."

"You're mestizo?" Pete asked.

"I guess. My mother is Spanish mestizo, says I have an American father. Anyway, I'm welcome at their parties."

Pete had broadened his expectations with regards to the world he lived in and found himself at ease in the Kitty Kat environment. The women were friendly but not openly soliciting, although he did observe couples going up a stairway to the second level. It seemed a person could pick their own poison.

It didn't seem too long before they needed to catch a Jeepney back to Sangley Point in order to beat the midnight curfew.

Marines in First Provisional Brigade board troopship in San Diego July 1950

This image is in the public domain.

8.

On War's Fast Track

Chris Engelson got off the bus with his duffle bag at the main gate of Camp Pendleton and watched as the bus pulled away and disappeared, carrying Pete to San Diego. Chris felt a pang of loneliness as his connection to his past moved out of sight. He wondered when he would see Pete again.

He showed his orders to the main gate guard who directed him to a commuter bus parked nearby. The bus driver looked at his orders. "Going to the Provincial Brigade formation area," the driver said, "like everyone else today." Chris was the first on the bus but was soon joined by half a dozen other young marines carrying duffle bags. When another bus pulled up behind them their bus pulled away and traveled along base roads for about half an hour before stopping in front a large warehouse looking building. A marine standing outside of the bus directed them into the large building. Inside the building it was crowded and chaotic. Long lines of men waited their turn to get to tables where personnel clerks worked. A person working the floor looked at Chris's papers and directed him to one of the lines.

A stocky, salty-looking corporal stood ahead of him in the line. Chris asked, "Got any idea why we are standing in this line?"

The corporal looked Chris over. "I hear they are forming a brigade to go to Korea, the First Provisional Marine Brigade, and are cleaning out the attics and closets to man it. Yeah, just re-upped for four more years, never saw this coming. Might have given it more thought if I had. How about you?"

"Fresh out of boot camp," Chris replied.

The corporal chuckled. "You may be getting some advanced combat training. I don't need any more of that shit."

Chris didn't want to seem dumb but asked the question anyway. "What's a provisional brigade?"

"A brigade is like a division, only less. An infantry division would normally have three rifle regiments, a brigade probably has just one. I heard it will be the Fifth Regiment. There will likely be some artillery, tanks, air support but not as much as a division. For you and me, division or brigade doesn't matter much one way or the other. For us the big thing is the squad, platoon, company. That's the world we live in."

When Chris reached the table at the head of the line, a clerk looked at a list of names, made a check mark, and handed him a paper to sign.

"You're checked into the First Provisional Marine Brigade."

As the words "First Provisional Marine Brigade" penetrated his mind, he realized he had been put on the fast track to war. When Chris heard about the Korean War, he knew the odds he would be going to Korea sometime in the future were pretty good. Now, suddenly, the future had arrived. For a moment Chris felt unsteady, lightheaded. He took a deep breath and felt physical normality return.

The clerk handed Chris a sheet of paper that located where he fit into the First Provisional Brigade: First Squad, First Rifle Platoon, Easy Company, Second Battalion, Fifth Regiment. On the paper were also the names of the Easy Company commander, Captain Wilson, the platoon leader, Lieutenant Ray Cleaver, and the squad leader, Sergeant Frank Teal. The number of the tent where Chris would stay in Tent City was listed at the bottom of the page. The tent city was a walkable distance from the building Chris was in.

Chris left the administration building carrying his duffle bag and saw the corporal walking ahead of him. Expecting that the corporal would know his way around, Chris hurried to catch up.

When he caught up with the corporal, he introduced himself. "PFC Chris Engelson," he said, holding out his hand.

"Corporal Brad Hautman," the corporal replied and shook Chris's outstretched hand. He asked which tent Chris was assigned to and found out they would be in the same tent. "Hey we're in the same squad," he said.

They found their squad leader, Sergeant Teal, with the other tent occupants waiting to go to chow at 1700. Sergeant Teal welcomed Corporal Hautman and Chris to the First Squad. "You're the last ones on the list. We now have a full complement of thirteen men. Bring your mess kit and we'll head to the mess tent. The food is bad but it'll keep your motor running."

While walking to the mess tent, the sergeant briefed Corporal Hautman and Chris. "You guys have some catching up to do. We'll be loading on ships four days from now."

"Jeez. That fast?" Corporal Hautman asked.

"It's been asses and elbows since I got here," the sergeant replied. "I'll have you two scheduled in for physicals and paperwork in the morning. Tonight we'll set up our fire teams."

Later that evening, Sergeant Teal designated who would be in the three First Squad fire teams. The First Fire Team would be led by Corporal Hautman. It included PFCs Adam Anderson, Les Green, and Chris Engelson. The corporal made Chris a rifleman, Adam a BAR man—he'd be handling a Browning automatic rifle. Les would-be a BAR assistant.

The next morning Chris and Corporal Hautman went to get their physical exams and shots.

Chris asked the corporal what the chances were that a person would fail the physical.

"Almost zero. They wouldn't have assigned you to the brigade if they didn't think you were fit. Just out of boot camp, you're fit."

During the physical, two medics hit Chris with hypodermics in both arms simultaneously.

Later in the day Pete and Hautman received new identification cards, checked their pay allotments, and verified their GI insurance recipients.

The next day the squad members went through their personal items, discarding non-essentials and drawing items they were short of, and stowed what they needed in backpacks that they would carry aboard ship along with a sleeping bag and their weapon.

On Wednesday morning, the Easy Company marines checked weapons out of the armory. The rifles had been packed in cosmoline, a greasy substance intended to prevent rust, and the men spent the morning disassembling, cleaning, and reassembling them.

Adam, the fire team's designated BAR man, got his Browning automatic rifle. "Never fired one of these things," Adam told Corporal Hautman.

"Maybe we can get some practice on the ship, shooting at garbage," Corporal Hautman replied.

In the middle of the afternoon, Sergeant Teal told the squad they could have the rest of the afternoon off. They could write letters or just relax, but they would be leaving on trucks at 1000 the next morning to board a ship in San Diego. He added, "You can do pretty much what you want, but you are confined to Tent City until we leave tomorrow."

"Jeez, kinda limits our options," Corporal Hautman muttered.

Chris decided to write letters to his folks and to Pete. It would probably be his last chance to write before they sailed. His squad had been given a return address to put on their outgoing mail that would follow the brigade. Since he didn't know Pete's current address, Chris included his letter to Pete with the letter to his folks so that Pete's parents could forward it to Pete when they knew how to reach him.

Les Green, the fire team BAR assistant, a short, wiry kid from Florida, worked at getting a poker game going. Corporal Hautman and Adam Anderson, the fire team BAR man, a tall, blond, muscular farm boy from North Dakota, took him up on the offer. They started to play while Chris wrote his letters. Everyone seemed a little subdued. The hurried schedule and a future full of unknowns weighed on the fire team.

The next morning, the First Rifle Platoon lined up with the rest of Easy Company and loaded onto trucks to be transported to the San Diego Naval Base. The convoy moved like a conveyer belt as it carried the provisional brigade's personnel and equipment down Highway 101 to the San Diego Navy Base where ships were anchored that would carry them to a war. In the process they messed up the traffic on the two-lane Highway 101 and down town San Diego for a couple of days. At the North Island naval base, they found ships lined up stem to stern along a quay being loaded with the First Provincial Brigade's cargo. Trucks and men scuttled about as cranes lifted load after load onto the ships. Tanks and artillery were parked nearby, waiting to be loaded. Easy Company boarded a ship named the *Clymer*. The First Fire Team followed Corporal Brad Hautman up the gangplank and down two levels into a compartment filled with bunks stacked five high. There was room for only one person at a time to move between them. Chris had never been on a ship before and hadn't even seen one up close, but he knew right away the *Clymer* wasn't a luxury cruise ship.

"Welcome to your new home," the corporal said. He traded his lower bunk for Adam's third level bunk, explaining that BAR's didn't make good bunk mates and Adam could store his weapon under his bunk. The rest of them would have to sleep with their weapon and back packs.

Chris wondered if he and his equipment would fit in the bunk. There was hardly enough clearance between his bunk and the one above to push his backpack in. He, his backpack, and his M1 would become very intimate during the voyage.

By evening the fully loaded Clymer moved out into San Diego Bay where it anchored for the night. Everyone in the compartment had been given a green meal card which indicated that they would line up for chow at 1800. At the scheduled time, Chris and the rest of the fire team found the chow line long and slow.

Les complained, "Damn, there's lines to piss, shit, and eat." Les had enlisted a short time after his seventeenth birthday and looked to be about fifteen. Besides being young, he weighed a little over 140 pounds and stood just five foot eight inches tall.

"Aren't you glad you joined the Marines?" Adam asked.

"You bet," Les replied. "Beautiful ship and quarters. Did you feel how thick and soft the bunk mattresses are? And I'll bet the food will be just as good."

Corporal Hautman laughed. "Hey kid, you're going to grow up to be a good marine. You'll really like sleeping in a hole in the ground and eating C-rations."

After the meal, which could be best described as adequate, the fire team decided to go out on the ship's deck to get some fresh air. The sun had set and the air had cooled down. It felt pleasant. The lights of San Diego and the naval base framed the bay where a large number of navy ships were riding at anchor.

The scene reminded Chris of "Harbor Lights," the song on the Houser Studebaker radio that had been interrupted by the announcement of the invasion of South Korea.

Adam, impressed by the scene, exclaimed, "Look at all the ships! Are they all part of this thing we're in?"

Corporal Hautman guessed that most of them would be part of the convoy that would be sailing the next day. He identified the ship types they could see. There were troop transports, LSTs—Landing Ship Tank—most likely loaded with tanks, and artillery.

The next morning the ships lined up and moved through the channel between Point Loma and the North Island Naval Base out into the Pacific Ocean. It soon became evident that conditions in the crowded troop compartments would not improve once they were underway.

Despite a relatively calm sea, motion sickness became common. During the peak of the motion sickness, the compartment became nearly unbearable but, unfortunately, lying quietly in their bunks offered the afflicted the only available relief. Chris had a mild case. Lying in his bunk alleviated the symptoms, and he soon felt normal again. Adam really suffered with a severe case that lasted several days. Even Brad Hautman had a touch. Only little Les seemed immune, and he made a big deal about it.

When Chris got his sea legs, he started spending much of his time on deck. One day while he and Corporal Hautman stood leaning on the rail watching the ocean, Chris noted that the convoy seemed to be moving at a pretty leisurely pace.

"Yeah, we are," the corporal replied. "The slowest ship sets the pace. I'd guess the LSTs are the ones. They weren't designed for speed. One thing, we aren't bobbing and weaving like they used to during the Big War. That slowed things down even more."

The marines occupied some of their time with training. As Corporal Hautman had hoped, Adam had a chance to fire his BAR off the side of the ship in several training sessions. Some of the people in the weapons platoon saw some of their machine guns, mortars, and recoilless weapons for the first time and got a hands-on orientation. All of the enlisted marines went through Korean information orientation where they were introduced to Korean geography, history, people, weather, things like that. Other than these activities and standing in lines, the marines had little to do aboard the ships that were transporting them to a distant place.

After watching the water and the other ships in the convoy for a day or so, Chris looked for other things to do. He scrounged books from marines who no longer wanted them, read them, and then exchanged them for different books from other marines. He found that standing in the chow line with a book made the wait seem shorter. He sometimes regretted having to put down the book to pick up a food tray. The weather remained consistently pleasant and he found a little nook in the fantail of the ship where he did most of his reading. He started writing a journal about things he observed on the ship. These activities filled his days and time moved quickly.

Originally the marines on the *Clymer* had been told the convoy would stop in Japan, but that didn't happen. They were informed a day before they were to dock in Japan that they were going directly to Pusan. The Pusan perimeter, located on the south-eastern tip of South Korea, thirty to fifty miles deep with a hundred-mile front remained the only part of the country not overrun by the North Koreans. Apparently, the U.S. Army was having trouble maintaining that small foothold and needed help as soon as possible.

On August 2, the convoy entered the Port of Pusan located in a large natural harbor surrounded by a sprawling city with several small mountains protruding from within its boundaries. Larger mountains filled the horizon beyond the city. The port teemed with activity and many ships were anchored, waiting their turn to unload. However, the marine convoy moved right in and the *Clymer* seemed to have hardly slowed down before docking and starting to unload.

After Easy Company disembarked, the marines marched to a warehouse where they exchanged their backpacks for "782" gear which included a field pack and cartridge belt, drew ammunition for their weapons, and were issued as many hand grenades as they wanted to carry. They also filled out burial information forms, a task that reminded Chris that this was no drill.

9.

Settling in at Sangley Point

Hut 21, the Quonset Pete and Tony lived in, had the capacity to house a tightly packed platoon, but since there was no shortage of Quonsets at Sangley, only two squads shared the hut. Hut 21 came with a hut boy named Chico. He was paid monthly from a hut assessment managed by the occupants of the hut. Chico's pay came to about 130 pesos a month, which varied a little as the marines, who contributed five pesos a month, came and left. For his pay, Chico swept the hut six days a week and shined the marine's boots and shoes. For an extra fee Chico took care of the laundry. Chico would pick up the laundry on any day but Sunday, his day off, and return it cleaned and neatly folded two days later. The hut boy job, a relatively easy job, paid better than many other jobs in Cavite.

It didn't take Pete and Tony long to learn their roles at Sangley Point. Their duties rotated between main gate guard duty, peripheral base patrol, and honing their kill skills in case the Huks got any crazy ideas.

Marines with seniority got the most sought-after main gate day shifts. There were no good peripheral patrol duty shifts. The patrol shifts ran from 1600 to 0800 and included most of the periphery of the base. The only area excluded from the peripheral patrol was a stretch of beach that ran in front of and for some distance on either side of the brig. The brig, with bright lighting and guards on duty twenty-four hours a day, provided all of the security needed for that part of the beach. Except for a fence that separated Sangley Point from the city of Cavite, the waters of Manila Bay formed the border of the naval base. Each marine on patrol duty would walk about a quarter mile of the base shoreline or fence. To relieve the monotony, they walked different parts of the periphery on different nights.

Pete learned that boredom was part of a non-combat marine's life. However, he wasn't usually bored on duty, even on peripheral patrols when he was alone on the dark beach. During those times, Pete could do a lot of uninterrupted thinking. He imagined accomplishing all kinds of important things and solved a lot of difficult problems in his head.

The off-duty hours were when time weighed heaviest. Sports, tennis, softball, and a swimming pool provided distractions, as did the officers' and enlisted men's clubs. Serious drinking provided relief for many servicemen. Some marines played endless hours of poker, usually with five or ten cent limits which used up hours of idle time without a lot of money changing hands. Liberty, subject to a midnight curfew, was another boredom-relieving activity for Sangley Point marines. Tony and Pete's duty and liberty schedules matched for the most part so they would often go on liberty together.

Mail was an important part of Pete's life as it was for most servicemen. Pete had no reason to be a letter writer before joining the Marines, but he now wrote home at least once a week and looked forward to getting newsy letters from his mother.

Pete located the base chapel, a Quonset hut distinguished by a fake front and a cross set in front of it, and attended a Sunday service the second weekend after his arrival at Sangley Point. A tall, skinny young navy man with a sallow complexion acting as the church greeter extended his hand when Pete entered the chapel to attend the service. "Good morning!" the greeter said. "Welcome to the Sangley Chapel Protestant service. I don't believe I've seen you before."

"Just arrived this past week," Pete replied.

"You didn't waste time finding the chapel," the greeter replied. He introduced himself as Jim Haskins.

Sangley Point Chapel, a Quonset with a false front

Photo by author

The nondenominational Protestant service, as expected, had not been memorable. The navy chaplain seemed eager to get through the service and back to the officers' club.

After the service, Jim approached Pete and asked if he had enjoyed the service.

"It was okay," Pete replied. "Okay, but not what I'm used to."

"Where you from?" Jim asked.

"South Dakota, Lutheran."

"I'm from Oklahoma, Baptist," Jim replied. "It's not what I'm used to either, but our faith, our morals will be tested here as they've never been tested before. Have you been off the base? It's a real sin hole out there. You need to be a strong Christian to maintain your morals in this place."

Pete admitted he had been off the base. "It's a little different than I'm used to."

Jim agreed, "A lot different. I've found being involved in this chapel and with a mission in Manila has helped me maintain my faith, even strengthen it. I've had an opportunity to put my faith to the test and bring more faithful into God's flock."

Jim's advocacy was a little overwhelming to Pete who, as a staid Lutheran, didn't flaunt his religion, but he had to admit that what Jim said had merit. Jim offered an alternative to becoming mired in behavior Pete knew his mother would not approve.

When Jim suggested that Pete accompany him for a weekend to the Manila mission, Pete recalled the midnight curfew. "I wouldn't be able to stay overnight."

"You can apply for an overnight pass for mission work. I'll give you the address, phone number of the New Gospel Mission. It'll work, guaranteed."

Pete agreed to accompany Jim if he could get a pass.

Tony and Pete regularly went to the chow hall together when their schedules allowed.

"Hey, just found out my car will be here the end of the month," Tony said one day while they were eating lunch.

Pete didn't know if he heard right. "A car, what are you talking about?"

"Yeah, a 'fifty Ford, has about fifty miles on it."

"You must be on a different pay scale than I'm on."

"My uncle paid for it."

"Now why in the hell would your uncle pay for a new car for you to take to the Philippines?"

"To make money, the car is worth twice as much here as in the states. The Marines ship cars for people whose deployments are longer than a year, also your wife and kids if you have them. I'll sell it after a year, split the profit with my uncle."

"Didn't you hear?" Pete asked. "They're going to ship you to Korea next month."

"By that time my car will be here, and I'll sell it to you, split my share."

The whole idea seemed weird to Pete. "We're sending people to fight a war in Korea and shipping their personal cars along."

Tony didn't think they were shipping them to Pusan. "Even the government wouldn't do something that dumb."

Pete had noticed cars parked in the enlisted men's Quonset hut area but hadn't thought much about it. "What will you do with the car? Cruise around Cavite?"

"We can drive around, go to Manila," Tony answered.

"What about the Huks?" Pete asked. "Heard they own a big part of this island."

"Only during the night," Tony replied

Late in July Pete received a letter from Chris inside one from his mother.

Hi Buddy

I'm sending this letter to my mother and hope it gets back to you. Once we get the addresses figured out we can write directly. Hope things are going well with you. Never did check in with the First Marine Division. When I got to Pendleton they had me check into a brigade being formed to go to Korea. It's been all assholes and elbows since I signed in. We got a physical, shots, new ID card, got rid of a bunch of personal things, got an M1 that's mine to keep. I'm part of a fire team and am getting acquainted with the other three members and the rest of the squad. Tomorrow we will be trucked to San Diego where we will board ships. We won't be going to some Pacific Island with soft breezes and sandy beaches or the Philippines. Looks like I drew the short straw.

Heard it's been hot and dry in South Dakota since we were there. Could be bad for the small grain that should have been in the milk stage about that time. Good for putting up hay.

Have you heard from Lyle? Wonder what he is doing these days. They could be starting up the draft again and he won't be acting so cocky.

Probably be a while before my mail catches up so won't know what is going on back home until it does. I now have a PO address for my mail that I will include at the end of this letter.

Hang in their buddy, things could be worse.

Chris

The Pusan Perimeter boundaries near the end of July 1950

10.

The Pusan Perimeter

Although there seemed to be a lot of confusion when the brigade first arrived at Pusan, Chris figured somebody must have a plan because things did seem to come together in pretty short order. After picking up field packs and ammunition, Easy Company moved out of the harbor area and dug a defensive position on a nearby elevated site. Although they were far from the front lines, they could hear artillery in the distance.

While digging foxholes, Les wondered what stunk. "Smelled it when we got off the ship."

"It's shit," Corporal Hautman replied. "It's precious stuff, they use it for fertilizer. You get used to it, won't smell it after a week."

"Can hardly wait," Les replied.

Not knowing what to expect, the young marines were on edge. During the night their untrained eyes saw bushes begin to move and they heard imaginary sounds. Once, shots rang out. Corporal Hautman, the awake person in the foxhole he and Chris shared, yelled, "You dumb shitheads, knock it off!" It seemed to work. Things soon quieted down.

Early the next morning, the Fifth Regiment's first battalion took off in trucks to act as an advanced guard. In the early afternoon, the second and third battalions boarded antiquated passenger trains. A shrill whistle sounded and the train hauling the second battalion began to move. Brad

Hautman and his team pulled off their packs, parked their weapons, and found seats in the crowded car.

"Where in hell are we going?" Les asked.

Hautman answered, "It'll be hell for sure, but you have to ask the generals what part of hell."

Lots of things new to Chris were happening. He wasn't surprised. Going to war isn't something that happens every day, and it would be a new experience for most of the men in the regiment. Corporal Hautman was an exception.

Chris asked the corporal, "You've done this before. Do you get used to this kind of thing?"

"Hell, no," Hautman answered. "War sucks but it's all I know. I went in when I was seventeen."

"Do you get over being scared?" Adam asked.

"You learn to cope. When we were going into Tarawa and Okinawa, I looked around the landing craft at all these guys and I'm thinking, a lot of these poor sons-a-bitches will be dead before tomorrow, but I never thought it would be me. I'm looking around this car and I'm thinking the same thing."

Hautman's remarks got Adam's attention. "You're not pumping me up."

"Don't worry, kid. For most of you, what they drilled and beat into you at boot camp will take over. You'll be scared shitless but would rather die than let your buddies down or act like a coward. Once we're engaged, you'll forget everything except what's happening around you. Some guys learn to like combat, the ultimate high. It's like a drug, gets addictive. There will be some that can't handle it. Don't know who until the moment of truth. Some big brash guy will cower, while some undersized meek-acting guy will stand tall in the trenches."

The train cars were hot and stuffy, and the marines opened most of the train windows. The tracks were in bad shape the train moved slowly and cars bumped and swayed. Chris took in the scenery. What he assumed were rice fields lay between ridged hills that had terraces running up their slopes until they got too steep to cultivate. From Chris's perspective, some of the hills would qualify as mountains. Farm country, he thought. But not farm country like South Dakota where the hills were smaller and crops were grown all over them. The tops of these hills weren't planted. They were covered with small trees, scrub grass, low bushes, and rocks.

After two hours of slow travel, the train stopped and the second battalion disembarked. A road ran parallel to the railroad, and a village stood some distance down the road. Artillery fire, quite loud, could be heard.

The men of Easy Company moved into an open grass-covered mostly flat area where the rest of the brigade would assemble the next day. Evening approached and the process of setting up a perimeter began. Sergeant Teal stepped off a line to mark where the First Squad would dig six two-man foxholes.

"We'll be on fifty-percent watch status with two-hour watches," he said. "We'll maintain blackout conditions. We're not too far from the enemy and the situation is fluid."

The First Fire Team started digging two foxholes about twenty feet apart. Corporal Hautman and Chris would occupy one hole and Adam and Les the other one. A machine gun crew from the weapons company started digging a hole to the left of Hautman and Chris. They were setting up a heavy 30-caliber machine gun.

It had gotten really hot, and Corporal Hautman and Chris soon worked up a good sweat. Les called out from where he and Adam were digging. "Hey, Corporal, is this where hell is?"

Hautman laughed. "If you need to ask, you ain't there yet." As they dug, the corporal told Chris that the foxhole would be their home in Korea until further notice, so you will be digging a lot of them. The deeper you dig the better." The corporal dug himself a little seat at one end of the foxhole. "Might as well be comfortable when on guard," he said. "We'll be doing two-hour rotations. It's hard to stay alert much longer."

By the time the First Fire Team had their foxholes dug, they began thinking about what they would do for dinner. Before boarding the train, they had been given C-rations intended to last two days. Now they investigated what they had to eat. Corporal Hautman predicted that they would learn to love C-rations.

After Les did an inventory of his rations, he proclaimed, "Beans and franks, love 'em. Somebody can have my cigarettes; don't use 'em."

Adam laughed. "Les is too young to smoke."

After eating, the squad tidied up their area, dug a latrine, and checked and cleaned their weapons. When it grew dark, they sat around and shot the shit for a while, finally settling into their holes after 2200.

Chris found sleep nearly impossible. The newness of his situation activated his mind, and his body wasn't adapted to sleeping with his butt in the dirt and his back up against the foxhole wall. It didn't feel at all like what he believed a bed should be. At 0200, it was his turn for another guard rotation. He stared into the dark. He knew an open field with a few bushes lay out there, but he couldn't see anything. Cloud cover blocked any moon or starlight, and like a dark night in South Dakota, there was little or no ambient light.

Something in the darkness caught his eye. He felt almost certain something had moved. He wasn't going to repeat the previous night's fiasco when the company shot into the dark for no good reason, but he couldn't deny his senses. He put his M1 on the edge of the foxhole and double-checked to be sure he had a clip in it and the safety off. Somebody to his right fired off a round. He raised the M1 to his shoulder and fired next. A fusillade followed. The 30-caliber machine gun in the next foxhole joined in, sending out a stream of tracers. A flare went up to illuminate the field. Visible in the glare of the flare were two very dead cows or oxen. Non-commissioned officers were running around trying to get the marines to stop firing. It took a while for things to settle down and for darkness to take over once again.

The next morning, the First Fire Team squatted near their foxholes eating C-rations and talking about the previous night's activities.

Adam congratulated Chris on killing a couple of cows. "We should be eating beef instead of these C-rations. What happened to those cows?"

Corporal Hautman said some gooks dragged them off early in the day when it got light enough to see. "Maybe they were their cows. Came to find them and there they were, looking like some kinda sieve."

Les hoped the North Koreans would hear that marines shoot anything that moves. "They might think once or twice about sneaking around here."

Adam said he hoped they already knew that.

Chris observed a lot of activity during the day as the brigade started to come together. Tanks, artillery, and transport moved in by rail. Artillery crews drilled and fired off a few rounds to shake out loose ends. Tankers, still sitting on flatcars, fired 90-millimeter guns into some nearby hills to verify their sighting. Helicopters began using an improvised landing site. Flights of F4U Corsairs appeared overhead. A field kitchen had been set up so they wouldn't have to eat C-rations for a while. The regiment command and support units set up tents.

It remained hotter than hell, and the site had no shade. Despite the heat, Lieutenant Ray Cleaver had the First Rifle Platoon out during the hottest part of the day doing some small unit exercises on a nearby hill.

Early that evening, the First Squad returned to the brigade site and lined up for a hot meal being served by the field kitchen. After the meal they went to their foxholes and did personal chores. Corporal Hautman stood gazing to the west where he knew the enemy would be.

"I'll be damned," he said. "Looks like a bunch of NK are digging in on the second ridge to the west."

Other men in the squad jumped to their feet and looked west, Chris among them. Chris picked out what the corporal was looking at. There appeared to be a bunch of people doing something, but they were so far away that he couldn't be sure who they were or what they were doing. They looked to be a mile or two away and in a place where one would expect to find the enemy.

The sight of what was likely the enemy gave Chris a strange feeling. He didn't know those people, didn't like or dislike them, but would kill them if he had the chance. He mused, "I wonder if they are looking at us?"

"If they have eyes, they are," Corporal Hautman replied. "Funny, I've never seen anything like this before. Why aren't we shelling them? Why aren't they shelling us? This ain't Okinawa!"

The next day word drifted down to the squad level that the Marine Fifth Regiment would be going on the attack. The next morning the Third Battalion moved forward in trucks borrowed from the army. Lieutenant Cleaver informed his First Platoon that the Second Battalion would be next. They would move up as soon as the trucks became available, which turned out to be late that night.

Chris took in the sights and sounds of men moving into battle in the middle of the night. He experienced an out-of-body sensation, observing himself in the darkness moving with the rest of the squad as forces beyond their control propelled them towards their destiny, whatever it might be.

As a new day dawned, the Second Battalion arrived at a clutch of buildings, the village of Chingdong. As they disembarked from the trucks, they heard a series of loud explosions. "Mortars," Corporal Hautman muttered. "Feels like old home week."

Les wanted to know how close they were to where the mortar fire was coming from.

"We are talking yards, not miles," Hautman replied.

The situation at the village seemed chaotic to Chris. A mixture of army and marine units were milling around. The easiest way to tell one from the other was the tan lace-up leggings the marines wore versus the boots worn by the army. An aid station had been set up in the village, and Jeeps—converted into ambulances that carried four stretchers each—were bringing in the wounded. A truck filled with corpses in body bags dropped them off near the aid station. Finally, the Second Battalion marines removed themselves from the chaos and to an unoccupied hill north of the village where they set up a defensive perimeter.

No sooner had the battalion gotten the perimeter set up when patrols were sent out to check out the neighborhood. Sergeant Teal's squad was assigned to check out a ridge coming down from higher ground north of the Second Battalion perimeter. The day had started out hot and became hotter. It felt like a hot summer day in South Dakota except they were near the ocean and the humidity made it seem even hotter. The Engelson family had a rule that if the temperature climbed above a hundred degrees, they didn't work in the fields. A hundred degrees in South Dakota didn't feel nearly as hot as this humid air did. Chris couldn't remember heat as uncomfortable as this was.

Les commented that this sure as hell had to be hell, and Hautman agreed.

The squad moved in a ragged line up the ridge over uneven ground covered with rocks and small bushes. Sergeant Teal had urged everyone to drink lots of water, but Chris soon found his canteen empty. Getting enough water became a concern. While shocking grain on the farm, they used to wrap gallon jugs in wet burlap, fill them with cold water, and would drink them dry. He remembered tipping up those jugs and letting the water gurgle down his throat.

The heat and the rough terrain diverted Chris's mind from the fact that he was on his first combat patrol and from the real possibility that they would encounter the enemy. As the squad approached a point where the ridge they were on merged into a large hill, a chatter of machine gun fire refocused Chris's mind. He had wondered how he would react to real combat. Would fear overwhelm him? He found himself focused on doing what he had been thought, what he was observing within his range of vision and how to deal with what he could see. At the same time, he felt the presence of his squad and his dependence on them and each other. And finally, the chain of command began to make some sense. This was no time to debate the decisions of those in the command, from squad to platoon, to company leaders and so on up the chain. At Chris's level, the squad leader gave the orders and squad members carried them out no questions asked.

Suddenly a machine gun opened fire ahead of them and the squad went to the ground. Someone yelled that the point man had been hit. The enemy machine gun continued to fire. Sergeant Teal ordered a withdrawal. Chris and the rest of the First Fire Team laid down small arms fire in the direction of the machine gun while the Second Fire Team dragged the marine that had been hit down the ridge. Chris lay behind a large rock and fired his M1. He couldn't see a target, just fired up the hill towards a place where the machine gun might be. The men dragging the hit marine away from the action passed near Chris's position and he could see the marine had been killed. Only moments earlier he had been alive, full of life and now dead. Dead, Chris felt the permanence of the condition in a way it had never occurred to him before. Chris had only seen one dead person up close before, his grandmother laid out in a fancy coffin. That seemed like a natural occurrence, life lived, then death. Not this.

That evening the Second Battalion lengthened and strengthened the line facing the hills to the north. During the night, North Korean patrols tested the Second Battalion perimeter but didn't mount a serious attack.

The next day the First Fire Team discussed the situation. Corporal Hautman said we and the NK are feeling each other out, probing and being probed.

Chris said he had heard Sergeant Teal and Lieutenant Cleaver talking about waiting for some junction to be cleared by the army taking longer than planned so now the marines were going to help the army get it done.

"Not surprised," Corporal Hautman said, "Marines are always cleaning up army messes."

Chris wasn't so sure. He remembered the village aid station where he saw army wounded and body bags. Those guys were fighting and dying.

That night while Chris had the watch, trip wires set off flares that revealed a mass of North Korean soldiers moving towards the Easy Company line right in front of him. Chris reacted, kicked Corporal Hautman to wake him. There was a standing order to challenge and fire at anything outside of their perimeter and he started firing his Garand into the approaching mass. This wasn't like the day before, firing at unknown targets. These were "can't miss" targets, and Chris knew his shots were killing men. His only emotion as he killed was a fear that they would not be able to kill enough of them before the attackers overran the perimeter. A wall of small arms and machine gun fire did drive the attack back before any NK could penetrate the marine defenses, and the marines suffered only minor losses.

The Hautman's fire team was quiet and subdued the next morning while eating their C rations. Hautman, broke the silence, complained about being woke up in the middle of the night by Chris. "I've got a bruise from where you kicked with that wake-up call. Maybe I can get a purple heart."

Hautman's remarks drew quiet smiles from the rest of the fire team. Adam finally opened up, said they ran out of BAR ammo and Less ran back to get more while he used a M1 to keep killing gooks. "God, unbelievable."

"Looks like we got ourselves a real war" Hautman said, "And we are likely to see a lot worse situations than we saw last night."

Less wondered how it could get worse. "I thought last night was on the high side of worse."

'We were in dug in positions firing automatic weapons at standing up men." Hautman replied, "Don't happen often, not any more. Even if a war is going great from a general's view, it might not be going so good for an infantry platoon's view if it is pinned down by the enemy with no good options. That war is between your platoon and those people trying to kill you while you are trying to kill them. That's war at its worst as far as your squad, your fire team is concerned.

In any case the episode gave the young marines involved a quick introduction to infantry warfare. For Chris the death and destruction he saw disturbed him while on the other hand it built his confidence in the platoon's ability to handle the enemy they faced

On August 8, the Easy Company and the rest of the Second Battalion moved to aid army units assigned to clear the junction so the marines could proceed with their planned attack. Hautman's First Team didn't know anything about the grand strategy involved but did know they would be attacking a hill facing them as the First Battalion maneuvered to get into position for the attack.

Hautman's fire team could hear artillery and see F4U Corsairs working the ground over as they approached the hill. Corporal Hautman told his fire team that they would be attacking today, not defending. It's a little tougher problem in the infantry business.

Les told the fire team that he had decided that flying one of those F4U's would be a better way for him to be fighting this war.

Adam agreed but in about half an hour we will be walking up that hill no matter what we think we would rather be doing

The terrain they faced consisted of grass covered ground with numerous flinty rock outcroppings, a few trees and low bushes slopping up to the top of the hill. The whole Second Battalion started moving forward. The day had already started heating up and the sound of the thump of mortars and small arms fire could be heard. Easy Company was on the right flank of the advance. The Second Battalion moved several hundred yards forward without incident. The First Platoon strung out at the end of the right flank could hear the sounds of heavy fighting further down the line of advance. Lieutenant Cleaver could be seen working the radio and soon ordered Easy Company to continue moving up the hill and flank the enemy behind a ridge. Easy Company continued the advance without any opposition for several hundred yards before turning to move into the flank of the enemy. Soon after making the turn Easy Company ran into resistance and went to the ground and began moving ahead one fire team member at a time while others provided covering fire.

Chris could see movement where the enemy was positioned, and he fired in that direction while Hautman, Les, and Adam took their turns moving forward. When it was Chris's turn to move again he swallowed hard, overcame his mental resistance to exposing himself, rose to a crouching position and dashed forward. He dropped to the ground, relieved that he had succeeded in dodging enemy fire one more time. Other marines weren't as lucky. He could hear cries of pain and calls for corpsmen as the advance continued. Apparently, the marine losses were not acceptable and after about an hour the word come down to back off, pull back and artillery started dropping on close in front of them and F4U's appeared and started dropping ordinance and firing rockets within yards of where Hautman and the First team crouched in the hot sun behind some rocks

While the artillery fire and air support were going on Lieutenant Cleaver had C-rations, and water distributed and more ammunition to anyone who needed it.

The Fire team bunched up to eat their C-rations. Les complained that the Lieutenant hadn't brought any umbrellas for shade.

"How about some lawn chairs so we don't have to sit on the hot, hard ground?" Adam added,

After a long softening-up period word came down to resume the attack. Easy Company found only sporadic resistance moving forward. Apparently, the enemy decided to find safer ground and had withdrawn. The Second Battalion occupied the hill and dug in for the night Lieutenant Cleaver had been wounded during the second attack and had to be taken out of action. The platoon reorganized. Sergeant Peters, leader of the Second Squad and a veteran of island-hopping battles in World War II, replaced Lieutenant Cleaver as leader of Easy Company's First Rifle Platoon.

The First Squad with a normal complement of thirteen men took a head count and found that ten men had survived the day in good enough shape to remain effective. Hautman's fire team hadn't taken any losses

That next day the First Fire Team learned that the junction that had been fought over for three days had finally been cleared and the marines would be able to do what they were supposed to be doing. An Army regiment relieved the marines on the hill and the First and Third Marine Battalions began moving off the hill. The Second Battalion would stay on the hill and hold the hill until the Army Regiment got fully dug in. It was toward evening before the Second Battalion began moving from the hill and were happy to see what looked like a like a mile-long line of trucks waiting to move the move them where ever they were going. Corporal Hautman said a truck driver told him they were heading south towards a town named Kosong. Knowing the name of the destination didn't help

Chris. Another spot on the map, another Korean village. The convey of trucks got rolling at 1800. The trucks ran with their lights on and moved over a poorly maintained paved road at a good pace.

At midnight the trucks pulled up and Hartman's squad dismounted along with the rest of the Second Battalion on a dark road. There was a lot of confusion as the platoons and companies lined up as a Battalion on a very dark night. After the battalion got moving it passed the First Battalion and took the lead.

While passing the First Battalion the First Fire Team heard bitching from some First Battalion grunts how they had been moving on foot all the previous day and half the night. They had done a lot of marching and a little fighting as they advanced, and they were about to collapse. Chris didn't dare tell them they had been taking it easy all day on the hill and had road trucks to catch up with them. Adam agreed it wouldn't be useful to tell them about that.

.

Although strung out in a long column and marching in the dark, it seemed to Chris the squads and companies had maintained their cohesion. At dawn's first light a dozen trucks, Jeeps, and three tanks passed the marching column of Second Battalion marines.

Adam stuck out his thumb. "How about a lift?" he yelled.

Hautman said they were likely moving up an advanced guard. "No use waiting for foot sloggers when there's no opposition."

At 0600 the Third Battalion showed up to take the lead. The Second Battalion now took the rear-guard position. Chris figured the First Battalion was still resting somewhere after their eighteen-hour march the day before.

Though bringing up the rear, the Second Battalion marines had to keep up with the advance. They were unlikely to engage the enemy, and they could take breaks that left some space between them and the next battalion in line, but they still had to cover the distance and not get too far behind.

As the sun climbed, Chris could tell they were in for another brutally hot day. By 1000, he had drunk all the water in his canteen, and the battalion had been on its feet since midnight. Les was walking ahead of Chris, loaded down with everything Chris carried, but as a BAR assistant, he also carried extra magazines of BAR ammunition. Suddenly Les lurched, stumbled, and went down with a thud. Chris hurried to help him up, but Les couldn't stand by himself. He tried but kept falling down. People often talked about heat stroke in South Dakota. Chris had never seen anyone with the condition, but he guessed that must be Les's problem. That and not having had any appreciable sleep during the previous two days.

A corpsman confirmed Chris's diagnosis but called the condition "dehydration." He waved up one of the Jeeps that had been fitted out to haul the wounded.

The rest of the fire team dropped out of the column and waited for the Jeep to pick up Les. When the Jeep arrived, the corpsman and Chris helped Les climb in.

The jeep driver said they had hauled two Jeeploads back to the field dispensary already, "Get a bunch of fluid in 'em and some rest and they'll be good to go in a few hours."

Before taking Les away, the driver handed the fire team a gallon of water. They filled their canteens and had a good drink from the water that remained in the container.

Soon after the Les episode, the column came to a halt. A fire fight could be heard somewhere up ahead. Chris caught himself falling asleep on his feet. Adam stretched out on a grassy spot and immediately fell asleep. After an hour's delay, the column began moving again. They marched past some 105-millimeter howitzer artillery firing in support of their advance, and a while later they saw a flock of F4U Corsairs and P-51 Mustangs attacking something up ahead.

"Damn, what's all the fuss about?" Adam wondered.

Chris didn't know but hoped to God whatever it was would slow down the pace of the advance. He felt about as stretched as he could get and was sure the rest of the squad was in the same condition,

Despite the ominous sounds and sights, it didn't slow down the advance but it wasn't too long before the Second Battalion reached Kosong where it held up and prepared a defensive position for the night. While the First Squad dug foxholes in their section of the perimeter, Les showed up, looking nearly normal after his bout with dehydration and ready to resume his role as BAR assistant. Said he caught a Jeep ambulance coming to get more dehydration victims. Sergeant Teal told Les they had reserved a place for him, and he could help Adam finish their foxhole.

"Gee, thanks," Les said. "I coulda stayed back there, had hot meals, no foxhole, nobody shooting at me."

"Why didn't you?" Adam asked. "Seems like anyone with even a little brain would've figured that out."

"I missed all you assholes." Les replied.

Chris knew that Les had honed sarcasm to a fine art, but believed there was a grain of truth in his remark. The bonds the fire team was forming in combat were running deep.

Les wondered why they were digging in, said he had been looking forward to another all-night march. Hautman figured the regiment had been pushed to the limit of its endurance and needed a rest. "Nah," Les replied. "The brass don't give a shit how tired we are."

Hautman got uncharacteristically serious. "Not true Les, marine officers take care of their men before they take care of themselves."

Les recognized Hautman's tone and concentrated on helping Adam finish digging their foxhole.

The next morning the First Battalion headed the advance. The Second Battalion, refreshed after the overnight halt, trailed them. After moving west of Kosong on the road to Sachon, the First Fire Team saw the reason for the air support activity they had observed the previous day. They found the road littered for miles with destroyed armored vehicles, trucks, Jeep-like vehicles, motorcycles, and the bodies of dead North Koreans.

"Christ!" Corporal Hautman exclaimed. "They must have been caught in the open in broad daylight. Must have been what all that air support was about yesterday afternoon."

As Chris gazed at the dead North Koreans he realized the sight didn't affect him emotionally. The sight of the bloated rapidly spoiling bodies was revolting, but other than that didn't register much differently than observing the other spoils of war. His lack of reaction to this horrific scene bothered him. Had he, within the span of a few days, become immune to the sight of human devastation?

The Second Battalion followed the First Battalion all morning with no delays and no sounds of enemy action. Again, the main concern became fatigue and dehydration due to the fast pace and an increasingly hot day. However, today the First Fire Team noticed that Jeeps hauling water seemed to be more plentiful then before.

Adam remarked that they finally figured out hauling water to the troops made more sense than hauling dehydrated marines back to the aid station.

Les thought adding a few cans of cold beer to the mix once in a while would be another improvement.

Adam laughed. "Les, you aren't old enough to smoke or drink beer."

"I'm old enough to kill gooks," He replied.

Les's remark caused Chris to realize that maybe ninety percent of the marines in Korea wouldn't be able to drink beer legally in most states. Too young to drink beer but old enough to die. Again, Chris pondered the permanence of death. This wasn't a game where one played dead. Dying at any age is a permanent thing.

They continued a fast-paced march with few breaks until 1100 when the sounds of small arms fire and mortars could be heard from somewhere ahead of them. The column came to a halt and the First Fire Team got a welcome break. Soon artillery rounds were passing overhead and exploding in the hills ahead of them near the village of Changchon. F4Us appeared and attacked the same hills. The Second Battalion marines relaxed along the side of the road, sitting, eating C-rations, smoking, and visiting. Ambulance Jeeps passed by on the road, soon returning from the front of the column with casualties, some wounded and some in body bags.

"At least they're ridin'," Les said.

Adam didn't think the ones in body bags cared much, one way or another.

Fighting continued through the afternoon on a narrow front in a narrow valley with high bluffs on either side. Only the First Battalion, at the head of the column, was involved. The Second Battalion dug in for the night on a low hill in the valley expecting that they would be relieving the First Battalion in the morning for the final drive into Sachon.

In the middle of the night, Sergeant Peters alerted the First Platoon that the brigade was beginning an immediate withdrawal and the Second Battalion would become the rear guard.

Hautman woke Chris and the rest of the fire team and informed them of the unexpected order. Chris thought he might be dreaming but soon realized the foxhole he sat in and the people around him were real. At the same time, he could hear a very hot fire fight underway on the hill where the First Battalion had dug in for the night. "What in hell is going on?" he asked, confused.

Corporal Hautman answered, "I can't make any sense out of it. We had the gooks on the run, we're winning this fight."

Adam suggested that Hautman talk to the generals about that. "Talking to privates isn't going to do much good."

Les agreed. "Gotta talk to the general, don't see any suggestion boxes sitting around." Les thought they should put up a sign telling the gooks they can have their damn hills, we're leaving. Chris appreciated the irony of the idea. A lot of dying was going on for nothing.

The next morning, men who looked haggard and drained were coming off the hill where the fire fight had occurred. A sergeant told Corporal Hautman that one of the First Battalion Baker Company platoons had been overrun during the night and had been decimated.

That afternoon the Second Battalion began loading on trucks to be transported to someplace but nobody seemed to know where. Rumors were rampart but nobody seemed to know why the Fifth Regiment stopped attacking or where it would be going. Neither Sergeant Teal, the First

Squad leader, nor Sergeant Peters, the acting First Platoon leader, had been informed of any deployment plans. Finally, Hautman found out where they were going from his usual source, the truck drivers. They were going to a place called Masan.

When they arrived at Masan, Easy Company was told to line up for a hot meal.

"Hot damn, a hot meal!" Les exclaimed. "What next, a hot shower, clean clothes?"

"Don't push your luck," Adam advised.

After a hurried meal, Easy Company boarded a train for Miryang, a staging center for a major battle taking place nearby.

11.
The New Gospel Mission

Early in August, Pete met Jim Haskins at the Sangley Point boat dock at 0800 where they would take a navy boat that ran regularly between the Sangley Point and the Manila Hotel further up the bay. They planned to spend the weekend at the New Gospel mission that Jim Haskins had described when they met at the base chapel a few Sundays previously. Both Jim and Pete were dressed in the civilian clothes favored by Sangley servicemen, white trousers and flowery sports shirts. Not too different from the clothing worn by natives, but the servicemen's size and shoes made them easily identifiable.

The boat ride lasted about half an hour. While they made the crossing, Jim described what they would do at the New Gospel Mission that weekend.

"We will be making up some flyers describing a mission rally coming up in three weeks. An evangelist speaker will be coming over from the states. It's a pretty big deal, and the mission wants to get a good turnout. After we get some flyers printed, we'll start distributing them. We'll be doing that for the next two weekends."

"Sounds like a big job," Pete replied in an absent-minded way. His attention had been diverted by the scene around the boat as it proceeded towards Manila. The boat's route took it through a shallow part of the bay where about a dozen destroyed Japanese war and merchant ships lay on the bottom. Their rusting superstructures protruded out of the water. Pete had followed the news during World War II closely by listening to the radio and reading *Life* magazine and the Sunday edition of the *Chicago Tribune* that his parents subscribed to. That he could see relics of the war that he had read about or seen in pictures with his own eyes excited him.

"How do you suppose all those ships were sunk?" Pete asked Jim.

Jim seemed about as interested in the sunken ships as Pete had been in the flyers. He replied with a non-committal "dunno" and then returned to his subject. "I wonder what would be the best way to distribute those flyers. Wonder what Reverend Beale is thinking." Then he moved to another matter. "Did you have any problem getting an overnight pass?"

"No," Pete replied. "Like you said, no problem."

"As I figured," Jim said. "The Marines would rather have its people doing mission work than whoring and drinking."

The Margaret docked in front of the storied and impressive Manila Hotel, the place General MacArthur had made his headquarters after returning to the Philippines and which had somehow avoided destruction during the war. Jim and Pete flagged a Jeepney to complete their travel to the New Gospel Mission.

Pete remembered pictures in *Life* magazine that showed Manila totally destroyed less than five years ago. It seemed to have been completely rebuilt, but much of the construction looked temporary and slipshod. They did pass one large Catholic cathedral, damaged and in disrepair, but still standing and still impressive.

Pete asked Jim, "Aren't the Philippines mostly Catholic?"

"Ninety percent," Jim answered. "But that's changing. The evangelists are gaining." The answer puzzled Pete. "Is the mission converting Catholics?"

"We aren't converting them. We are giving them a choice, a different way to worship."

Pete thought about Reverend Rickman, who had been the minister of the Lutheran church his family went to for as long as he could remember. He remembered how Reverend Rickman told Pete's confirmation class that the Catholic Church had deviated from the teachings of the Lord and its members would have a problem entering the Kingdom of Heaven. They were Christians, but were being led down a false path. So, Pete knew the issue went deeper than just a different way to worship, but he didn't press Jim any further.

When they arrived at the New Gospel Mission, Pete observed that the large, almost new mission building that appeared more substantial than most of the other buildings in the neighborhood. Jim introduced the missionary, Reverend Beale, and his attractive wife, Diana, to Pete. The Beales, tanned and trim, looked young, maybe thirties or early forties. Reverend Beale said he had to go to an event sponsored by the mission that morning and needed someone to take pictures, so could Jim and Peter join him? He drove them in a sporty new MG with the top down to a small hall where a group of mostly women and young children had gathered. Beale handed out some pamphlets and then talked about the information in the pamphlets in the native Tagalog dialect. As Reverend Beale talked, Jim took pictures with the mission's new 35-millimeter Leica camera. Two native volunteers set up a large bowl of warm rice on a table at the front of the room. After Reverend Beale finished talking, the people in the group lined up and each was given a small bowl of rice sprinkled with cinnamon and sugar.

While driving back to the mission, Reverend Beale talked about the event. "The bowl of rice is what draws them," he said. "Without the rice we wouldn't get very many. If we start getting too many, we will restrict the rice to only the children. Jim, did you get any good pictures?"

"Think so," Jim replied. "Took a bunch of them."

"Good. We'll send some of the good ones to our sponsors."

Pete and Jim joined Reverend Beale and his wife in the mission for lunch. The missionaries' living quarters in the large mission building were up-to-date in every way. The meal prepared by a Filipino cook and served by a Filipina maid proved to be a substantial improvement over navy fare. Pete found it difficult to reconcile his previous image of missionary life with what he witnessed at the New Gospel Mission. He had imagined missionaries occupying huts in the jungle, living the life of the people being converted. It seemed his image needed updating.

Preparing and printing the rally flyer took up the afternoon. That night, Pete and Jim slept in the mission dormitory where they found six neatly made up bunk beds. They were the only people in the dormitory. Jim said the dormitory was used almost exclusively by U.S. servicemen.

The next day, stacks of flyers were delivered to Filipino volunteers who were to distribute them. Jim wanted to be involved in the distribution, so decided that he and Pete would go out and put flyers directly into the hands of people on the street. Jim decided they should roll the flyers into tight cylinders and put rubber bands around them so that people would be more likely to unroll and read them. The cylinders could also be fired out of a Jeepney like missiles. Pete felt uncomfortable with personal proselytizing, but he didn't want to offend Jim so didn't object.

By ten o'clock Sunday morning, Jim and Pete had rolled up a bunch of flyers and put them in a satchel. They went out on the street and Jim began pushing the flyers into the hands of people, saying, "Tanganan bumasa. Take read." Jim and Pete, both stark white and at least a head taller than any of the natives, stood out like bright lights. Pete wondered what the natives thought of these strange-looking people and tried to look as small as he could.

After Jim had approached most of the people in the immediate area, he hailed a Jeepney and they piled in. There were already four passengers in the Jeepney. Jim thrust flyers in their hands and instructed them to "Tanganan bumasa." The passengers looked at him strangely and then off into space, acting as if he weren't there. Jim turned his attention outside the Jeepney and started firing the flyers from the Jeepney at people on the sidewalk. Having run out of Tagalog phrases, he shouted in English, "Come to the rally! Be saved!"

Pete sensed that the Jeepney driver and the other passengers wished Jim would disappear. Pete had similar feelings. The Jeepney stopped at a square where an open market had attracted a large number of people. Two of the Filipino passengers got out.

Jim punched Pete on the shoulder. "Hey, we'll get off here, too. Lots of people."

Pete's inner self took over. "Go ahead," he said. "I'm going back to Sangley."

Jim looked surprised. "What! Why?"

"I just can't do this kinda thing."

"What kind of Christian are you?" Jim asked. "A fake, afraid to show your faith?" Jim swung off the Jeepney and headed into the crowd.

On the boat back to Sangley, Pete pondered his decision to return to the base. The decision was a spontaneous reaction to his discomfort with spreading the word of God. Was he what Jim described, a fake Christian? Weren't real Christians supposed to spread the word as part of their faith?

A person reading a book sat next to Pete. Although he wore civilian clothes, Pete identified him as a sailor by his highly polished black shoes.

The sailor put down his book and asked Pete what he had been doing in Manila. "Spent the weekend at the New Gospel Mission," Pete replied.

"You're an evangelical?" the sailor asked.

"Lutheran," Pete replied.

"Same thing," the sailor said. "I used to be an evangelical, Baptist. Now I'm a fanatical atheist."

Pete looked at the sailor. He knew about atheists, but had never known anyone who said they were one before.

The sailor expanded on his views. "I come from a small town where everybody was, or at least claimed to be, a Christian. Except for a few misguided renegades, everybody in the town was headin' for heaven. At the time, I thought that was normal, that the earth is occupied by Christians and a few heathens who were headed for an eternity in hell.

"After being around a while, after being in the navy, I realized half the people on the earth hadn't heard about Jesus, and another quarter of the people who had heard of him had other ideas about God. My church had taught me that anyone who didn't accept Jesus would burn in hell. I began to think about that. What about all those people living or dead that hadn't ever heard of Jesus? What about those that lived and died before Jesus showed up? Will they burn in hell through no fault of their own?"

Pete listened, hardly comprehending what the sailor had said. "You're talking beyond me," he said. "I figure that's what preachers are for, to figure out those kinds of things."

"You're right," the sailor answered. "That's why I figure most preachers and priests are stealth atheists. They think about these kinds of things all the time. Most of them grow up sheltered until they are ordained, pumped full of Christian doctrine and beliefs. Most of them are intelligent and learn about things not taught in the seminaries. They learn things that would cause them to question what they've been taught."

When Pete got off the boat at Sangley Point, he was overwhelmed by the thoughts churning through his head. He had been called a fake Christian and then introduced to atheism during the past few hours. One of the pillars of his life had been shaken, and he felt confused by what he had done, seen, heard, and felt during the day.

F4U Corsairs, Marine air support workhorses during the Korean War

A Marine M26 Pershing tank

Browning Automatic Rifle (BAR)

Images on this page are in the public domain downloaded from Wikimedia Commons.

12.

The Naktong Bulge

Miryang appeared to be a semi-permanent base to Chris, and it looked like good farm land had been appropriated for the base site. The type of land that was not too plentiful, from what he had seen.

A large tent city of squad-sized tents with wood floors made a welcome change from the foxhole accommodations Chris and the rest of the squad were becoming used to. There were showers and a place where they could wash their clothes by hand and hang them to out to dry.

Adam said he could get used to this, then added, "Les, you got the rest of your wish list filled, showers and clean clothes."

"Don't get too used to it," Corporal Hautman warned. "Hear we are we are moving out tomorrow."

"What?" Adam protested "Won't have time to dry my clothes."

After a night of uninterrupted sleep, the First Squad waited for Sergeant Peters to return from an early-morning briefing. He confirmed that they were to be ready to move out in the early morning hours the next day. He had found out the reason for the quick redeployment. The North Koreans had crossed the Naktong River about a week ago, punching a hole in the Pusan Perimeter., The army had been trying to contain them and drive them back without much success. "Our job is to push the NK back across the Naktong."

They did have mail call, the first since arriving in Korea. They cleaned their weapons, washed or replaced hard-worn clothing, and ate hot meals for one whole day.

Chris received a handful of letters from his mother and two from Pete. The grain crops around Milbank were ready to harvest and looked better than expected, and recent rains had raised hopes for a decent corn crop. Pete's letters were mostly about what Pete had been doing on liberty, not much about what he did as a marine. Pete's letters reminded Chris he had only been on liberty once since joining the Marines and that was when he and Pete visited Tijuana with Tony and Sam after the four of them got out of boot camp. His original vision of life in the Marines had been more like what Pete was doing rather than what had been happening in Korea. Circumstances matter. Chris suspected that some of his experiences were probably more exciting than what Pete had to endure, if getting shot at could be considered exciting.

He had time to write a letter to his folks to let them know that, though the scenery was different, Korea's summer weather reminded him of South Dakota. He also wrote a letter to Pete.

Chris, who had been immersed in reading and journal writing while the *Clymer* carried a portion of the First Provisional Marine Brigade across the Pacific Ocean, he had hardly had time to blow his nose since landing in Korea two weeks earlier. Before leaving the ship, he had placed a small notepad for journal entries and a paperback copy of Hemingway's *A Moveable Feast* into his backpack. But once he reached Korea, he hadn't opened the book and had made just three short entries in the journal that recorded only his location and the date.

On the evening of August 16, the Fifth Marine Regiment began to move to a forward position. To Chris it looked like everything the Fifth Regiment owned was moving, supporting artillery, tanks, Infantry

Sergeant Peters informed the First Platoon that because of a shortage of trucks the infantry would be moving up one Battalion at a time. The Third Battalion left first in the middle of the night. The Second Battalion, which would be leading the attack on a number of hills known as the Obong Ridge, loaded into the trucks at 0400.

Corporal Hautman became a little perplexed when they were dropped off at the U.S. Army garrison at Yongsan, about a forty-five-minute march from where the attack would begin. "We don't need a warm up" he complained.

Chris couldn't forget Hautman's earlier words about going into combat when he looked at the young men forming up to march off to battle: "Some of these poor bastards will die today, but it won't be me." The words now had a deeper meaning to Chris since he had experienced battle and the death of fellow marines.

The Second Battalion moved up to the line of departure at 0730 as a barrage of artillery announced their intention to attack the Obong Ridge. The Obong Ridge stood out from the surrounding hills by being higher than other terrain in the surrounding area. The ridge was covered by dry grass a thin mixture of shrubs and small pine trees. The artillery preparation only lasted a short time, maybe fifteen minutes. Corporal Hautman thought the artillery attack was pretty meager. "Like a warning shot across the bow," he said.

A follow-up attack by a swarm of F4U Corsairs seemed more intense and lasted longer than the artillery barrage, but it didn't impress Hautman who expressed the opinion that artillery is the way to prepare for an infantry attack.

Chris thought the Corsairs were doing a pretty good job.

"Can't replace artillery," Hautman replied authoritatively.

After the air attack, the Second Battalion headed across a series of rice paddies on foot to attack the ridge. The setting caused Chris to remember reading about marines in World War I who advanced through a wheat field swept by machine gun fire in the battle of Belleau Wood. The rice in the paddies stood waist high and had started to turn golden like wheat ripening in a South Dakota field.

However, where wheat grew on dry land, the rice stood in water. Les let out a yelp when he stepped into a pond and sank into water and mud over his ankles. "Snakes," he yelled. "Big snakes."

Adam confirmed Les's observation that the paddy water provided a home for some healthy-looking snakes. Adam also reminded Les what the farmers used for fertilizer.

"Shit!" Les exclaimed, "And no showers."

The fire team tried to stay on the dykes bordering the paddies, but they were narrow and not designed to provide a dry crossing for a marine battalion. Fortunately, unlike Belleau Wood, machine guns were not sweeping the paddies.

When they reached the ridge, the Second Battalion started up the base of a hill when sniper fire was encountered. Calls for Medics began to be heard. The sniper fire was ignored as Easy Company continued to move up the hill. Easy Company had advanced nearly half way up the hill when machine guns from intersecting positions began raking the location and took an immediate toll of standing advancing marines. The First Squad went to the ground. None of Hautman's First Fire Team had been hit in the first bursts of machine gun fire. They hugged the ground, not sure where the enemy fire originated from or what to do about it. The small shrubs and pine trees scattered about made it difficult to locate enemy emplacements. Chris pointed his M1 Garand rifle up the hill and fired in the direction of where he thought the enemy might be. Machine gun fire continued to sweep the slope, keeping the marines pinned down. More of them were hit, and the wounded could be heard calling for help.

Sergeant Teal exposed himself, ran crunched over to where the First Fire team lay on the ground firing at the unknown. He shouted, "I see one of the guns. Follow me!" Bent down low, Sergeant Teal started forward and as if pulled by a magnet, the First Fire team followed. Sergeant Teal sprinted forward in a crouched position. He suddenly stopped, stood erect and then fell forward. The fire team went to the ground and Chris could see they were very close to the machine guns position. He pulled a hand grenade off his belt and heaved it towards the target. He saw two machine gunners scramble when the grenade landed in their dug-in position. The grenade exploded, and the First Fire Team ran forward firing into the emplacement as they moved and tumbled in on top of two dying North Koreans. The next thing Chris saw were hand grenades tumbling down the hill towards them. One of the grenades fell into the emplacement. Hautman picked it up and threw it back towards where it came from, and it exploded in mid-air. Another grenade exploded on the edge of the emplacement, and Chris felt a sharp pain in his back. The grenade throwers then charged down the hill towards the fire team, but Adam blew them away with his BAR.

After the attack subsided, Les exclaimed, "Chris, the back of your shirt is all bloody!"

Chris had forgotten the pain he felt when the grenade went off on the edge of the hole. Hautman suggested Chris go back and find a corpsman, but Chris declined. "Hell no," he said, I'm not leaving this frigen hole. I might get killed.

The First Fire Team took stock. Sergeant Teal lay on the ground badly wounded or dead while the fire team members had survived the melee intact except Chris who had a bloody back. Although ahead of the line of attack they were in a dug-in position capable of holding all of the fire team members and Corporal Hautman said they would stay put until the attack got moving again. They tidied up their position by removing the two North Korean bodies growing cold. They placed them on the uphill side of the hole to give them further protection from down-slope fire. Chris noted that each of the NK had taken multiple bullets during the First Fire Team charge in addition to grenade shrapnel. They had not suffered a slow death.

They removed the enemy machine gun which had been damaged beyond repair during the attack on the position. Adam had his entrenching shovel out and was making some emplacement improvements.

Enemy mortar shells were falling on the marines stalled on the slope of the hill below them. Friendly mortars were plowing up the landscape ahead of them. The First Fire Team's position seemed to be in a "no man's land" with both friendly and enemy mortar rounds passing over them.

On the other hand, friendly artillery and F4U ordinance was hitting the ground uncomfortably close in front of them. All this activity seemed to be keeping the North Koreans hunkered down in their holes. Hautman complained that they were doing the softening up now they should have done this morning. Chris didn't much care when the mortars, artillery, and planes pounded the enemy. Anytime seemed like a good time to him.

Despite the pounding the enemy was taking they continued to rake the slope where Easy Company found itself stuck. Their attention turned to Sergeant Teal, laying a short distance from their hole. Although he hadn't moved they didn't know if he was badly wounded or dead. If he was wounded they could try bringing him into their hole since there didn't seem to be any medics this far up on the hill. Hautman questioned whether or not to take the risk. In their situation Hautman didn't want to lose any more men. While considering the situation Les suddenly crawled out of the hole and down to where Sergeant Teal lay. A short time later he returned. "Sergeant Teal is turning cold," he said.

The softening-up barrage and air strikes let up around 1600 and the NK machine guns had also quieted down. "Did the NK pull back?" Corporal Hautman wondered aloud." Chris noted everything seemed to have gotten awful quiet. "What's happing? He asked. They soon could hear and see marines moving up the hill and the NK machine guns were still quiet. They made themselves visible as the advancing marines bypassed their position. They found out that the advancing marines were from the First Battalion and were reliving the Second Battalion.

Corporal Hautman said they better get out of their hole and see if they could and find their platoon. "That might take a while. Chris you go to an aid station, get your back taken care of or at least get a clean shirt. That's an order, stay at the aid station until someone from our fire team comes to lead you back to the platoon."

As Chris headed for an aid station he went through the area where the Second Battalion had stopped their advance and where medics were working on wounded and where others had begun picking up those beyond the need for medics. It appeared to Chris that the Second Battalion had taken heavy losses during the clash with the NK.

Chris asked a corpsman working on the wounded where the nearest aid station was.

"What's your problem?" The corpsman asked.

"Grenade shrapnel in my back." Chris explained.

The corpsman took a look at Chris's back and told him to go to the bottom of the hill and check into the Brigade Aid station. "You've got a bunch of shrapnel in there, not deep. While you're going down, could you help carry a litter down to the aid station? We have a backlog of wounded and KIA (Killed in action)."

Because of the distance and terrain four men were being used to move litter wounded down the hill. Chris helped two corpsmen and another walking wounded carry a marine that looked like a teenager down the hill. The poor kid moaned all the way. The corpsman said he couldn't give him morphine because he had been wounded in the stomach. The aid station had men on litters lined up waiting for attention. Chris, classified as walking wounded, waited at the end of the line. Filled body bags were stacked off to one side of the aid station. Helicopters were carrying out the more seriously wounded two at a time.

Chris tried to stay out of the way of as corpsmen and doctors worked sometimes methodically and sometimes frantically on the seriously wounded. Chris had time to reflect on what he was seeing while he waited. He had read a lot about war in magazines and newspapers during WWII which had ended only a few years ago. It looked exciting, Men charging a beach, formations of bombers battling enemy fighter planes, navy ships steaming in formation. This was real war, dirty, bloody, young men wounded, dying. That charge on the machine gun emplacement this afternoon, following the Sergeant into deadly fire without hesitation, without thinking. What had happened to him, who he had become?

It was getting dark when Les showed up and said they had found their platoon and squad. It was a while later that a that a very tired young doctor looked at Chris's back and pronounced it to be a minimal-cost Purple Heart wound. A corpsman cleaned Chris's back with some alcohol smelling stuff and then dug out the shrapnel, applied bandages and told Chris to have the platoon corpsman change the bandages as needed. Then the corpsman told Chris he was free to go. Before leaving, Chris talked the corpsman into getting him a clean shirt.

Les waited as Chris was being cared for and then led him back to where the First Squad had dug in. He was given a C-ration and wolfed it down, realizing he had not eaten since very early that morning.

The Second Battalion had been put in reserve status, giving it a chance to lick its wounds and reorganize. Corporal Hautman had the numbers. Nearly half the members of Easy Company had been killed or wounded in the morning fighting. Every fire team had at least one casualty, including the First Fire Team if Chris's minor wounds were counted.

Corporal Hautman replaced Sergeant Frank Teal who had been killed when he led the charge on the machine gun emplacement early in the day, and Chris became the new leader of the First Fire Team. This left the First Fire Team short of a rifleman.

That night, shortly after Chris had assumed the watch at 0200, he heard the sounds of a furious fire fight going on high on the ridge. After about a couple of hours things quieted down. In the morning the First Fire team found the Second Battalion would be moving up at ten hundred to occupy some hill. When they moved up they had to pass through the ridge top to get to the hill they were to occupy. As the First Fire Team moved through the ridge top Chris noted that the top of the ridge had been reshaped by the pummeling of exploding ordinance the previous day and unrecovered bodies of unburied North Koreans and dead marines lay everywhere. Apparently, all of the wounded had been removed. Chris noted the smell, a mixture of spent ordinance and flesh. The Engelson family butchered every year in the early winter, and Chris recognized the slightly sweet smell of newly killed flesh and also the putrid smell of animals that had died and not been disposed of soon enough. What Chris smelled was a combination of the sweet and putrid.

Les, not familiar with the smell, wanted to know what it was. Corporal Hautman, the newly appointed squad leader who still dug in with the First Fire Team, answered, "Dead people. That's the smell of a good day's work by an infantry regiment. It'll get stronger after the day warms up'"

Les said that seemed to be another good reason not to get killed. The Second Battalion found the hill they were to occupy abandoned and with lots of fighting holes already dug and ready for use. The hill provided a good view of the Naktong River and which was within the range of some of their heavier weapons. That afternoon the marine heavy weapons made life hazardous for North Korean stragglers attempting to retreat back across the river.

Corporal Hautman joined the First Fire Team when they broke out C-rations for dinner. Talk turned to why the marines were here getting eaten up in the fight for this ridge of dirt.

Corporal Hautman had an opinion, said it's a wonder why the army ever lost these hills, high ground looking down on a narrow valley cut by a wide river. I guess it can be waded, but it's still a pretty big barrier. The army has been trying to get these hills back for over a week, and the marines got up here in a day. Well, a day and part of another day. What's wrong with those guys?"

One of the letters Chris got from his mother brought the news that Arnold Schultz, a neighbor boy who had gone to the same one-room school he and Pete attended, had been killed in Korea. Chris was shocked by the news that this little boy, as Chris remembered him, had been killed here in Korea. Arnold had joined the army right out of high school, probably for the same reason he and Pete joined the Marines. Arnold had been stationed in Japan and was among the first to go to Korea.

When Chris responded to Corporal Hautman's question, he had Arnold in mind. "I don't think those soldiers are any different people than marines. They grew up in the same kinds of places, did the same kinds of things we did."

Corporal Hautman agreed. "Can't blame the dog faces but you can question the training and leaders."

Chris suggested that maybe all the fighting the army had done during the past week had knocked some of the piss and vinegar out of the NK before the marines took them on.

Adam disagreed, noting that the NK seemed to still have plenty of piss and vinegar when we ran into them yesterday.

The Second Battalion had barely moved into their new bivouac when the First Fire Team heard they would be moving out the next day to parts unknown.

Les said he had hoped they would be staying where they were for a while. Nice view of the river, foxholes dug by the NK, nicer than we would ever dig.

Adam agreed, bet the army will move back in after we cleaned out the NK.

Chris admonished, "Stop thinking, remember all we have to know is how to salute, say yes sir and that payday is going to happen someday."

Adam laughed, "That is supposed to be my line. Stop using my fucking lines.

The next morning as the First Fire Team prepared to leave, a unit of the Army Twenty-Fourth Division began moving in.

"See," Adam said, "What'd I tell you?

Chris answered that one didn't have to be a psychic to figure that one out.

Les raised his eyebrows, "Stop using fancy words like psychic to confuse normal people. You mean mind reader, right." They were interrupted by Corporal Hautman ordering the First Squad to get in line to move out.

The next day the First Fire Team along with First Provisional Brigade found themselves at a base near Mason to refit and fill its depleted ranks with replacements, A reserve marine corporal named Dan Fleming became the First Fire Team's rifleman, the position held by Chris before he became the First Fire Team leader. Corporal Hautman made the decision to maintain PFC Chris Engelson as the First Fire team leader rather than the higher-ranked Fleming because Chris had three weeks of combat experience and Dan had none. Dan was okay with that having joined the Marine Reserve to help pay for college and had little interest in rank. The Marines must have been running low on first and second lieutenants because Sergeant Peters had not been relieved of his acting platoon leader assignment.

Chris and Dan hit it off right away. About the same age, neither was excited about fighting a war but would do what had to be done. Dan stood less than six foot, didn't look athletic but had no trouble doing what a rifle man does. He had grown up in northern California where his family ran a small grocery and convenience store at a rural intersection where there were a few houses and a fruit-packing plant

When the First Fire Team arrived at their new location they had hoped to have some real rest and relaxation. The had large floored squad sized tents, running water, real bath facilities, ate hot meals and got two cans of beer a day. Pretty close to heaven for marine infantry coming out of combat. However, the First Fire Team was disappointed about the rest and relaxation part when Sergeant Peters informed the Platoon that revelry the next morning would be at 0500, and they would have two hours to shit, shin and shave, have breakfast and be ready to begin four hours of combat training at 0700, "Fuck," Les said, "I need combat training like a hole in the head."

"It's not for assholes like us," Adam explained. "It's for the new guys like Dan."

"Yeah," Dan agreed. "It's for us fat, dumb replacements."

"Maybe," Les said. "But you're not going to learn about combat from any kind of training anyone can think of."

There were no real liberty opportunities. The nearby town had few attractions other than some prostitutes who, for a price, serviced a large portion of the brigade.

Chris got letters from his mother and he wrote letters to his folks and Pete. He also had a chance to update his journal.

The brigade had been in the area a little over a week when on September 1 First Fire Team learned the First Provisional Brigade had been ordered to return to the Naktong Bulge that they had recently cleaned up and do it again.

"What the fuck is going on?" was Les's question when he heard where they were going and for what reason.

It also seemed incredible to Chris. Once, okay, but twice in the same place?

Adam thought the army would be to embarrassed, no fucking shame.

Chris had defended the army during discussion like this previously. He couldn't this time.

On September 3, the First Marine Provisional Brigade launched a repeat attack on now-beat up terrain above the Naktong River. After two days of intense fighting, often in pouring rain, and after heavy losses on both sides, the marines again pushed the North Koreans out of the bulge.

Chris and Dan were foxhole mates, and Chris, now the combat veteran, became Dan's mentor. Chris passed on some of the wisdom he had learned from experience and from Corporal Hautman. After two days of combat, some of it pretty intense, Chris pronounced Dan combat ready.

Dan commented that it was a skill he hadn't planned to acquire. "I knew the reserves could go active but who would think another war would be coming along so soon?"

Chris could sympathize. "I wasn't thinking about war when I joined. I thought the world had gotten war out of its system for a while. So here I am, too-late smart. What can I say? I'm a volunteer."

On September 8, the First Provisional Brigade moved directly from the Naktong River front to Pusan where the marines learned they would be loading on ships and sailing in five days.

While in Pusan, Chris picked up a copy of the military newspaper *Stars and Stripes* where he read that the GI Bill had been extended to include Korean War veterans. Chris didn't see this information as significant to him, but mentioned it to Dan.

Dan said it sounded like a hell of a good idea, if he lived to collect. "Sure as hell better than the active reserve."

On September 13, the First Provisional Brigade loaded onto ships and became part of the First Marine Division headed for an unknown destination.

Les quipped, "I'll bet we're going to Japan for R and R."

Chris guessed they wouldn't be hauling tanks and artillery on an R and R trip to Japan.

Les had to admit it wouldn't make much sense.

13.

A Long Way from the War

In late August, Pete received a letter from Chris.

Hi Buddy

We are in Miryang, a place sometimes called the Bean Patch. This is just a stopover while moving from one battlefield to another. Just time enough to take a shower and write a letter to lucky you.

I'm learning firsthand what war is about. Let me tell you, it's a bitch. Pitching bundles don't compare. The ship I came over on is the George Clymer. It and a bunch of ships made up a convoy that hauled the whole First Provisional Marine Brigade, men, tanks, artillery with all their stuff across the big lake. The brigade has an air support wing too which came over on a carrier. We were on the cramped Clymer for almost three weeks. The most exciting thing to do was go up on deck and look at the ocean. Besides the ocean we could see how big a convoy it takes to haul a brigade somewhere. It's big, lots of troop ships and ocean-going landing craft.

I read a dozen or so books while on the ship and started writing a journal. It really helped make the time pass. I'm still trying to maintain a journal but it's been pretty much hit and miss since arriving in Korea. Seldom enough sleep, some days no sleep.

First, they said we would land in Japan before going to Korea. Guess they were having problems in Korea that couldn't wait and we went straight to Pusan. There are limited dock facilities at Pusan and ships were waiting to unload but we must have had priority and started unloading as soon as we got here.

We took a beat-up train to a place thirty miles west of Pusan and after a few days saw our first fire fight. It's confusing and can be life threatening. Actually, I felt more scared before getting into a shooting situation than when we were in the middle of it. I don't believe you ever become fearless in this business, but you learn to cope. We had the NK on the run when we were suddenly pulled out and regrouped in the Bean Patch, getting set to fill some holes in the line the army is having trouble maintaining.

Besides the war, not much going on here. Hope the battle for Cavite is going well.

Your buddy

Chris

Pete read the letter half a dozen times. In a way he envied Chris, doing what marines are supposed to do. Doing guard duty when real marines were fighting a war seemed like being something less than a man. Pete realized somebody had to do the guarding, and also, he wasn't sure how he would handle combat. Knowing Chris pretty well, Pete could tell from his letters that Chris had adapted to the situation. Pete also sensed that Chris had matured pretty fast in the past few weeks.

Tony had been busy. For one thing, his car had arrived. He also seemed to be spending a considerable amount of his free time with Maria, the mestiza hostess at the Kitty Kat.

"What's going on with you and Maria?" Pete asked one day when they were eating lunch in the chow hall. "You seem to be spending a lot of time with her, ignoring your friends. How about all this driving around Luzon we were talking about before you got your car?"

"Given a choice between spending time with Maria or driving around Luzon with you, what do you think I should do?" Tony asked.

"Really, whatta ya got going there?"

"The best piece of ass in Cavite," Tony answered.

"How do you know?" Pete asked.

Tony laughed. "You know, it just kind of happened. Maria asked me if I could get her something at the commissary. Sure, why not? She invited me to her place. She shares a place with her younger sister not too far down the street from the Kitty Kat. Before you know it, we're in the sack. Once you get a taste it's hard to leave it alone. Pretty soon I'm bringing more stuff from the commissary, helping pay the rent."

"You asshole, you're shacking with Maria."

Tony agreed. "Somebody has to do it. We'll have a party sometime so you can meet the sister. Pretty nice except for the soldier thing."

"Whatta ya mean, soldier thing?"

"The sister has something going with a soldier, but he's never around. Off on some island doing some kind of survey."

The following Sunday, Tony hailed Pete as he returned from church. "How'd you like to go to the beach, have a picnic with the Mendez sisters? You can meet Alisa."

"I got a really busy schedule," Pete replied. "Go to the club, have a couple of beers, take a nap, but I maybe I could squeeze it in."

"Good," Tony said. "I'll pick you up around 1600."

Pete liked Tony's car. The 1950 Ford had the same no-fenders design as the Houser family Studebaker Pete had wrecked before joining the Marines. "I need one of these," he told Tony. "Gotta start saving some money."

Pete's first impression of Alisa, Maria's younger sister, exceeded Tony's description of her as "pretty nice." Alisa had many of Maria's attributes, but in a more refined sort of way. She was smaller and shorter, but with a well-developed female form, a doll-like face, large brown eyes, and dark brown hair with a natural curl.

At the beach, they emptied the contents of a picnic basket, two bottles of local rum and sandwiches, onto a blanket. The sun dropped below the horizon while they were eating, and darkness enveloped them suddenly as it does in the tropics. After they finished off the last bottle of rum, Maria suggested they go swimming.

Manilla Bay's water is far from clear blue and Pete had doubts about swimming in it.

Is it safe?" Tony asked.

"It's okay, just don't drink it," Maria replied, "Philippine's swim in it all the time."

Pete still had some doubts "Maybe Philippine's have a tolerance," he said.

"Oh come on" Alisa said as she peeled off her dress and revealed a swimsuit underneath. Tony said he hadn't brought a swimsuit and neither had Pete. Maria said they could wear their underwear, if they had any. They took Maria's advice and stripped down to boxer shorts.

Alisa waded out and Pete followed her into the shallow water that seemed to extend a long way into the bay. There was a large rock protruding out of the water and they decided to move toward it. The water was about chest high at the rock and they decided to crawl onto it. The rock was roomy and had a flat top where they sat and enjoyed the warm tropical air. Alisa started talk about her family. "Our mother moved us to Cavite from Manila after our house and just about every other house in the city was destroyed during the Battle for Manila. We lost everything except our lives. Seems like a long time ago, but it's only been five years. Things can change fast in a war."

Pete realized the Mendez sisters knew more about war than he did or probably ever would. "How is your mother?" he asked.

"She died two years after we moved to Cavite. Maria and I were teenagers on our own. I want to go back to Manila someday. Maria and I have applied for airline hostess jobs with the Philippines Airlines. They fly around the Philippines and to Los Angeles. We speak Spanish, English, and Tagalog. Maybe I'm dreaming, but I want to believe we have a good chance."

"How soon will you know?" Pete asked.

"We just put in our applications, but soon, I hope. What about you? What's happened in your life?"

Good question, Pete thought, nothing as difficult or stirring as the Mendez sisters had experienced, and his future was still a mystery. "Not much, sort of drifting."

Alisa slipped into the water and called for Pete to join her. He joined her. Alisa was going through some gyrations, came up with her swimsuit and laid it on the rock. Pete forgot about the quality of the water and just about everything else. He pulled off his shorts, Alisa pressed against him. Pete lost his virginity while standing chest deep in Manila Bay's dirty water and with his back pushed against a rock. After the picnic, Pete visited Alisa at every opportunity, with or without Tony. He found himself bringing things Alisa wanted from the commissary and helping out with the rent.

The foursome started doing things together. Tony and Pete would bring the sisters onto the base as their guests to spend evenings at the enlisted men's club where different things were going on almost every night. There were dances, and the Mendez sisters loved to dance. They tried to teach Pete how to dance, with some success. Other diversions the club offered were movies, bingo, and, for many of its patrons, a lot of heavy drinking. In the evening when the day cooled down, the foursome enjoyed sitting on the large patio at the back of the club while drinking cold San Michaels. The patio protruded out into the bay and overlooked the Sangley Point sea plane facilities. Live bands from Manila replicating "big band" sounds would sometimes perform on the patio. Pete enjoyed watching native folk music and dancers in costume performing native dances. While watching these activities one evening, Pete mentioned how weird it seemed to be sitting drinking beer in the company of attractive women and being entertained while other marines in Korea were being shot at and feeling thankful when they got an occasional hot meal, shower, and change of clothes.

Maria didn't think there was anything strange about the situation. "It's always been that way, men in wars always fight hard, play hard, drink hard, love hard. But not all marines do all those things. Some fight hard, some drink hard, some play hard, some love hard, some die."

Tony said he liked the part he had, wouldn't trade it, especially for the fighting and dying kinds of things.

Pete often had an urge to be in Korea in the middle of things with Chris, but kept it private. Would he feel the same way if they tapped him on the shoulder and told him he was going to Korea?

The foursome began traveling to Manila in Tony's car. The trip took about an hour over a bumpy paved road. In Manila, they attended mestizo activities and ate at good restaurants that were too expensive for ordinary Filipinos but affordable for even low-ranked U.S. servicemen. They also went to Jai Alai games, a sport the Mendez sisters were fans of because they had become acquainted with some of the players through their mestizo and Spanish connections. Pete had never heard of the game but had started to get into it after watching a few times. Jai Alai games and some mestizo community activities presented a problem. These events took place in the evening so they had to travel back to Cavite after dark. The marines had been warned that the Huks were active in the area at night, but after a couple of uneventful trips, Tony and Pete's concerns waned and the foursome often drove to Manila for evening events.

Pete's world had settled into a satisfying routine. He often thought about Chris and how chance, or the luck of the draw, had determined their different circumstances. Pete hadn't gotten a letter from Chris in over a month, and he had become worried about his well-being. The Inchon landings and the fighting in Seoul were in the news, and marines were doing the bulk of the fighting.

Early in October, Tony, Pete, and the Mendez sisters traveled to Manila for a Jai Alai game. Before the game, they stopped to eat at the Más Grande, a Mexican restaurant Tony had discovered. At the game, Pete felt especially adventurous. He risked five pesos at the pari-mutuel betting window and ended up winning fifteen. He bet five pesos on the next game and won seven more.

"Keep going," Tony advised. "You're hot."

Pete felt the excitement, but also sensed that he had moved out of his comfort zone. "Nah," he said. "It's too easy."

"You sound like a damn Mexican," Tony replied. "It isn't real money if you haven't worked your ass off earning it. Here, I'll give you five pesos. Bet it for me."

Pete did, and lost it on the next game.

Tony philosophized. "Pete's money, Pete's luck. My money, my luck."

After the games, Maria and Alisa wanted to congratulate Enrico, a Jai Alai player they had developed a speaking friendship with and who had had a good night. They met Enrico outside the player's dressing room and Alisa introduced the two marines to him in Spanish, calling Pete "Pedro." The Mendez sisters and Tony carried on a spirited conversation with Enrico in Spanish while Pete remained mute on the sidelines. Alisa, and for that matter, Tony and Maria had been trying to teach Pete rudimentary Spanish but with mixed success. He had picked up quite a few words and phrases, and in a bar or at a mestizo party he could almost fake it, but in a noisy hallway with a three-way conversation going on, there was no way. Pete figured he had little or no natural language ability and didn't fight it.

As usual, darkness had set in before they headed back to Cavite, and, as usual, very few vehicles were traveling on the road from Manila at that time of night. They passed through a few small communities where subdued light from dwellings relieved the darkness, but otherwise it was cut only by the headlights of Tony's car. Tony had grown familiar with the road and drove at speeds only limited by the poorly maintained roads.

Suddenly a parked truck appeared in the Ford's headlights, blocking the road in front of the car. The tires screamed as Tony mashed down on the brakes, stopping the car just short of the truck. Armed men surrounded the car, gesturing to the occupants to get out. One man held a Coleman lamp. The light revealed their captors to be little brown men who were wearing a variety of semi-military and civilian clothing and armed with AK rifles and machetes.

A man that acted like the leader started talking in Tagalog. Maria responded. A long back and forth ensued with Alisa joining in at times and with the apparent leader consulting with some of his ragtag followers. Finally, Maria turned to Tony and Pete, saying, "Dig out any money you have on you and take off your watches. Don't try playing games. Give it to me."

Pete dug out the money he was carrying, including his Jai Alai winnings, and took off his watch. He gave it all to Maria. Tony did the same thing, and Maria handed everything to the leader. The leader nodded at someone who got into the truck and drove it to the side of the road.

"Okay," Maria said. "Get into the car and drive away, slowly."

The leader waved as they drove away.

"Whew." Tony exhaled a big breath. "I could see my uncle's Ford in a Manila car lot early tomorrow morning."

"I worried more about my neck than your car," Pete said. "Machetes give me the heebie-jeebies, more than guns."

Once they were underway, Maria gave them a rundown of the negotiations. "We were lucky. The road block wasn't intended for people like us. We convinced them that we would bring them a lot of trouble with little benefit if they detained us. But since they had us in their net, they wanted something to show for it. The cash and watches filled the need."

"Were they Huks?" Tony asked.

"That's them," Maria replied. "Now you know what they look like."

"They look like every other Filipino I've seen," Pete commented. "What's their problem? What are they trying to do?"

Maria tried to explain. "It's a communist organization called the Hukbalahap, trying to take over the government. When elections were held in 1946 after independence, they didn't do so good, so they are trying to win in a different way. They just might. They have been getting stronger and control big hunks of Luzon."

"Pete wanted to know what they would if the Huks won. "Keep on living, hopefully," Maria replied. "What else can one do?"

Marines go over the seawall during Inchon landing

As a work of the U.S. federal government, the image is in the public domain.

14.

Inchon

Chris and his fire team found themselves on the USS *Henrico* heading out to sea as part of a very large convoy heading to somewhere unknown to the First Fire Team. The *Henrico* was one of the troopships that had originally brought the First Provisional Marine Brigade across the Pacific to Korea. The ship reminded Chris of the *Clymer* down to the finest detail—the crowded, stinking troop compartments, the long chow lines, and the lack of any organized diversions. Despite a rough sea, Chris did not suffer sea sickness. He must have become immune after the Pacific crossing.

The convoy that the *Henrico* became part of was larger than the earlier Pacific convoy in part because the full First Marine Division was being transported and because of the presence of a large number of capital ships and two aircraft carriers.

Corporal Hautman and Chris went up on deck the first day to get some fresh air. They found the air very fresh, driven by a strong wind whipping across the deck. Even with the rough sea and limited visibility, they could see many ships from where they stood. Hautman pointed to a large ship in the distance. "A battle ship!" he exclaimed. "Been a long time since I saw one of them."

"Have you ever seen anything like this?" Chris asked.

Hautman replied. "One pair of eyes can't see everything. But I can tell you that when we went into Okinawa, there were ships everywhere as far as you could see. Our country pretty well disarmed after WWII. What we have now is a little piece of what we had at the end of WWII but it's still a pretty impressive sight."

During the first afternoon at sea, information had been passed to the platoon leaders that answered the question on every marine's mind: where were they going?

Sergeant Peters passed the word to the platoon. "You guys have been wondering where we are headed. Me too. Well, on September 15, three days from now, we will be making an amphibious assault on Inchon. They tell me it's a seaport with a population of over two hundred thousand a short distance west of Seoul and near the North Korean border. Should be interesting landing on the beach of a large city. Don't know if that has ever been tried before. Another thing, it has one of the highest tides anywhere. Very narrow window of time to get to an eight-foot seawall that borders the beach. Any questions?"

Les wanted to know how they will get over that sea wall. "I'm not very tall and can't jump very high." The question raised nervous laughter. Sergeant Peters replied, "They had a bunch of Japanese carpenters make wooden ladders. There will be two ladders in every landing craft. Hope they work."

Someone in back piped up. "Never had any amphibious training."

"Welcome to the party," Sergeant Peters said. "I never had any when we went into Guadalcanal. There's not much to know. Getting down the rope ladder with your gear and then getting into a boat that's going down when the ship is going up is the hardest part. The landing craft will be the Higgins boats hanging from davits on deck. After you get into the boat it's pretty much up to the navy to get you to the beach. Once you get to the beach your job begins."

The good news for Chris had been that they would only be at sea for three days. The sea had been stirred up by something and motion sickness soon affected many of the marines in the crowded troop compartments. Chris would have liked to go back to the fantail where he spent much of his time during the Pacific crossing, but heavy seas spraying the deck eliminated that option.

On the second day at sea, despite the poor lighting and hardly enough room to lift his head, he lay on his bunk reading Steinbeck's *Grapes of Wrath*, a book he had scrounged while in Pusan. In some ways the book reminded Chris of the Depression years in South Dakota, but it sounded like it had been even worse in Oklahoma. While he read, the possibility of going to college occurred to him. Why not? The GI Bill made going to college possible for any veteran who qualified. Did he qualify? No high school. That could be a problem, but he had heard there was some kind of test he could take that would be equivalent to a high school diploma if he passed it. He wondered how difficult that would be. He needed to get answers to these questions. In the meantime, there was this war to fight.

On the morning September 15 the fleet warships began pounding the beach the marines would be invading. Sergeant Peters briefed the First Platoon on the plan for the day as the bombardment proceeded. Sargent Peters said the Third Battalion would be attacking the Green Beach this morning, neutralizing a threat to the Red Beach where we will be landing at 1600 this evening. So, relax, we will have breakfast and lunch on board.

Sergeant Peters went on to describe the plans for landing on the Red Beach at 1600. "Normally," he said, "in an amphibious landing, a battalion will hit the beach all at one time. But this beach is narrow, and both the First and Second battalions will be going in side by side, one company at a time. So, three LCVPs (Higgins boats) will hit the seawall carrying marines from Easy Company while three other landing craft full of a company of First Battalion marines will hit the wall at the same time. "You all know your disembarking order. I will be first up the portside ladder with the Second Squad and Corporal Hautman's First Squad will be first up the starboard ladder. Squad leaders will lead their squads and fire team leaders lead their fire teams. We will meet on the beach and join the other Easy

Company platoons. Our objective will be Observation Hill." Sergeant Peters pointed to a map he had hung on a bulkhead. "You can see we will be passing through part of the city to reach the hill. Regiment tells us resistance should be light and we will be on the hill in time to dig in for the night. Hope they're right. It'll be getting dark so don't get lost. Squad and Fire Team leaders, be sure you have maps before we launch."

Sergeant Peters First Platoon and the rest of the Second Battalion stayed below deck that day and waited for orders to move up to the deck and climb down the rope ladders to enter the Higgins boats.

At 1500 the *Henrico* started to launch its landing craft. It would take most of hour for the LCVPs to get into the water get the marines loaded and get into line for the landing. Chris and his fire team went over the side to load into the third landing craft. Chris found that hanging off the side of the ship on a rope ladder loaded down with a field pack, M1 rifle, all the ammunition he wanted to carry, and four hand grenades was at least as much of a challenge as he had expected it to be. He sympathized with Adam, who carried the twenty-seven-pound Browning automatic rifle and Adam's BAR assistant, Les, who carried two canisters of BAR magazines in addition to all the equipment Chris carried. Chris got both his feet off the rope ladder and onto the landing craft running board almost simultaneously, released his hands, and dropped to the deck standing up. Adam and Dan also successfully transferred to the landing craft from the rope ladder. Les, apparently overwhelmed by all the weight he carried, lost his balance when he descended to the landing craft deck and made a full body crash. Chris and Adam helped him to his feet.

"Are you hurt?" Adam asked.

"Only my fucking pride."

Chris offered to carry the BAR magazine canisters up the ladder when they got to the sea wall.

"Bullshit," Les replied. "You can fire me, but as long as I'm the BAR assistant, I'm lugging those canisters."

"Okay," Chris replied. "Be a stubborn asshole."

When fully loaded, the landing craft had standing room only. The training manual said the marines should be in a kneeling position coming into shore so they would be protected by the landing craft's bullet-proof exterior. Obviously, such a nicety wouldn't be possible.

After the first landing craft were loaded they circled until all of the *Henrico* landing craft were launched and loaded. Then the landing craft got into a three abreast formation and headed for the beach. A brief rain squall wet the First Rifle Platoon as they stood in the landing craft. Fire and smoke from the ongoing bombardment of the beach added an ominous quality to the already darkening sky.

When they reached the seawall, the coxswain held the boat's bow against the wall while the marines scrambled to set up the ladders. Chris and Corporal Hautman set up the starboard ladder. Hautman went up the ladder first, followed by Chris and the rest of the First Fire Team. Les followed Chris, carrying the extra weight of the BAR magazines. He came off the ladder and onto the beach with a little swagger in his step and a smile on his face as if to say, "I guess I showed them I could handle my job."

Sporadic small arms fire could be heard, but no organized resistance greeted Easy Company as the marines came over the seawall. The company conducted an informal head count after landing and started moving towards their objective, Observation Hill. The company moved through deserted city streets and climbed up Observation Hill as it grew dark. While Chris and Dan dug in for the night, they could hear what sounded like a fire fight breaking out nearby on Cemetery Hill, which was being occupied by the First Battalion. After less than half an hour, the sound of the fire fight faded and the rest of the night remained quiet. The next morning, Easy Company began moving with the other Second Battalion companies through the streets of Inchon to search for and eliminate any resistance. To Chris it looked like a parade, a single-file line of marines spaced ten to twenty feet apart walking along each side of a street. Occasionally the sound of an encounter could be heard in the distance, but the Easy Company First Platoon moved through Inchon all day without encountering enemy resistance. By the end of the day, the marines controlled all of Inchon.

Corporal Hautman found it hard to believe how easy and successful the landing had been. "I'm not used to this kinda war," he told Chris. "On day two I'm used to being in a fighting hole on a strip of beach hoping we won't be pushed into the ocean."

The next day a Korean marine battalion took over the occupation of Inchon, and Easy Company and the rest of the Second Marine Battalion headed for Kimpo, the largest and finest airport in Korea. They found it undamaged and, for the most part, undefended.

Chris and the rest of the First Rifle Platoon would have liked to spend the night in one of the big Kimpo hangers but, as expected, they were ordered to prepare a defense perimeter. Easy Company First Platoon was assigned to a remote position in front of the main perimeter for reasons not clear to the First Fire Team.

Adam wanted to know why they were digging in forward of what looked like the Easy Company perimeter.

Les made a guess. "They've run out of trip wire. They're using us for trip wire."

After Chris's fire team finished digging their foxholes, Chris asked Corporal Hautman what the plans were for the next day.

"Be ready to move out at 0630."

"Where we going?" Chris asked.

"The division isn't telling me what the plans are," Hautman answered, "or asking me what we should do tomorrow."

"What about Seoul?" Dan asked. "It's big and not far from here."

"Nah," Hautman replied. "Marines wouldn't know what to do in a big city. Jungles, hills, beaches is what we do."

Les showed up carrying some extra C-rations. "Hey, heard we will be heading for Seoul," he said.

Chris laughed, "What were you saying, Corporal?"

Hautman gave Chris a mean look but didn't answer the question.

During the night there was some probing of the Easy Company

perimeter and one halfhearted attack. The First Fire Team had become seasoned fighting men and weren't rattled or impressed by the night's activities.

The next morning, marine air units were already moving into Kimpo and Korean marines assumed occupation duties. Easy Company spent the day clearing villages around Kimpo. Dog Company marched off to the east with a platoon of tanks in the direction of Seoul. The following day the rest of the Second Battalion followed Dog Company. There were no flank patrols which suited the First Fire Team since they didn't have to move off the road into the rough terrain, but the lack of patrols made Corporal Hautman uneasy. Later in the day they saw Corsairs and artillery bombarding a hill near the road which indicated somebody must be watching the flanks. By the end of the day, all the Marine Fifth Regiment battalions had taken up positions on the bank of the wide and deep Han River.

The next morning after artillery preparation, the Third Battalion made the initial crossing of the Han River. The First Fire Team could tell from the noise that the crossing had been opposed. At 1000 the Second Battalion formed up to load into Landing Vehicles, Tracked (LVTs). Two squads crowded aboard each LVT, leaving standing room only.

Chris wondered if the thing would float. There were no life jackets, not that the heavily loaded marines could have been kept afloat with life jackets. The LVT the First Fire Team boarded lumbered down to the river and wallowed into the water. Much to Chris's surprise it floated, but the free board appeared to be less than a foot.

Unlike the Third Battalion crossing the Second Battalion crossing was unopposed. A flotilla of LVTs made several trips to move the Second Battalion across the river without incident. After crossing the Han, the LVTs carried the marines up the opposite bank a thousand yards and dropped them off on the road to Seoul. The Third Battalion had already secured the nearby hills. The men of Easy Company were less than eight miles from Seoul, a short day's hike the way things had been going.

Other than the weak attack during the night at Kimpo, the First Fire team had seen little serious enemy action since landing at Inchon. During a break as they proceeded down the road to Seoul, Les remarked that things were getting a little boring, nothing like the Pusan Perimeter and the Naktong Bulge.

"Be careful what you wish for," Adam warned. "There's worse things than being bored."

"Yeah," Dan agreed. "I wouldn't mind being bored right up to when I'm discharged."

Chris mentioned that he had a friend doing guard duty in the Philippines. "He thinks I'm the lucky one, doing what marines are supposed to do."

Adam laughed, "Your friend better wish he never gets lucky."

Les said he thought the friend was fucking lying.

That afternoon, the battalion approached a ridge of knobby hills that lay between the Second Battalion and Seoul. It halted and prepared a defense perimeter for the night. When Corporal Hautman came by to admire the holes the First Fire Team had dug, Adam asked, "What the hell is going on? There's hours of daylight left. We could make Seoul if we kept going."

Hautman pointed to the hills in front of them. "Those hills are crawling with camouflaged dug-in NK. Looks like the picnic is over. Sergeant Peters said to be ready to move out and up the hill in front of us after the artillery and air support pounds it in the morning."

Chris remembered what looked like a similar hill in the Naktong Bulge called the Obong Ridge that hadn't turned out well. The artillery preparation in the morning lasted nearly an hour, much longer than it had on Obong Ridge where Easy Company had taken heavy losses.

Rice paddies, flat and open, filled the approach to Hill 105 South, their objective. As the Second Battalion spread out and entered the paddies, Chris felt relieved when he realized the paddies had been drained. He thought, likely getting ready to harvest. No mud, no snakes. In a way it reminded Chris of wheat fields back home, ready to be harvested.

Chris called out to Adam, "This remind you of North Dakota?"

"Yeah," Adam replied. "It sure does. I'll bet we're as welcome as a hail storm to some gook farmer." Corporal Hautman overheard the conversation. "Hey, you farmers, get your fucking minds outa the fields."

Spread out and exposed, the Second Battalion took casualties from sniper fire soon after they began advancing across the rice paddies. The platoon leaders shouted and signaled the marines to advance on the run. The First Fire Team didn't need to be prodded. Chris felt fear but also exhilaration as they rushed forward to where they could find cover in foliage and irregular terrain. The First Fire Team ran until they flopped down, unscathed, among some brush and boulders on the hillside. They lay breathing hard to catch their breath.

"Hey, Les," Dan called out. "You still bored?"

A voice answered, "Shut the fuck up."

The battalion formed a rough line on the lower part of the hill and started advancing. Heavy automatic and mortar fire coming at them from the hill made progress costly and slow. U.S. artillery and close air support continued to rake the hill but it wasn't enough to suppress the enemy fire.

During the morning advance, Corporal Hautman's First Squad assisted in locating and taking out two heavy machine gun emplacements, but with casualties. One BAR man was killed and two riflemen wounded. The First Fire Team had no casualties. In the middle of the afternoon, the squad got the chore to quiet another heavy machine gun that was methodically tracking back and forth across the hill. Its exact location hadn't been determined. The machine gun had dug in well enough to survive repeated U.S. artillery and air strikes.

Corporal Hautman noted that the machine gun fire seemed to stay a couple of feet above the ground. "Probably dug in with an embankment in front of it," he said. "We can work our way up closer by staying under its fire." What about the NK infantry? Chris asked. Hautman seemed to ignore Chris, continued, "We'll move up on our bellies, one fire team at a time."

They started moving forward, searching for their objective. The Third

Fire Team went first. The Second Fire Team had crawled forward a hundred feet when one of its men screamed. Then it was the First Fire Team's turn to move up.

After they completed their move, Dan tapped Chris on the shoulder. "I see it," he said. "I see where the bastards are." Chris looked in the direction Dan pointed. He could make out a well dug-in position behind some scrub bushes and camouflage.

When the Second Fire Team moved up the next time, someone yelled for a corpsman. Another marine had been hit.

Suddenly, Dan jumped to his feet and ran towards the machine gun with a grenade in each hand. He was hit, staggered, but kept running and at short range, threw both grenades into the machine gun nest. Explosions ripped the nest while Dan spun around, shredded by more hits. The squad rose instinctively and charged the emplacement, routing the infantry defending the machine gun.

The First Squad didn't take time to assess the damage. With the enemy giving ground, Easy Company moved to take advantage of the moment, advancing a hundred yards before being pinned down by another set of dug-in machine guns. By then the sun had dropped below some nearby hills, and the Second Battalion's three companies tied it in for the night.

After things settled down, Chris went back down the hill and found Dan dead from multiple wounds. The two Second Fire Team marines who had been hit were seriously wounded and were being evacuated. Chris had hardly gotten to know Dan. He had only been with the fire team a few weeks. Chris had seen enough combat to know death came suddenly and unexpectedly, but apparently Dan had deliberately chosen to die because he didn't want to see other marines die. Chris had never seen that happen before.

He mentioned this to Sergeant Peters who said that he would write a recommendation for Dan to receive a medal.

Chris thought, a medal isn't going to do anything for Dan, but the Marines like to have heroes, and it might make the family feel better.

The next morning the regiment renewed its attack on Hill 105 South.

During the fighting, a mortar round exploded near the First Fire Team and Les caught several pieces of shrapnel in his left arm. A corpsman bandaged him up and had him go back to an aid station where most of the shrapnel could be picked out. Before leaving, Les chided Chris, "Going to be getting a cheap Purple Heart like yours."

"Not good enough to get a ticket home," Chris replied.

Les said he didn't want one of those or a body bag to go with it.

With Les gone, the First Fire Team consisted of only Chris and Adam. Chris assumed Les's role and carried the extra BAR ammunition magazines for Adam.

It wasn't until the middle of the afternoon that the marines finally occupied the crest of Hill 105 South and Chris and Adam standing on the hill could see the city of Seoul spreading out before them. It looked huge. "We are supposed to take that?" Adam questioned. "We had problems taking this little hill."

Adam remembered how a million men, Germans and Russians, fought for months over the carcass of Stalingrad, a city smaller than Seoul. Chris agreed. "Don't seem like a job for a few marines." he replied.

Remnants of NK remained in the hills northwest of Seoul, but the city itself took priority. Dog and Easy Companies prepared to enter the city before nightfall while Fox Company would remain to occupy the crest of Hill 105 South and deal with any of the NK remnants.

Before Easy Company departed the hill, Les returned, patched up and ready to rejoin the First Fire Team. Chris greeted him. "Thought we were rid of you."

"Wrong again," Les replied. "Nobody else wants me."

Actually, despite their regular put-downs, the bonds between the First Fire Team's core members had become stronger over the past two months as they shared experiences as infantrymen in almost constant combat. Their trust in each other, a trust involving their very lives, had become unquestionable. Besides that, the First Firing Team had a crying need for a BAR assistant.

Easy Company soon learned the kind of war they would be fighting in the streets of Seoul. The next day, the company had orders to move along a main boulevard towards a group of government buildings. The First Rifle Platoon moved down a side street to the boulevard with no opposition. However, they found that the first main intersection on the boulevard had been barricaded with sandbags and rubble from nearby buildings. While the company's platoon leaders assessed the situation, sniper fire hit a rifleman in the First Platoon. The Easy Company commander, Captain Wilson, ordered the clearing of nearby buildings of snipers and any other NK defenders.

Corporal Hautman's squad was given the chore to check out a small three-story building where the front and back of the first floor had been blown out. Chris figured the first level had been some kind store. Empty shelves that had probably held goods for sale still lined the side walls. Hautman laid out the plan for moving up to the second and third level. The Second Fire Team would hold on the first level, the Third Fire Team to take the lead to the next level, the First Fire team would follow and then move up to the third level. Hautman shouted "let's go" and led the third and First Fire teams up the stairs. As Chris moved up the stairs, he wished for the first time that he could trade his M1 for a carbine or even a burp gun. Rifles weren't designed for close-quarter street fighting. Hautman reached the second level door, fired a couple of shots into it and kicked in the door. There were three rooms on the second level. The marines kicked in the doors of the rooms and found them unoccupied. The Third Fire Team held up on the second level and Chris, Adam and Les followed Corporal Hautman up the stairs to the third level. Corporal Hautman pumped three shots into the door and kicked it open. A shot rang out and Hautman fell backwards down the stairs. Chris pulled a hand grenade off his belt, armed it and threw it though the open door. When the grenade exploded, Chris rushed through the door firing his M1 from his hip emptying the clip on two men firing back at him. Adam and Les found two dying North Koreans when they entered the room behind Chris.

Chris could feel his heart racing and also the sense of high alertness, almost euphoria, which he now associated with combat. Had he become a combat junkie? God forbid.

A member of the Third Fire Team bent over Corporal Hautman and checked his condition. "Other than a few bruises from falling down the stairs, can't see anything wrong."

Corporal Hautman felt around. "I think you're right. Good, I sure as hell don't need another Purple Heart."

By the time the First Squad returned to street level, the marines had begun an attack on the barricade in the intersection. First, artillery and Corsairs dropped ordnance on it. Then engineers moved in, sweeping the approaches for mines while Easy Company and a weapons company poured small arms fire, smoke grenades, 81-millimeter mortars, recoilless rifle fire, and rocket rounds into the obstacle. After the mines were cleared, two Pershing tanks rolled in and blasted the barricade at short range with 90-millimeter cannons. Sherman flame-thrower tanks and bulldozers were held in reserve to be used if necessary. After all this preparation, the Easy Company fire teams charged the barricade and found only a few survivors in the rubble. All were anxious to surrender.

Easy Company's attack on the barricade had worked as planned. Before darkness settled in, the next three barricades down the street met the same fate.

Chris didn't understand why the North Koreans bothered to build barricades. He remembered reading about the battle for Stalingrad, where rubble provided all the cover either side needed. He shared his thoughts with Adam and Les.

Adam agreed. "They're building targets. It's not hard to figure out where they are. By the time we get to them, most of the fighters are dead or traumatized."

All the next day Easy Company moved down the Boulevard continuing to smash barricades and assault associated buildings, averaging about one every two hours. Marine casualty rates were high. Hautman said it reminded him of routing the Japs out of caves on Okinawa.

Late that same day the men of Easy Company learned that the allied command had declared the city of Seoul liberated, and that General MacArthur and Syngman Rhee, president of South Korea, would visit the city to mark the event. Adam said somebody should tell them gooks in the barricades we're attacking that the city has been liberated. The following day, enemy resistance had slackened noticeably. North Korean forces were observed to be actually withdrawing in large numbers. Except for scattered resistance, the enemy seemed to have evaporated. Easy Company was able to move down the boulevard and occupy their objectives without further opposition.

"What's happening?" Chris asked Corporal Hautman.

"I haven't been told but suspect the gooks are getting out while they can. Heard the Eighth Army is into North Korea."

"Good fucking thing," Les said. "Otherwise we might all have retired before we finished this job."

Hautman reminisced, "It's been less than two weeks since we landed in Inchon. MacArthur says we have liberated one of the biggest cities in Asia. I thought that might be a stretch yesterday but looks truer today. Not bad for a bunch of amateur street fighters."

"What's next?" Chris asked.

Les suggested a victory parade in San Francisco.

The marines who landed at Inchon didn't have to wait long for an answer to Chris's question. After a few skirmishes north of Seoul, the First Marine Division returned to Inchon to load on ships that would take them to their next assignment, destination unknown to the First Fire Team.

While waiting to embark, Chris updated his journal and wrote letters home and to Pete. There was a mail call, but apparently his mail had not caught up with him. He had not gotten any mail since leaving Pusan.

15.

The Present and the Unknown Future

Late in September, not long after the Huk encounter, Pete received another letter from Chris. Recent news from Korea had been upbeat, with the landing at Inchon turning the direction of the war solidly in the United Nations Coalition's favor. The letter revealed that Chris had once again been in the middle of the action but had survived unscathed.

Hi Buddy

Been busy. I'm beginning to feel like a combat veteran, a lucky one. Only minor scratches so far. In early September they took us out of a heavy combat engagement in the middle of the night and a pouring rain and moved the brigade back to Pusan where we spent about a week getting everybody and everything on ships to go somewhere to do something. After we were at sea we found out we were going to do an amphibious landing at a place called Inchon. Amphibious landings, that's something me and a lot of other marines on board had never done or practiced before. Some of the officers and non-coms are veterans of landings in WWII and they told us not to worry, you'll be getting on the job training.

We had the usual stinking crowded ship and a rough couple of days at sea.

Fortunately, we had a short distance to travel and spent only three days aboard the troopship which included the convoy assembly, time in route and waiting to disembark. The troop ships converged with just about every kind of ship the navy has at Inchon and we laid off shore for the better part of the day while the navy ships and planes blasted the landing site.

The troop transport had a bunch of Higgins boats on board which they dropped into the water, and we climbed down rope ladders to board them. We were all carrying about eighty pounds of gear, the BAR men and their assistants even more. It's not bad until you get down to where the Higgins boat is bobbing and the ship is rolling. At that point I'm thinking, I'm not liking this on the job training. If you end up with one foot on the boat and one on the rope ladder, you are in big trouble. You have to make up your mind, both feet on the Higgins or both feet on the rope ladder.

The beach where we were landing is known for its high tides that come in fast and strong and go out just as fast. We had about an hour to get people on shore before the tide goes out, like pulling the plug in a bathtub.

We had two eight-foot ladders in the boat. The Higgins boat was run up against a high seawall at the beach and we used the ladders to get over the wall. When we got on shore there were explosions and shooting going on but our platoon didn't run into anything. Seoul is a different story.

We did a lot of marching and a little fighting the first couple of days heading towards Seoul. Some units met heavy resistance but we mostly marched. Things changed when we entered some hills on the outskirts of the city. The NKs were in those hills, well dug in and well equipped.

We found another kind of war in Seoul: fighting in buildings and in the streets. The NK constructed barricades at the intersections of the city's major streets and boulevards. It took a lot of time and fire power to remove them one at a time. After butting our heads against the barricades for a couple of days, the NK began withdrawing. I guess the NK were more worried about being trapped than losing the city. Good thing because Seoul is a huge city and we could have been busy there for a long time if they hadn't withdrawn.

In less than two weeks the war has turned around, the NK's are on the run everywhere. It seemed longer than two weeks to me, a lot of things happening, some good, and some bad. We lost many good men, almost thirty percent in our platoon, KIA and wounded. As a rifleman you are one of war's expendables.

Right now we're back in Inchon getting a little breather while preparing to embark once again on another project the thinkers have in mind. We are getting replacements to fill our ranks. We have a new rifleman for our fire team and the platoon is back to three full squads.

Changing the subject, I've heard they are reviving the old GI Bill for Korean veterans. Strange as it might seem, I have been thinking about the future, if there is such a thing for a marine rifleman in a combat situation. So guess what I have been thinking? I'm thinking of going to college after finishing this job.

I can hear you laughing, "Going to college, you dumb fart, remember you didn't go to high school."

"Look, smart ass," I answer, "You ever heard of the equivalency test?"

The test evaluator who talked to me in boot camp said I'm pretty damn smart for somebody with only an eighth-grade education, better scores than most high school grads he sees. Besides, I'm an experienced, certified, skilled killer. How many high school grads can say that?

Seriously, I've figured out what I want to do with this life. I want to write, be a journalist or something like that. I always did a lot of reading, a bad habit I picked up from my mom. She always did a lot of reading. Sometimes the housework would get in the way but she made time to read. Reading and writing are related and I've figured out writing is something I'd rather do than milking cows.

I find writing these letters to you is something I really like to do. But instead of writing them to you, which you have to admit is sort of a dead end, I would, in my fantasy world, be writing them for the Associated Press. On hindsight, when crunched down in a foxhole trying to stay alive, joining the Marines does seem to have been a dumb thing to do, but it did cause me to become aware of a bigger world and to imagine my future in ways I never considered before. So, my future is planned. College after the Marines, work towards a career in journalism.

Thanks for the letters. I do appreciate hearing about the details of your difficult dull duty. Remember, my offer to trade places anytime stands.

Your buddy Chris

Good old Chris, Pete thought. Dodging bullets and planning his future. More power to him. Pete hadn't heard about the GI Bill being resurrected. He had an uncle who had gone to college using the World War II GI Bill and who had recently enrolled in the University of Minnesota veterinarian school.

Pete had never thought of college being in his future. Besides ministers and doctors, he didn't know many people who had gone to college. Those were people on a different level than him and people with his background. But if Chris could get into college, why couldn't he? He knew Chris was no dummy. He did dumb things, but he wasn't a dummy. At the same time, Pete always figured he was just as smart as Chris, and he should know, having been in the same class with him for eight years in their one-room school.

If he did get into a college, wouldn't it be neat if he and Chris went to the same college? However, Pete wouldn't want to go to journalism school. He knew that, but didn't know what he would want to take.

After the Huk encounter, Tony stopped driving his car on the Manila-to-Cavite road at night. Pete agreed with the decision. Tony worried about the car, and Pete worried about his neck. The Mendez sisters agreed that it had become too dangerous to travel the rural roads around Manila after dark.

Near the end of September, Maria and Alisa brought up the subject of moving to Manila. Some of their mestiza friends who worked as hostesses at an upscale bar in Manila called the Blue Note thought Maria and Alisa should apply for jobs. All the hostesses were mestizas who could speak Spanish and selected for their looks and social skills.

In early October, Pete stopped at the Mendez home in Cavite and found Alisa excited. "We are moving!" she exclaimed. "Moving to Manila."

"You got into the Blue Note?" he asked.

"We did," Alisa replied. "Start working in November."

"We need to mark the occasion," he said.

They found an unopened bottle of rum in a kitchen cabinet, pulled the cork, and poured a toast.

Pete proposed, "To better times in a bigger town."

"Hope so," Alisa responded. After tasting the rum, she added, "Won't take much to be better than the Kitty Kat."

"What happened to the airline job?" Pete asked.

"We heard. They said they had all the applicants they needed right now."

"Too bad, sounded like a really super job."

"They said we could keep applying, but this Cavite bar girl isn't going to wait for a dream job that's not likely to happen."

Pete asked if they had found a place to live in Manila.

"We'll share a house with two of our friends, girls who work at the Blue Note. We get the upstairs, two bedrooms and a bath, and share the kitchen. It's a good neighborhood. We move the end of November."

After having absorbed Alisa's plans, Pete began to wonder how these changes would affect him and their relationship. He had grown comfortable with the situation and realized he had developed a fondness for Alisa that went beyond physical desire. Had he fallen in love with a prostitute?

Maybe prostitute would be too strong a word. The tips Alisa earned as a hostess were legitimate, but he knew that the Mendez sisters depended on special men to supplement those earnings and that he was one of those special men.

Pete wondered if he could afford to be a special man for a woman living in Manila. He had been spending every dime of his payday money to do things with or paying for things for Alisa, not saving a penny for the new car he wanted to buy when he got back to the states. Sometimes when he ran short, he even borrowed from the detachment slush fund, a member-funded money pool that earned 250 percent per annum on payday loans.

"Is it expensive?" Pete asked.

Alisa seemed to sense Pete's concerns. "It won't cost more than the house in Cavite. We have to share, but it's a big house."

It soon became apparent to Pete and Tony that their arrangement with the Mendez sisters would survive, at least in the short term, when Maria asked if Tony could move some of the sisters' stuff in his car. Tony, always ready to help, agreed, and Pete volunteered to do some of the heavy lifting. The sisters were moving from one furnished house to another, but still had a lot of stuff to take. Their belongings filled the car, leaving only room for Tony to drive. Pete and the sisters took a bus to Manila, carrying suitcases and bags that wouldn't fit into Tony's car.

Alisa's description of the house in Manila had been accurate. The house, a good-sized, two-story stucco set back from a busy street by a wall and patio, seemed more than adequate to fill the Mendez sisters' needs. The neighborhood appeared better than average and bordered an even nicer residential area.

The Margaret, the boat that traveled between Sangley and Manila, followed by a Jeepney ride became Tony and Pete's favored way to visit the Mendez sisters. They also used the Margaret and Jeepney ride combination to bring the sisters back to the enlisted men's club as their guests. When their duty schedules allowed, Pete and Tony would often make the trip together, although sometimes Pete went alone. Occasionally Pete or the two of them would stop at the Blue Note where Maria and Alisa worked as hostesses.

Located on prestigious Escolta Street, the Blue Note attracted an upper-scale eclectic male clientele. It occupied a relatively small space, being only thirty feet wide and extending back about twice its width. A long bar stretched halfway down one of the side walls, and small tables and chairs filled the remaining space. The Blue Note's big draw was its mestiza hostesses. The Blue Note hostesses, much like traditional geishas, maintained a platonic relationship with customers while working in the bar. What they did on their own time was their business.

On a Saturday afternoon early in December, Alisa had the day off while Maria worked at the Blue Note. On his way to see Alisa, Pete stopped at the Blue Note. Maria wasn't busy, so she pulled up a stool across from where he sat sipping a beer at the bar.

"How do you like working here?" he asked.

"Tips are better than at the Kitty Kat, lots better," Maria said. "American servicemen aren't famous for tipping, and everything's a prelude to sex."

Pete laughed, "You're hurting my feelings."

Maria modified her statement. "Present company excluded, at least the part about tipping."

"Alisa is the only woman I've ever had."

"You're a liar!" Maria exclaimed. "Marines hump everything wearing a skirt."

"I never kissed a woman before Alisa."

"Get off. Quit while you are still ahead."

"Swear to God, hope to die."

Maria marveled, "You are a rare bird or a good liar. Oh, something you should know. Bill is back at the Cavite army base."

"Bill?" Pete questioned. "Who's Bill?"

"You don't know about the army guy? He's been down on some southern island on a survey, been gone since before you showed up. One of our

Cavite neighbors said he'd been asking around the neighborhood, trying to locate Alisa."

Tony had mentioned something about an army guy, but Alisa had never said anything about the person. Pete wouldn't have considered it a problem in any case in the early stages. Alisa introduced Pete to sensual pleasures he had fantasized about for years, and he found them better than he had even imagined. Alisa had satisfied Pete's immediate desires, and if it had ended then he would have moved on with a smile on his face. More recently, however, their relationship had evolved into something beyond sensual, and Pete found the news about an army man disturbing.

"Has Bill found what he's looking for?" he asked.

"Not so far. You worried?"

"I don't know. Should I be?"

"Alisa likes you. Not to worry."

After leaving the Blue Note, Pete pondered his dilemma during the Jeepney ride to the Mendez sisters' apartment. Should he reveal his true feelings to Alisa? What were his true feelings? He didn't understand them himself, so how could he communicate them? Were his emotions getting ahead of his ability to handle them? I'm only twenty years old. Besides, Alisa is a tainted woman. If not in my eyes, she certainly would be in my mother's eyes. Yes, but she seems to care for me and is the first woman to have ever given me any attention. Maybe that's my problem, a lack of experience with women.

When Pete reached the house, Alisa hugged and kissed him.

"Oh, I've missed you!" she exclaimed.

Pete noted that it had only been a week.

"It's been a long week," Alisa said as she unhooked a catch on the back of her blouse and pulled it off, revealing bare breasts. A half hour later they lay panting and perspiring on her bed.

Later Alisa took two San Michaels out of the refrigerator, and they carried them out to the front patio where the house blocked the rays of the setting sun. The air had cooled, and it felt comfortable where they sat at a small garden table.

They made small talk for a while, Alisa about the Blue Note, Pete about a letter from his friend Chris telling how things were going in Korea. Then Pete asked, "Who is Bill?"

Alisa gave Pete a questioning look. "You hadn't heard about Bill?" she asked.

"No," Pete replied.

"Bill is someone I've known for about a year. Before I met you, he was sent to Mindanao Island where the army is doing some kind of a survey. We hear he is back now, but he's been gone for four or five months."

"Sooo, now what?" Pete asked.

"Nothing," Alisa replied. "Bill drinks too much and gets mean. I don't want him around."

"Was he around before the army sent him away?"

Alisa stood up, put herself on Pete's lap, wrapped her arms around him and kissed him. "You are what I want. You are the kind of man I want. I love you, Pedro. I love you so much it hurts."

Pete realized his feelings were being reciprocated. They loved each other. It might be wrong, it might be awkward, but none the less, it was a fact.

Pete told Alisa he loved her, too. "I have the same feelings, Alisa. I can't keep you out of my mind. It feels wonderful and hurts at the same time. I want you so much, to have, to hold, to never let go."

Thoughts whirled in Pete's mind. Now what? We love each other, now what? What do people do when they are in love?

Alisa answered Pete's thoughts. "I want to marry you, have your baby," she said.

Pete stopped breathing. The answer stunned him. Should it have? What baby? What does she mean exactly? Whatever she meant wouldn't work for a lot of reasons, his mother being one big reason. He was twenty years old and no way prepared for what Alisa suggested.

After a long while he replied, "I can't do that. I'm not ready for anything like that. It's not possible."

Alisa got off Pete's lap and stood up. Pete saw a look in Alisa's face he had never seen before. Contempt.

"Oh, high and mighty," she said. "You screw my ass off, but that's it. Is that what love is all about? What if I told you I'm pregnant, what would you say to that? Hey, that's what happens when you screw, that's what it's for. I thought if we really loved each other we could find a way to do it right. Love will find a way. All that shit. We would find a way to be together and to love and nurture a child. I can tell you right now, I'm not pregnant with your child, and I'm not going to be."

Alisa got up and walked into the house. Pete sat alone at the garden table for a long time. It had grown dark when he finally walked out into the street, hailed a Jeepney, and started the trip back to Sangley Point.

Over the next few days, Pete concentrated on Alisa and their broken relationship. At the same time, he began to hear disturbing news about China intervening in the Korean War. Pete's thoughts turned from the turmoil he felt over his relationship with Alisa to Chris and his very different circumstances. Chris had more serious things going on in his life than woman problems. News reports were describing how hundreds of thousands of Chinese soldiers had crossed the Yalu River and were engaging

United Nations forces in North Korea. Only a few weeks before, General MacArthur was talking about having the troops home for Christmas. Now the talk had changed to concern about the very survival of United Nations forces in Korea. Pete feared what might be happening to Chris and the other marines in Korea. There were reports of U.S. marines fighting in a place called the Chosin Reservoir.

PBM flying boat, used by the navy for patrol duty in the Far East during the Korean War

This image is in the public domain.

Mountains on Bataan

Photo by author

16.
A Diversion

Pete had observed the comings and goings of navy patrol squadrons at Sangley Point during the time he had been there. There were nine P2V land-based patrol planes operating out of Sangley when he arrived, but they had been replaced by a squadron of ponderous PBM flying boats. There were four other land-based patrol planes parked in a restricted area. They had their own guards and were involved in some secret activity. Base personnel had started calling the secret outfit the 50-footers because of a rumor that if you got closer than within fifty feet of their area, they would shoot you.

Pete figured that the only reason Sangley Point Naval Air Station existed was to provide a base for and to service navy patrol planes. All of the administration and service people, the infrastructure, and the marine contingent were there for that purpose.

While talking to navy patrol types at the enlisted men's club, Pete found out something about their operation. The patrol squadrons were based on the West Coast, in California and Washington state, and deployed about once every year or year and a half for a six-month tour to the Philippines, Japan, Okinawa, or Adak Island in Alaska's Aleutian chain. The Philippines were a favorite deployment destination, and it had nothing to do with the weather.

The 50-footers didn't rotate. They just hunkered down in their own little restricted area and didn't come from anywhere or return to anywhere. Their planes came and went regularly. Sometimes one or two of the planes would be gone for a week or two and then reappear. Pete could tell by the sound when one of them took off. They had jet engines in addition to regular prop engines and made a hell of a racket on takeoff.

Pete liked to sit on the patio at the back of the enlisted men's club and watch PBM flying boats take off and land. While they waited to take off, PBMs sat low in the water like bobbing turtles. When a plane started a takeoff run, it plowed a lot of water, but after a while it would get up on what they called a step where the plane started to act like a speed boat and gained enough speed to fly.

The same weekend that Pete and Alisa's relationship crashed, the PBM squadron suffered an extraordinary tragedy. Two of the squadron planes drove into mountains, one on Bataan Peninsula in the Philippines and another in Japan. All the crewmen, eleven in each plane perished; an unprecedented catastrophe for the nine-plane squadron.

At the platoon muster the following Monday morning, Pete learned the platoon would be contributing ten men for a crash site team to investigate the Bataan PBM crash site and retrieve bodies. Those interested were asked to volunteer. Pete volunteered, welcoming any opportunity to divert his mind from the abrupt end of his relationship with Alisa. Tony also volunteered, welcoming a change in the everyday routine, even if it promised to be a grisly task.

Pete and Tony had discussed Pete's sudden fallout with Alisa when he returned from Manila on the previous Saturday.

"It happened so sudden, I didn't know what to think," Pete had said.

Tony guessed Pete and Alisa were on different pages of the same book. "So, what're you going to do now?" he asked.

"Save my money to buy a new car," Pete replied. "A Studebaker."

"No more wasting money on women?"

"Alisa made me realize this woman thing is a serious life-changing business. I'm not ready for that."

Tony agreed, "You gotta love 'em and leave 'em. That's where we're at. You just can't get too serious. It'll spoil your weekend."

"It sure as hell spoiled mine."

Pete and Tony learned that Sergeant Kolowski, the sergeant who had traveled to Sangley Point with them from the states, would be the senior non-commissioned marine on the crash site team going to Bataan and would be in charge of the marine contingent. They had seen Sergeant Kolowski around the base but hadn't had any direct contact with him since he introduced them to the wonders of Cavite. Sergeant Kolowski scheduled a briefing for the marine volunteers on Tuesday. He greeted Pete and Tony by name when he saw them among the volunteers.

He gave the marine contingent the details of their task. "Officer in charge of the operation will be LTCD Richards, the PBM squadron executive officer. Two navy crash site investigators will be part of the team and two navy corpsmen. The corpsmen will help identify victims and put the pieces together. This won't be a picnic. Six Philippine army soldiers that know the terrain and environment will also come with us. The Philippine soldiers will carry their weapons. Everyone else will carry a sidearm. Don't expect to run into any Huks, but could run into some aggressive scavengers. We'll sail on a Landing Craft Utility, an LCU, to get close to the site. There're no roads. It's estimated we will have to cut through a couple of miles of jungle from the nearest good beaching site. We'll use the LCU as a command center. There is a lot of room on the LCU but limited accommodations. It can haul tanks and over a hundred men, but it isn't a hotel. Any questions?"

Tony asked, "How long is this going to take?"

"Getting ready, the job itself, and then cleaning up is expected to take about a week."

"Will we be spending nights in the jungle or on the boat?" someone asked.

"Both," the sergeant replied. "We won't be returning to the LCU to sleep. If we are at the boat at the end of the day, we'll sleep there. If we are in the jungle, we'll sleep there."

"How do we get the remains out?" someone else asked.

"In body bags carried by two men on a stretcher."

"Won't that be kinda heavy, down the mountain?"

"The doctors say most of the body fluids will be gone, animals will most likely have consumed some of the remains, shouldn't be too heavy."

Pete began to feel queasy just thinking about it.

The crash site team boarded the LCU on Friday. While they waited to get underway, Pete and Tony visited with Sergeant Kolowski.

"My normal tour for this place is up in three months," Kolowski said. "The way things are going up north, could be sooner. The First Division is getting pretty beat up in the Chosin Reservoir. Can you imagine fighting when the temperature is minus forty degrees? Jesus. War is hell in decent weather. You can thank your lucky asses you are in the Philippines living the good life."

The conversation steered Pete's mind to Chris. Very likely Chris was in the middle of those hellish conditions. God, Pete thought, women are my biggest problem.

After two hours of cruising, the LCU reached the entrance to Manila Bay and passed between the tip of the Bataan Peninsula and Corregidor Island. Pete recognized those places as the focus of early World War II news reports and remembered the names of some local people from his home town that had been there at the time. Now the war news focused on Korea.

They cruised along the west coast of the Bataan Peninsula for about an hour when they passed Subic Bay a large US Navy facility, which Sergeant Kolowski noted was about three hours from their destination. As predicted the LCU slowed down about three hours later and turned towards a large sandy beach where landing craft pushed its nose up on the sand and stopped. It had started to rain, so the retrieval team rigged up a tarpaulin on the back half of the open deck to shelter their cots where they would sleep that night.

In the morning Pete, Tony, and the rest of the team headed into the jungle to make their way to the crash site. They were loaded down with everything they would need to live in the jungle while they worked at the site. Their gear included shelters, rain wear, and water and food for three days in addition to eleven body bags, six rolled-up stretchers. The two-tiered jungle was covered by a high canopy which grew above thick, almost impenetrable undergrowth. Five marines at a time were set to work with machetes in half-hour shifts to hack a path through the undergrowth. When a team started a shift, they slipped off their heavy packs and took the machetes from the marines who had the previous shift. Pete, familiar with hard work, had no doubts that he could handle cutting a path through the jungle with a machete. Since age sixteen, he had been throwing around feed sacks weighing a hundred pounds and pitching heavy bundles of grain during threshing season in the hottest part of the South Dakota summer.

After only a short time of chopping the undergrowth, Pete's T-shirt became soaked with sweat. Every whack of the machete raised a swarm of biting insects. The thickness of the jungle prevented any breeze that might help relieve the stifling heat. Pete and Tony weren't doing much talking, saving their energy for the work at hand. About halfway through their shift, they came upon some unnatural mounds and holes in their path. "You know what?" Pete said between deep breaths as he worked. "These must be World War Two earthworks. The Americans and Filipinos fought the Japanese in this stinking jungle for about three months at the start of the war."

"You think so?" Tony answered. "Can you imagine fighting in a place like this? Didn't take long for the jungle to cover it up."

Pete did the math. "'Bout nine years," he said.

After finishing their shift, the team walked back down the path they had cleared to retrieve their packs. Tony recounted all of the reasons it had been such a mean job, including that they were working on a steep incline.

Pete agreed. "The hills I know go up and down, not up and up. How high you think this hill is?"

"Mountain," Tony replied. "This is a mountain, not one of those South Dakota hills you're used to. I think I heard its two thousand feet high. I've been on mountains higher than this in Mexico that were a lot easier to climb. No jungle, just rock and sagebrush. The plane crashed about halfway up the side of this mountain so we only climbing a thousand feet."

Pete speculated that the plane had to have been lost. "They should have known they were flying lower than some of the hills around here."

"Mountains," Tony corrected. "I heard they had lost an engine and were flying in a rainstorm. We'll probably never know all the answers."

By the time the team took a noon break, they were more than half the distance to the crash site. The party opened C-rations for lunch but had little time to relax. After half an hour, Sergeant Kolowski put the next team of trail-breakers to work. "We need to get to the site in time to set up camp before dark," he said. "Tomorrow we'll get started on the job we're here to do." That afternoon the usual tropical shower developed, and the men donned rain gear and kept going. They arrived at the site of the crash in the early evening. The plane had flown straight into a mountainside that inclined about forty-five degrees so the area of impact was relatively small. The navy investigators established a perimeter around the site and the team set up camp just outside the perimeter.

The investigators spoke to the team members who would be removing the bodies, described the plans for the following day. The investigators would first do a walk-around with the marines and navy medics to find the downed airmen's bodies and identify things the investigators didn't want to be disturbed during the bodies' removal. During the walk-around, the marines would hack down any foliage that might impede the work. The walk-around would take most of the following morning.

It had grown dark by the time the team ate their C-rations, and many of them turned in early. It had been a long day, and the following day would be no exception.

The next morning was not a pleasant experience for Pete nor any of the rest of the group. Pete had seen dead people before: a cousin who died young of leukemia and his grandmother on his mother's side. They were laid out in fancy coffins, dressed in their best, looked like they were sleeping. These bodies didn't look anything like that. He had tried to prepare himself for what he expected to be a difficult experience, but reality overpowered his imagination. The crash had occurred almost a week before, and the bodies were infested with maggots and insects and had been mutilated by feeding animals. An appalling odor pervaded the site.

At lunch time, Pete couldn't eat. He lay in his hot pup tent and tried to prepare himself for the afternoon ahead. After the mid-day break, the medics and marines split into two teams. They donned face masks, rubber gloves, and aprons and went to work. Each five-man team worked with a body until they were satisfied they had identified the crewman and had bagged the body and all of its parts. Pete and Tony were on the same team. The first body they worked on had been torn apart at the torso. There were dog tags identifying the upper torso, and the medics identified a lower torso with a missing leg to go with it. A partially eaten leg was linked to the one-legged torso by shoes on the two feet which matched in size, type, and amount of wear.

Pete found the actual bagging of the bodies didn't bother him as much as the walk-around had that morning. The initial shock must have prepared him for what had to be done in the afternoon. By evening, eleven body bags were laid out along one side of the crash site. The next morning, the marines and medics teamed up to carry six of the bodies to the LCU. Each pair of men would carry a body on a stretcher two miles down the jungle path the team had cut two days earlier. Pete and Tony found the two-man carry possible though difficult. Ten-minute breaks every half hour made the task bearable. The route that had taken a day to cover when they were cutting the path to the crash site took only two and a half hours to navigate when they were carrying out the crewmen's bodies. After reaching the LCU and placing the bodies below deck, the marines returned to the crash site and picked up the last five body bags. When these had been placed aboard the LCU, the marines returned a third time to collect any gear they had left at the campsite. The navy crash investigators, who had spent the day at the crash site, returned to the LCU with the marines on the last trip.

It had become dark by the time the LCU backed off the beach and started the six-hour trip back to Sangley Point. Pete and Tony relaxed and rested their aching muscles as the landing craft pushed its way through a calm sea. Pete, although tired after the day of taxing physical effort, felt satisfied. He tried to communicate his feelings to Tony. "I think we did something important the last few days," he said.

"What's that?" Tony asked.

"Well, you know. We identified and retrieved the remains. The families will get the remains, have a decent funeral. That's important."

"I suppose," Tony replied. "I wonder if the families will see the mutilated, decaying flesh we picked up. More than one marine lost their cookies picking them up."

"So you think we should just leave them up there?" Pete asked.

"I'm sure the dead airmen wouldn't care one way or the other. If the families saw what we picked up, maybe just covering them up for sanitary reasons would be preferable. We confirmed that they died, that's good, but beyond that, I guess I don't understand the need to haul the remains back to Tim Buck Too or wherever."

Pete didn't buy it. "That seems immoral, against Marine tradition."

"The wounded, sure," Tony replied. "The dead, what's the point?"

Pete didn't think it was a matter that needed to be pursued and dropped the subject.

When he considered what had happened over the past few days, Pete realized that while the crash site effort was dominating his mind and energy, he had little time to think about anything else. It had made his breakup with Alisa irrelevant, at least for a few days.

When Tony and Pete returned to their Quonset hut they found that Chico, the hut boy, was gone. He hadn't left voluntarily. He had been caught trying to get a stolen camera off the base in some laundry. The camera had been recovered and Chico hadn't been charged, but he wouldn't be allowed access to the base in the future. There had also been a watch missing earlier in the month. Pete had gotten along well with Chico and felt disappointed when he heard the news. Chico never missed a day, always had a smile on his face, and did a good job keeping the hut orderly and the shoes shined.

Bitter Cold, Bitter Fight

This image is in the public domain.

17.
Chosin Reservoir

After the Fifth Marine Regiment returned to Inchon, it became common knowledge that they would be making yet another amphibious landing. However, only a few high-ranking officers in the division knew when and where the landing would occur.

While waiting to embark on their next campaign, the First Fire Team received a replacement for Dan Fleming, the rifleman who had been killed during the approach to Seoul. The replacement, PFC John Dillman, came from a small town in central Kansas. He had just finished boot camp, having joined the Marines shortly after graduating from high school at the start of the Korean War. Of average height and a little on the skinny side, John acted pretty innocent. As the only son in the family that ran the hardware store in his home town, he had apparently led a rather protected life before going to Marine boot camp and becoming a fire team replacement.

With the exception of PFC Dillman, Chris and his team now felt they were amphibious-landing veterans and weren't too concerned about any future amphibious plans. They had been paid some of their back pay in scrip that the local Inchon bars and prostitutes would accept so were enjoying the lull. Besides, General MacArthur had said the troops would be home by Christmas and that only some mopping up was left to be done.

One day, Adam asked John why he had joined the Marine Corps when a war was going on. "Don't think I would have done that."

"I wanted to impress my girlfriend. "Got a Dear John from her before finishing boot camp."

"That's the funniest thing I've heard since breakfast," Les said. "Did you thank her for getting you in the Marines?"

"Never thought of that, think I should?"

Adam offered an opinion. "Wait till you've been in a couple of fire fights before you decide whether to thank her or kick her in the ass."

John looked a little apprehensive. He asked, "You guys seen much action? What happens?"

"People shoot at each other," Adam explained., "People get scared, killed, wounded. They use real bullets. That's about it." After explaining what fire fights were, Adam changed the subject. "Hey Chris, you've been around long enough to figure these things out. Where in hell are they sending us now?"

"Somewhere in North Korea," Chris replied.

Adam laughed. "You're so damned smart they made you a team leader. Pretty soon they'll make you a corporal if you don't get killed first."

When John Dillman filled the First Fire Team's vacant rifleman position, other vacancies and leadership deficiencies in the First Marine Division were also being addressed. This included bringing Easy Company's First Rifle Platoon up to full strength and replacing acting platoon leader Peters with Lieutenant Lewis. Sergeant Peters became the leader of the reconstituted Third Squad. Corporal Hautman got a promotion to sergeant and remained the leader of the First Squad.

On October 15, the men of the First Marine Division's Fifth Regiment loaded onto troop transports and LSTs—for the third time in less than three months.

The First Fire Team learned their destination soon after sailing. They were on their way to Wonsan on the east coast of North Korea. They had been at sea for a few days when someone noticed that the convoy had turned and was heading south. The north star had been ahead of the them and now it was behind them. A rumor swept through the ship that the war had ended and they were sailing back to Pusan.

However, the next day the fleet turned around and headed north again. The rumors finally honed in on the truth. The Wonsan harbor approaches were heavily mined and had to be cleared before the convoy could land.

As the days passed, the First Fire Team grew less and less happy with the situation. Les worried that they wouldn't be home for Christmas if they kept sailing in circles. The ship became as foul as it could get. The galley, stocked for a three-day voyage, ran short of food, and the turbulent sea caused the ship to pitch and roll at a sickening level. Rice, the only food that never became scarce, began to appear morning, noon, and evening. Les said it feels like we at the end of a big yo-yo string. Adam agreed. "It's not so bad when the NK messes up your day, you expect that, but when our fearless leaders screw up, it pisses me off."

Chris wondered who had come up with this half-baked plan. "I heard the South Korean Marines drove into Wonsan a week ago, our own Marine Air Wing is using the airfield, an army regiment is there, and the Bob Hope Show played there last night."

Adam was incredulous. "Missed the Bob Hope Show. Now that really pisses me off."

The convoy introduced John Dillman to the ocean and to life on a troop ship. Surprisingly, he didn't succumb to motion sickness, possibly because he didn't care for the galley food and didn't eat much of anything.

Finally, on October 26, the First Division marines were able to go ashore at Wonsan. They were welcomed by the South Korean Marines and U.S. Marine Air Wing personnel.

"Where in hell did those South Koreans learn the single-finger salute?" Les asked.

John guessed they practiced it while the First Division sailed back and forth in the Sea of Japan.

Wonsan sat on a narrow coastal plain backed up by the Taebaek

Mountains. Chris shivered as a cold north wind coming off the Mountains cut through his summer fatigues. It reminded him of the late October weather he experienced while growing up in South Dakota, and he knew it only hinted at what to expect in the near future. The mountainous terrain, though scenic in its own way, didn't look to Chris like a good place to fight a war. He had learned that fighting in hills could be difficult, and mountains had the potential to increase that difficulty to a new level.

The second day in Wonsan, Easy Company lined up to be issued winter-weight sleeping bags.

"Thank the Lord for small favors," Adam said. "I don't want to seem ungrateful, but I'd appreciate some winter-weight clothes to go with these bags."

"Put in your order," Les suggested.

After two days in Wonsan, Lieutenant Lewis informed the First Rifle Platoon that they would be transported by train the following morning to a place about forty miles north called Hungnam. The next morning, they joined the rest of the Fifth Regiment and boarded vintage trains manned by U.S. marines.

The Second Battalion filled a train which Les described as shot to hell. Chris had to agree. The engine looked like it had been used for target practice. He wondered how they kept steam in the boiler.

The train's appearance didn't bother Adam. "Might not be pretty, but it's better than walking forty miles."

The marines reached Hungnam after a slow and bumpy ride. Hungnam, like Wonsan, was a port situated in the narrow plain backed by low mountains. Soon after disembarking from the train, the Second Battalion began moving north on foot up a road into the Taebaek Mountains. The next day the First Squad of Easy Company's First Platoon received orders to patrol the right flank of the advancing column by proceeding to the top of Hill 415, occupying it until the following morning, and then returning to the main body of the battalion as it proceeded up the road.

"How do they come up with the names for these hills?" John asked.

"They pull them out of a hat," Les answered. "Or throw darts, something like that."

"Don't believe him," Adam advised. "It's the number of meters above sea level. Sometimes hills are the same height, so they add something like north or south to the name. Remember Hill 105 South on the edge of Seoul? That's where we lost Dan."

The squad moved off the road and followed the valley that paralleled the road. Chris soon felt the strain on his legs and body as they moved through the irregular terrain, up and down small hills, dodging rocks and trees and shrubs while carrying nearly a hundred pounds of gear, weapons, and ammo. Two weeks at sea with little physical activity had taken its toll. Towards evening they climbed up Hill 415. By the time they reached the top, all of the men were showing signs of exhaustion.

The temperature had hovered around freezing all day and some wet snow had fallen. Chris wondered how cold it got in these mountains. It didn't normally get this cold this early in the year in South Dakota. He knew it would get colder as they climbed higher.

Although they hadn't encountered any hostile activity during their patrol, Sergeant Hautman set a two-hour watch schedule so there would always be someone awake and alert in every foxhole.

Chris took the first watch, and his foxhole partner, John, unrolled his sleeping bag.

"Man, this feels good," John said as he crawled into the bag. "Payback time for carrying this thing all day. Didn't see anything today; think there're any NK around?"

"I'd guess the North Koreans aren't able to do much of anything anymore, otherwise we would be fighting our way up these mountains." Chris replied. "We're not paid to worry about these kinds of things, but having a division strung out on a narrow mountain road, the only road around, doesn't seem like a good place to be fighting anybody. Hope the decision-makers know more than I do."

John wanted to know why they were going up this road. "Guess it's the shortest route to the Yalu River." Chris replied. "Some planners in Tokyo looked at a map, saw a road going through the mountains almost straight to the Yalu, said, 'We'll just drive up this road to the border.' Like it was some Sunday afternoon outing."

"What about the rumor about Chinese joining the fight?"

Chris had also heard the rumor. "I don't think our fearless leaders would be dumb enough to push us up this road if they thought that would happen."

"Who's these fearless leaders?" John asked.

"Damn, you're a curious one," Chris replied. "Most marines talk about things they don't know anything about and no one believes them and that is alright. The fearless leaders are those marines blame when something goes wrong. They most likely don't know who that is and don't have to know. It's just somebody, anybody whoever it is, at the head of the chain of command that affects them. That's all they need to know."

John didn't seem satisfied. "That don't tell me anything."

Chris laughed, "You gotta get used to that when you are in the marines. But you know, everybody knows the fearless leader of this operation. It's MacArthur the head deity who resides in Japan. He has a bunch of generals in Japan and they run this show. Our division commander, General Oliver Smith, reports to some general at MacArthur's headquarters. That's where all the strategy comes from."

In the morning, the First Squad returned to the road. Chris considered it generous to call the single-lane path that grew narrower as they got further into the mountains a road. It had a variable surface that consisted mostly of whatever was uncovered when it was first cut into the mountainside. It was hardly wide enough for oxcarts to pass. Everything the First Marine Division owned was going up this road and Chris was aware that there were a number of army and Korean units also going up the same road. To Chris it seemed everybody going up this road wondered what to hell we were doing. Sergeant Hautman had heard that General Oliver wasn't happy about what was going on and was slow walking the column up the road. The road became rutted, and the wet snow and near-freezing temperatures made it slippery. Easy Company's men walked either on the road or doing flank patrol. Pete figured he would rather be walking than riding in a truck on the slippery road, which had sheer drop-offs in places.

Daily patrols and overnights off the road became routine for the squads in Easy Company platoons and within a few days they had their legs back in marching condition.

Easy Company had reached a small village called Sudong when, on the 2nd of November they were held up because of the leading Seventh Regiment ran into trouble. The Second Battalion Easy Company and the rest of the rest of 1st Marine Division sat on their haunches for two days while the Seventh Regiment dwelt with whatever was going on up ahead. The First Squad kept a fire going near their foxholes, used it to heat up C-rations and stayed in their winter sleeping bags as long as possible in the morning, shot the shit a lot and generally enjoyed the delay. Patrols were out every day but the Frist Squad lucked out and never had to go out.

After the column got moving again rumors quickly circulated that the delay had happened because the Seventh Regiment had run into the enemy ready to fight and got engaged in a battalion sized battle with a bunch of Chinese at a place called Funchilin Pass.

The First Fire Team heard the rumor after returning from an overnight flank patrol and discussed it that evening while eating C-rations and a cup of coffee. Sergeant Hautman joined them. The word Chinese in that rumor is what had their attention.

John Dillman remembered Chris telling him that we would never be going up this so-called road if our fearless leaders thought we would get involved with the the Chinese.

Chris agreed. "That is what I said. I was wrong. I'm beginning to wonder if the brass in Tokyo knows what is going on."

Les jumped in. "Hey," he said, "the brass knows. They know more than you'll ever know. Next month we'll be doing an amphibious landing south of Shanghai and you'll be saying, 'What da fuck,' and it won't matter what you say or think. So, stop thinking and do what you're told."

Adam wondered how we know they are Chinese.

"I hear they confirmed it three ways," Les replied. "The South Korean marines said 'Them's not Koreans,' some of the whoever they are surrendered and said they were Chinese, and papers on some of the dead ones said they were Chinese."

Adam laughed "MacArthur will need more proof than that."

Sergeant Hautman said this is a whole new ball game. We aren't goina be home for Christmas this year and maybe not next year.

"Maybe there's just a few of them," John said hopefully.

Adam laughed, "The words `few` and `Chinese `can't be used in the same sentence."

Chris knew that if the Chinese were really in this fight, what Sergeant Hautman was saying about this Christmas was certainly true and the First Marine Division was moving slowly into big trouble.

"As the First Fire Team approached a town called Koto-ri, the hills got steeper and more treacherous. The trucks drove in "granny low" all the time in order to get up the hills and to help brake on the way down. In many places, truck tires and tank tracks drove right on the edge of steep drop-offs into the valley below.

When the First Fire Team reached Koto-ri, the marines were issued cold-weather footwear called "shoe-pacs." The First Fire Team appreciated the chance to replace their summer shoes because they were already having problems with cold feet. The shoe-pacs were supposed to keep their feet warm, but instructions for their use seemed a little weird to Chris. The shoe-pac boot had a rubber outer layer with an insert designed to absorb moisture from perspiration. At the end of a day, the insert and socks had to be removed and dried out. For infantry in the field, that meant they had to carry spare inserts so they could dry the wet ones by wearing them somewhere on their body, like under their armpits.

"Like wearing a damn bra," Les said.

After a couple of days' experience with the shoe-pacs, the fire team found that wearing inserts like a damn bra to dry them was only a small part of the shoe-pac problems.

While humping hills on patrol, running and walking, the marines' feet would perspire and the shoe-pac inserts would get wet. When they slowed down, their feet stopped perspiring and started to get cold. With temperatures around zero, the wet inserts became ice packs.

Adam thought he would rather freeze his feet in his summer shoes than in shoe-pacs.

Les told him he didn't have that choice. "You hafta freeze them in shoe-pacs."

John Dillman wondered why they didn't test these things before they issued them.

Adam laughed. "They're being tested. You're a fucking guinea pig."

While on a patrol near Koto-ri, the First Rifle Platoon encountered two Chinese soldiers who seemed half-frozen, half-starved, and anxious to surrender. They were probably stragglers from the fighting at the Funchilin Pass. They wore bulky quilted coats and pants, quilted caps with ear flaps, and canvas sneakers with cotton socks. They had no mittens. Their feet were likely frozen. It made Chris realize there were things worse than shoe-pacs.

Easy Company passed through Koto-ri and kept going without any extended stops until November 16, when they reached Hagaru-ri, a village that sat on a high plateau at the south end of the Chosin Reservoir. As they climbed higher, the snow got deeper. It was piled into drifts two or three feet deep in places.

The men of Easy Company were still wearing summer fatigues when they reached Hagaru-ri, and the temperature had dipped below zero the night before. The marines starting wearing all the summer clothes they owned, two pairs of pants, shirts, but it wasn't enough. Cases of crippling frostbite and hypothermia began to occur. Trucks loaded with winter clothing had begun arriving at Hagaru-ri at about the same time as Easy Company, and the first order of business for the First Platoon was to get their issue of warm clothes.

They hardly had time to get into the warmer clothes before being assigned to occupy a hill named East Hill that dominated the area. The sides of the hill were very steep and difficult to climb. When they got to the hilltop, it was time to dig in for the night. The exposed ground was frozen several inches down and made digging difficult. Fortunately, snow had insulated the ground in places and made digging in those spots relatively easy so they were able to dig in adequately. During the night it snowed, filling foxholes and covering sleeping bags with about five inches of snow. The bright morning sun revealed a valley below that was magically transformed by the new snow. The First Fire Team men, all flat-landers, admired the view.

"Damn pretty," Adam commented. "Almost makes you forget it's twenty below zero."

"Not me," Les complained. "I'm from Florida. Didn't know it could get this cold."

Being from South Dakota, Chris had experienced weather with temperatures of twenty below but had never had to live in it twenty-four hours a day or fight a war in it. He shivered as they tried to figure out how to eat their frozen C-rations for breakfast. Sergeant Hautman solved the problem by allowing fires to be built to warm up the C-rations.

Later that morning, Sergeant Hautman came around to check on how well the First Squad was dealing with the cold. He found that the Third Fire Team rifleman's feet were so swollen he couldn't get his boots off and sent him down the hill for medical attention.

When Hautman asked Chris about the condition of his fire team, Chris reported that all were well but all were bitching about the shoe-pacs. "Just about everyone has had some frostbite on his face or hands, nothing to get excited about. We're learning to recognize it and deal with it. The feet are something else."

Sergeant Hautman agreed. "Can't feel frozen tissue. It's visible on the face and hands, not the feet."

Sergeant Hautman had all of the squad check their weapons and fire a few rounds. John Dillman had kept his rifle in his sleeping bag. Apparently, the rifle picked up moisture during the night and when it hit the outside air, froze up and wouldn't fire. He faced the task of disassembling and reassembling to get it to work. Adam found his BAR wouldn't fire. After injecting a few rounds that didn't fire, one round fired. After that it worked normally. Adam guessed it needed a little priming; the one round that fired warmed it up enough to work.

Sergeant Hautman said they were having big problems with starting vehicles. Vehicles that had to be ready to go were kept running.

The conversation wandered. Chris asked Hautman what he thought about sending a reinforced Marine division and an army regiment fifty miles up a cow path in the mountains in the winter with no alternate routes coming or going and with Chinese buzzing around.

Sergeant Hautman laughed. "We don't get paid to worry about that kind of stuff, but I would guess General Smith isn't too happy about it. We've been taking our time, very methodical, keeping our flanks secure. Air strips are being built at Koto-ri and here at Hagaru-ri. General Smith is following orders, but there's no rush to glory."

Some communications people with their own security moved onto East Hill, and Easy Company moved out to the edge of the Hagaru-ri perimeter. From there they were sent out on patrol on a daily basis.

The weather kept getting colder. The temperature dropped to more than thirty below zero one night and only got up to fifteen below during the day. It snowed often. One day snow fell in combination with wind gusting up to forty or fifty miles an hour. The First Squad had a patrol assignment and pushed out early before the snow and wind had picked up. By 1000 a complete white-out occurred, and the squad couldn't move. They spent the night outside the perimeter.

The next morning, Chris realized he was completely buried in the snow and couldn't tell up from down. The good news was that he hadn't suffocated and could still breathe, so he couldn't be buried very deep. He started yelling and pretty soon he could hear digging and muffled voices. Adam,

Les, and John soon dug him out of the snowdrift that covered him.

"Hey asshole, you missed muster," Adam said, "and breakfast."

"Bet I missed a great breakfast." Chris knew that the C-rations would be frozen solid and they wouldn't want to build a fire outside the perimeter so there probably hadn't been any breakfast for anyone except maybe the dry crackers in the C-ration. It remained extremely cold, but the wind and snow had died down and the squad returned to Hagaru-ri.

The rifle companies were doing patrols every day and the First Fire Team would see tracks in the snow, lots of tracks, enough to pack the trail down, evidence of large numbers of men moving along trails and ridgelines. Spooky. Chris didn't like the hide-and-seek game. Something was going on and the Chinese weren't telling anyone what it was. Sometimes Chris or other marines on patrol would spot people in the distance dressed in quilted green or white coats. The First Fire Team speculated that the coats were reversible, green on one side, white on the other. Les suggested they should hunt down some of the whoever they were, shoot a couple, and check out those coats. Adam agreed they would have to hunt them down because they seemed to be avoiding contact. "Whatever they are up to," Adam guessed, "it won't be helpful."

While back at the perimeter the First Fire Team observed a lot of equipment start to build an airstrip on a large open area on the Hagaru-ri plateau.

Adam noted the activity said it looks like we are going to hang around here for a while. The next day the First Fire Team watched as the Seventh Regiment and a section of the Eleventh Artillery Battalion on a road heading north.

Chris suggested that Adam's prediction that the First Marine Division was going to settle down in Hagaru-ri might have been a little premature.

On November 23, 1950, Thanksgiving Day, Sergeant Hautman's First Squad got in line for a traditional turkey dinner. "Can't believe it!" John exclaimed. "Haven't had a hot meal since Wonsan."

The First Fire Team held out their mess kits to be filled with turkey, stuffing, cranberries, and mashed potatoes and had hot coffee poured into their cups before sitting down on a frozen snow bank to eat their meal. Chris lifted his cup to sip his coffee, but found it already turning cold and a skim of ice forming on the surface. Same thing happened with the potatoes and turkey. Adam said he would give the cooks an "E" for effort. "But a heated-up can of C-rations would have done as much for me."

Chris commented, "At least somebody's thinking about you."

Adam agreed that it might have been a good idea but any dumb cook could have told them it's going to be a lot of work making something that'll be frozen before it can be eaten.

Lieutenant Lewis called a muster of the full First Rifle Platoon after the Thanksgiving meal. After putting the men at ease, the lieutenant, standing in a foot of snow and with the temperature at fifteen degrees below zero and a stiff wind blowing was struggling to communicate with the platoon through stiff lips. The fact that he had the wind at his back made it at all possible. Lieutenant Lewis informed them that their holiday at Hagaru-ri would be ending. The Fifth Regiment would move out and head north along the east side of the Chosin Reservoir at 0930 the next morning. As usual, the First Squad, First Platoon, Easy Company would be on flank patrol.

"Really sorry to hear we will be leaving this great vacation spot," Les said. "I'm expecting we'll be going to an even better place, more remote, more exclusive, and even colder."

"Sounds great," Adam responded, "except for the colder. I'm from North Dakota and this is too damn cold for me." He paused, looked at John, and then said, "Hey John, the tip of your nose is frozen white as a turnip. Pull up your scarf."

John had learned the drill. He pulled up his scarf and in a few minutes his nose thawed out, although the once frozen, skin tissue wouldn't revive and he would have a scar. Just about every marine sported frostbite scars on their faces after experiencing the constant below-zero weather at Hagaru-ri.

As the Fifth Regiment proceeded to move up the east side of the Chosin

Reservoir the men in the First Fire Team didn't see any enemy but felt its presence. It seemed like the Chinese were shadowing them but avoiding interaction. They heard that about two dozen Chinese had blundered into a Third Battalion perimeter which resulted in a fistfight that had been settled by a marine machine gun. The event seemed so weird that everyone in the regiment had soon heard about it.

On the morning of November 26, Sergeant Hautman informed his squad that the Fifth Marine Regiment would be relieved by an army unit and the regiment would be transported by truck to Yudam-ni on the west side of the reservoir. They would be moving one battalion at a time, the Third Battalion going first, the First Battalion second, and the Second Battalion last. The First Fire Team liked the words, "transported by truck."

Les wondered who in hell couldn't make their minds up about which way to go.

John having learned the source of all screw ups from Chris said it was our fearless leaders. Chris smiled, satisfied that John had taken his lecture about fearless leaders to heart.

They would be moving without having to patrol the column's flank. However, they were a little disappointed when their transport dropped them off north of Hagaru-ri at a place called Toktong Pass, a high point on the MSR (Main Supply Route) between Hagaru-ri and Yudam-ni. After dismounting from the truck and starting down a steep grade on foot, Chris had a good idea why the trucks didn't take them into Yudam-ni. The drivers didn't want to drive down the steep, narrow, winding road and cared even less to have to come back up it to return to Hagaru-ri.

As they marched down the steep pass, Sergeant Hautman said if anyone wanted to block the road, this would be the place to do it. Chris asked if anyone besides him felt like they were walking into a big trap. Adam wasn't sure about a trap, but they were sure as hell getting further out on a shaky limb.

It started getting dark as the Second Battalion, Fifth Marines marched into Yudam-ni that evening. Yudam-ni sat on a high oval-shaped plateau surrounded by low mountains. A few village buildings were surrounded by tents sheltering the regimental command centers for two Marine regiments, regimental support and supply functions, and medical facilities. Stockpiles of materials to supply the infantry regiments and a major part of the Eleventh Artillery Regiment could be spotted around the village, along with hundreds of parked trucks, Jeeps, bulldozers, and prime movers (tractor/truck vehicles) used for pulling artillery pieces. Not visible but certainly in place would be a perimeter line of defense running for miles through the hills surrounding the Yudam-ni plateau. Viewing all this equipment and defensive caution reminded Chris that General Oliver was being cautious as possible considering the existing conditions. Chris wondered if that would be cautious enough.

The Seventh Marine Regiment and Eleventh Marine Artillery Regiment had established themselves in the Yudam-ni valley and staked out some of the best real estate before the Fifth Regiment arrived. Easy Company found their bivouac would be in an old corn field on a flat piece of ground near a road junction. There were no natural features or manmade works that could be used for defensive purposes and they couldn't penetrate the deeply frozen ground with their trenching tools. Adam wanted to know how in hell they could defend flat ground with no fighting holes. "We'll be sitting ducks. If I had an old pick axe, I could dig a hole."

Someone in the squad did scrounge a heavy pick axe from some engineers and passed it around. After breaking through the solidly frozen top soil, the trenching tools could be used to finish the job. The squad was able to dig in somewhat adequately.

That evening, Lieutenant Lewis had his platoon gather around him in the dark, windblown corn field and briefed the men on the plans for the following day. The Fifth Regiment would be advancing out of Yudam-ni valley to the west from the junction in the road near where they were encamped. The Second Battalion would lead the advance out of Yudam-ni, followed by the Third Battalion and then by the First Battalion. As they advanced, the battalions would be alternating the lead. They would advance approximately forty miles along a primitive mountain road to where they could link up with the Eighth Army that would be advancing along the same road from the west. Chris could hardly believe what Lieutenant Lewis was telling them. Even a PFC could figure out that sending the First Marine Division further into these mountains tied to a single mountain road in unbelievably terrible weather was not a good idea, especially when they were seeing increased signs of enemy activity every day.

Dog Company, supported by Fox Company, would lead the Second Battalion advance along the road going west. Easy Company would follow in reserve to be used where needed.

As Easy Company followed the advance of Dog and Fox Companies the next morning, heavy fighting could be heard in the hills bordering the road. The Seventh Regiment had been assigned to clear those hills in order to protect the advance of the Fifth Regiment, and it sounded like there were already people on those hills that wanted to stay there. To Chris, the sounds suggested a major battle starting up. The Chinese were finally showing themselves Not a good omen for the planned forty-mile advance. Chris mentioned his concerns to Sergeant Hautman. Hautman agreed. He felt uneasy about what they were getting into. "We've been seeing those people in quilted jackets on the horizon for a long time. They weren't here to enjoy the weather."

By midmorning the advance stalled as both Dog and Fox Companies became engaged with a large number of dug-in enemy soldiers. By this time any doubt about the identity of the enemy had been erased; they were Chinese.

As evening approached, it was apparent that Dog Company would have to clear a fortified hill before they could advance further, so the Second Battalion elected to dig in for the night. The battalion formed a perimeter that included all of its companies. Easy Company was positioned facing a long draw bare of trees. Hill 403, the crest of which was occupied by marines from the Seventh Regiment, was on Easy Company's right and Fox Company was on its left.

Sergeant Hautman's First Squad found roomy, ready-to-use fighting holes near the middle of the Easy Company line which the squad quickly occupied. The First Fire Team claimed two of the holes and made them homey by lining them with pine boughs they cut from the small trees that covered the slope of the hill. John Dillman, the fire team's new rifleman, said he never thought seeing a ready-made hole in the ground would make him so happy. Sergeant Hautman had his squad test-fire their weapons to ensure they would work in the intense cold.

Chris took over the watch from John at 2100. As Chris crawled out of his sleeping bag, the cold hit him. He thought, God, this cold is unbelievable. John told him he had heard the temperature was twenty-five below. Chris could remember the temperature being that cold in South Dakota but not very often. This cold weather seemed relentless. He was wearing everything he owned and couldn't stop shivering—long johns over skivvies, wool pants over the long johns and foul-weather trousers over that, a T-shirt, a wool shirt, a wool sweater, a field jacket, a long wool pea coat and mittens with wool liners. He had a fleece-lined cap with ear lappers on his head with a helmet on top of that, and he tied a scarf around his neck that he could pull over his face. Despite being cold all over, the thing he really worried about was freezing his feet in those damned shoe-pacs. Other than boots, mittens, and cap, Chris hadn't taken off any clothes since arriving at Hagaru-ri. For that matter, he hadn't showered since taking a saltwater shower on the ship before landing at Wonsan. Then there was the problem of finding his shrunken-up dick among all those clothes before pissing in his pants. He hadn't had to do number two for over a week, thanks mostly to not eating much of anything. Hanging his butt out in thirty-below weather didn't appeal to him. Not that everyone hung their butt out. Men with diarrhea weren't able to get it out in time even if they wanted to. Some didn't even try for number one. After a certain point, the smell and lack of hygiene couldn't get worse. Chris occasionally sucked snow to get some water into his system, even though he knew from living in South Dakota not to eat snow to quench his thirst. What's worse, dying of thirst or sucking snow?

Chris hadn't been on watch for long when a friendly machine gun opened up to the left near where the Fox and Easy companies joined. The machine gun fired a couple of bursts and then became quiet. A little later Chris heard activity in front of his position and saw moving shadows. Adam, in the hole about five yards to Chris's right, fired a burst with his BAR. The shadows disappeared. Chris had had enough combat experience to realize the enemy was probing the line, drawing fire in order to establish the extent of the perimeter, discover the types of weapons they had, and look for weak points. All this activity put the company on a hundred percent alert without any prodding from higher command. The combat-wise marines knew what would likely follow the probing.

At 1100 bugles and whistles sounded off in the distance. Chris wondered how the Chinese kept from freezing their lips when they used those things.

Although the only available light was from a weak moon, the snow reflected the light and provided visibility for two or three hundred yards out in front of the perimeter line. Sounds could be heard from beyond the visible limit, shouts in a foreign language, more whistle blowing. These weren't the sounds of further probing. These were the sounds of men assembling for an attack on the Second Battalion perimeter. More machine gun and small arms fire erupted from the area where Fox and Easy companies joined.

Lieutenant Lewis moved around behind the First Platoon and ordered the men to commence firing. "At what?" Chris wanted to know. He couldn't yet see anything in front of the platoon's position. He shouted, "We need light!" As if in response, an 81-millimeter mortar flare lit up the area. What it revealed took Chris's breath away. Masses of men on a wide front strung out in long columns were advancing towards their position. Every weapon on the line began firing, but the columns of men kept coming. Chris fired his M1 at easy targets as fast as he could pull the trigger and shove new clips of ammunition into the rifle. He could hear Adam's BAR pouring out a stream of lead, as Les slapped in fresh magazines as fast as they were emptied. Heavy machine guns on either side of them tracked back and forth. A building in the draw behind the advancing Chinese caught fire and helped illuminate the scene. Additional columns of the enemy could be seen moving into the draw and advancing towards the perimeter line.

When survivors in the enemy columns got close enough, they started throwing hand grenades as they advanced. One grenade bounced just in front of Chris's foxhole. He caught it on the bounce and threw it back at the attackers. Grenades were going off like firecrackers. A grenade bounced off Chris's helmet and exploded on the edge of the foxhole. He felt shrapnel hit his left arm. Oh shit, not again, he thought, but soon forgot the minor wound as the enemy penetrated the line.

Attackers swarmed around the marines, throwing grenades and firing burp guns into fighting holes. Chris jumped out of his hole and emptied his clip on half a dozen of the enemy as they stormed the line. His M1 ejected the empty clip just as an enemy with a burp gun in his hands loomed in front of him. With no time to reload, Chris used the M1 as a club. He knocked the burp gun out of the quilt-clad person's hands and with the next blow smashed the head of the attacker.

The attackers who breached the perimeter and were still standing passed through the line and continued to the rear. The Second Battalion line must have been a barrier to them, not their objective. The nearest advancing columns were petering out, but the light of the burning building revealed more clusters of the enemy moving up as if preparing for a renewed attack despite the mortars falling on their ranks.

While they waited for the enemy's next move, a comparative calm settled over the First Fire Team. Chris realized he had not seen John during the attack. What happened to John? Chris did not have to look far. He felt something with his boot in the bottom of the fighting hole. It was John in a fetal position. His body shook violently, but not like he was shivering from the cold. Chris asked, "Are you wounded?" John didn't answer. "Can you sit up?" Chris asked. Again, John didn't answer. Chris grew impatient and called to Adam and Les, "You guys all right?"

In the faint light, Chris could see that Adam was bending over Les. Adam yelled for a corpsman. Chris crawled over to them. "You'll be okay, you'll be okay," Adam kept saying. "A corpsman is on the way to take care of you. You'll get a ride out of here to a warm hospital, you lucky stiff."

Chris got closer and pulled off a mitten and reached out to find Les's carotid artery and check his pulse. He jerked his hand back. He could feel that half of Les's face had been blown away. He was undoubtedly dead. Chris put his arm on Adam's shoulder, and Adam began to sob. Chris and Adam had seen a lot of death in the past three months, but this seemed different. Tears froze on Chris's face, his grief driven as much by Adam's grief as by the death of Les. The three of them had been together since San Diego. They had been through a lot together these last few months, a lifetime of experiences.

Chris went back to John, still huddled in the bottom of their fighting hole. He managed to get John to stand up, asked again if he was wounded, where did it hurt? Sergeant Hautman came by and checked John's condition. John had started sobbing, still not saying anything. "Sorry, John," Hautman said. "You just flunked the infantry finals. Get your ass to the rear and make yourself useful."

Chris knew it happened, and now saw it happen. Not until real combat would those who could cope be separated from those who couldn't. Hautman said he should detain John and write him up but didn't have time for that shit.

After Chris mentioned he had picked up some grenade shrapnel in his left arm, Adam said he had also taken some in his back. Sergeant Hautman guessed grenade shrapnel wounds would be as common as frostbite after what had happened that night. Chris and Adam knew the corpsmen and doctors and medical facilities would be overwhelmed and didn't bother to get their minor shrapnel wounds looked at.

Lieutenant Lewis appeared out of the dark looking for men to mount an attack to shrink the salient that the Chinese had driven between the Easy and Fox companies. "Jeez, Lieutenant," Hautman replied, "we've gotten real thin." Lieutenant Lewis sympathized, but ordered the Third Fire Team, First Squad to follow him.

The First Squad's ammunition was nearly depleted, and Sergeant Hautman took off in the dark in search of a resupply. He soon returned with a case of BAR and two bandoliers of M1 ammunition. He said a Jeep carrying ammunition and grenades was being unloaded and had half his squad go back to pick up as much as they could carry.

After the lull, bugles and whistles were heard again. The enemy columns that had been assembling near the burning building could be seen moving towards them for another go at the Second Battalion line.

A blaze of fire from the marines' line erupted as the second wave of attackers approached the perimeter. Chris acted as Adam's BAR assistant and slammed magazines into the BAR as fast as he could. The heavy machine gun next to them tracked back and forth, cutting down the advancing columns like a mower cutting weeds. This attack did not seem to have the intensity of the first attack. The enemy seemed to be going through the motions without great expectations and the attack petered out. Good thing, because the First Squad had only six men left on the line.

Sergeant Hautman guessed the enemy had shot their bolt for the night; that they had been used up. "They took roll call and nobody showed up. Those columns coming at us were whole companies taking a hundred percent losses. Can't keep doing that."

Chris thought about the First World War, where the generals learned the hard way that infantry advancing in the open against automatic weapons didn't work. Apparently, the Chinese hadn't gotten the word.

Sounds of the ongoing counterattack against the enemy lodged in the salient between the Fox and Easy Companies could be heard as the light of a new day appeared and as the last wounded were rounded up and the grisly business of moving dead marines to the rear got underway. Simply enduring the bone-shattering cold again dominated the survivors' lives as their adrenaline levels returned to normal.

As the new day dawned bright and cloudless, welcome flights of

Corsairs appeared, and the wreckage of the previous night's battle became visible. Piles of dead Chinese lay in front of the perimeter. Chris noted that many of the bodies were stacked in lines, like windrows of harvested grain. Numerous dead Chines lay in the vicinity of the marine fighting holes, victims of close-in fighting when they breached the perimeter. Chris and Adam inspected a few of the dead. Many looked like boys too young to shave. They all wore quilted white coats; many of them had wrapped cloth "puttees" around their lower legs and wore canvas shoes over heavy cotton socks. Some of them had wrapped cloths around their feet for extra warmth. "Jeez," Adam said. "I'll never complain about shoe-pacs again. I'd say the dead Chinese are the lucky ones."

"There's lots of lucky ones," Chris replied. He noticed frigid air being condensed from the mouth of one of the bodies. "There's a live one!" Chris exclaimed. They rolled the man on his back and frightened eyes looked at Chris and Adam. Crimson frozen blood on the front of the white quilted coat marked the location of his wound. Chris realized there were many enemy wounded lying on the ground in front of their perimeter, either dying from their wounds or freezing to death. Some of the wounded could be heard moaning. He also knew the regiment would be overwhelmed by its own wounded. Looking at the man in front of them, it seemed cruel, but neither Chris nor Adam, nor the regiment for that matter, had the capacity to help him. Adam wondered if putting him out of his misery would be the right thing to do. Chris couldn't bring himself to make that decision and turned away, wishing he could forget the poor man's misery.

Sergeant Hautman said it would be all right to build small fires to heat up C-rations and make coffee. He also said Lieutenant Lewis had been wounded in the fight to clear the salient, and Sergeant Peters would again assume command of the First Platoon, Easy Company.

The First Squad, First Platoon survivors gathered around a warming fire, sad-eyed and bone-tired, and talked about what had happened the previous night. The two-man crew that had manned the heavy machine gun on their right joined the coffee klatch.

During the conversation, Adam said he had begun to question the "home for Christmas" shit.

A member of the machine gun crew guessed the only way to make it home for Christmas would be if you were severely wounded or in a fucking body bag, not good options.

Sergeant Hautman agreed, adding, "Enjoy the day. The sun is shining, the Corsairs are flying, and the temperature is up to twenty below."

At noon, acting First Platoon leader Peters relayed orders for the First Platoon to prepare to withdraw to new defensive positions at 1300. A BAR man asked Sergeant Peters what happened to the Fifth Regiment's plan to advance west and connect with the Eighth Army.

Sergeant Peters told him the Second Battalion wasn't the only target of last night's attack. The entire Yudam-ni perimeter had been under a massive attack. "We found the enemy and they have us surrounded. I suspect any ideas about going further west on this road are on hold while we try to figure out how to save our own asses."

After seeing the columns of Chinese solders coming at them like ocean waves the previous night, what Sergeant Peters said crystallized Chris's thinking about their situation. His fear that they were being led into a trap had come true. They had fallen into a baited trap, and now the Chinese were attempting to kill their prey. "How in hell are we going to get out of this mess?" he asked.

"You're talking to the wrong crowd," Sergeant Peters advised.

"Yeah, Jesus Christ isn't around," a bleary-eyed rifleman added.

At 1300, mortars and a flight of F4U Corsairs began hitting preselected targets in front of the Second Battalion line in order to keep the heads of the Chinese down while the battalion began its withdrawal to a smaller and tighter perimeter. Easy Company moved to a hill 1426 that rose out of the flat Yudam-ni valley fully expecting the Chinese to come at them again during the next night and dug in as firmly as possible. The First Platoon was re-formed with Third Squad being eliminated and its survivors filling in losses in the First and Second squads. Sergeant Hautman remained leader of the First Squad. The First Fire Team, had two Third Squad survivors assigned to it. Nick Albano, a reserve corporal who was a second-generation Italian from Philadelphia, became the fire team leader. Bert Holberg, a Minnesota Swede, became the new rifleman, and Chris, happy to be relieved as team leader, elected to become Adam's BAR assistant. Nick and Bert had joined the platoon before the landing at Inchon and had become combat veterans. Nick with s muscular stocky body and Bert, a tall gangly person with blond hair fit the stereotypes their names implied.

That night, the expected continuation of the full-scale attacks did not occur. There were isolated clashes with probing patrols but no large-scale attacks.

The next day, Chris and Adam worked on improving the foxhole they now shared. They found some frozen sand bags and piled them on the side of the hole that faced out from the perimeter. Nick and Bert did the same thing with their foxhole located adjacent to where Chris and Adam had set up housekeeping. Their position offered a good field of fire with open ground that sloped downward in the direction of enemy positions.

Chris wondered why the attack on the Yudam-ni perimeter had not been resumed the previous night. Sergeant Hautman thought that the Chinese had been bled white. Chris wasn't so sure. He equated China with inexhaustible human assets. Later in the day, Chris's assessment seemed to be confirmed when, while working on their foxhole, Nick in their nearby foxhole let out a yell. "Look at that shit." He pointed to the valley between their hill and the mountains that rose further back. "Looks like a battalion at least."

Chris looked where Nick was pointing. What he saw took his breath away. It did look like a battalion of what had to be Chinese soldiers marching in a column in broad daylight. As they watched, mortar rounds started to fall on the marchers, followed by artillery and, finally, strafing Corsairs.

Chris guessed there's still a few Chinese around."

Adam agreed. "Like mice, if you can see them scurrying round during the day, there's a lot of them,"

Later in the day, the men of the First Squad learned that Hagaru-ri had been pummeled the previous night and the Main Supply Road between Yudam-ni and Hagaru-ri had been firmly blocked at the Toktong Pass. Even the men at Chris's level could figure out that if Hagaru-ri fell and the only escape route remained blocked, the Chinese could deal with the regiments at Yudam-ni in their own way on their own schedule. To Chris, the future of the marines at Yudam-ni appeared as bleak as the winter landscape. Sergeant Hautman had stopped by while checking on the squad's readiness preparations.

Adam asked him what he thought about the situation at Yudam-ni.

Sergeant Hautman thought about that for a bit, then said, it reminds me about what a French General said about their situation during the battle of Sudan in the Franco-Prussian war. "We are in the toilet and the Germans are about to shit on us. I'd say that's about where we are"

Adam laughed. "What happened?"

"Of course, they got shit on."

Chris asked Hautman how he knew about that bit of old history, "Did you read a book once?"

Me and a couple of other marines were sitting at a table in Panama one day and this marine that was always reading books opened a book and read the paragraph about the occasion. We thought it was really funny.

The First Fire Team agreed that was a pretty good description of their situation.

Yudam-ni remained quiet again the following night. The next day the marines of the Second Battalion were informed of a plan to break the First Division out of Yudam-ni and that their role would be to act as rear guard. During the day, they watched preparations for the breakout unfolding from their vantage point on top of Hill 1426. A huge caravan of hundreds of vehicles began to form up. Anything that couldn't be driven, hauled, or carried out of Yudam-ni was being destroyed. To lighten the load that would be transported or carried, the Second Battalion was ordered to discard everything not needed. The marines in the First Squad carried or wore everything they owned and, other than parts of their mess kits, couldn't think of anything to discard.

Knowing that there was a plan to get out of the trap the marines found themselves in had an immediate positive effect on the morale of the First Squad. They were no longer on mission impossible. They would fight their way out of the mess they were in and eager to get going.

During the day the marines on Hill 1426 watched as U.S. Air Force and Marine Corps made massive airdrops providing the regiments at Yudam-ni with critical items and some not so critical. Sergeant Hautman had heard but hadn't confirmed that one dropped a container of condoms. Adam wondered what in hell supply thought we were doing with these Chinese. Nick guessed that supply took it literally when the marines said, "Fuck the Chinese."

One thing that was dropped turned out to be a good idea. Tootsie Rolls. They could easily be carried in a pocket, where they froze. When put in one's mouth they thawed out and provided precious calories. Chris, like most marines, depended on syrupy canned fruit for most of his nutritional needs. Marines carried the cans in an inner layer of clothing where they eventually semi-thawed and became a quick source of energy. The marines also learned that dry food K-rations could be eaten even when the temperature was minus twenty degrees,

Later in the day, Chris and other First Squad members observed bulldozers digging a ditch where the dead had accumulated. What to hell is going on a rifleman asked. Corporal Hautman guessed they were going to bury the dead. That idea didn't sit well with some of the marines watching the activity. "What about the Marine tradition of bringing out the dead and wounded?" another rifleman asked. "Covered up by bulldozers in this God forsaken place don't seem right. Why not stack them in some of those trucks lined up to leave?"

A wounded BAR assistant who had just returned from the regiment aid station answered the question. "There isn't room for the wounded. I watched them loading the wounded into trucks. They put a layer on the truck floor, then put a floor on top of them and then put in another layer. I saw trucks with five layers. Those poor bastards won't be able to move out of their sleeping bags until we get to Hagaru-ri, and who knows when and if that will happen. I got the hell out of that aid station before they loaded me into one of those trucks. Every vehicle that can carry wounded will be loaded. And then, somehow, they'll have to find room to carry those who are wounded or killed on the way out."

All day long, fighting in the hills bordering the MSR could be heard. Chris, any marine for that matter knew those flanking hills would have to be controlled in order to move out of the hole they were in. Fourteen miles of hills infested with Chinese lay between Yudam-ni and Hagaru-ri. Chris remembered hiking in from Toktong Pass, a narrow path between high mountains that would create a formidable obstacle if it was defended by resisting Chinese. This would not be a quick and easy fourteen-mile hike.

The next morning the First Fire Team, gathered around a small fire between their foxholes making coffee and improvising a breakfast of canned fruit and K-rations.

At 0800 they observed tank D23, the only tank at Yudam-ni, and the Third Battalion, Fifth Marine Regiment headed south on the MSR towards Hagaru-ri in a column of companies that were supported by engineers with bulldozers. Following the lead units were vehicles of every description, fully loaded with supplies and wounded men. Any able-bodied men who were not attacking at the point or in the hills guarding the MSR or driving vehicles, or Second Battalion acting as the rear guard, were interspersed throughout the column and walking. All the withdrawal commotion gave Chris a feeling of being left out, of being abandoned as a sacrificial lamb to be offered up for the greater good. He voiced his thoughts to the other First Fire Team members. Adam agreed. "All's going to be left is us and a bunch of friggin' hills crawling with Chinese. 'Course, MacArthur said there's only a few Chinese volunteers up here and we'll be home for Christmas." Chris wasn't surprised by the direction the conversation had taken. By this time, all the grunt marines knew for sure that the hills around the Chosin

Reservoir were filled with Chinese, regardless of what MacArthur thought, and sending the First Marine Division up to Chosin on a tenuous mountain road had been a strategic blunder.

While the column moved onto and up the MSR sounds of fighting could be heard of Marines struggling to control the skyline bordering the MSR. Vehicles and men waiting in Yudam-ni filled in the back of the column as room on the MSR opened up. The column moved ahead slowly but steadily for about an hour when all movement stopped for another hour then started inching forward again. The artillery remained in their pits and fired at targets to the south of Yudam-ni and intense air cover added further support.

By 1300, the withdrawal column had moved out of sight of Hill 1426, and Easy Company received orders to move further down the valley to Hill 1276. From Hill 1276, Chris could see the tail end of the column sitting, not moving, a few hundred yards south of the hill. The column had moved, but not much.

Easy Company spent the remainder of the day building up their defensive perimeter on the new hill. The men were becoming expert perimeter builders, using barbed wire, trip wires, and anti-personnel mines as part of the routine. They had acquired a quantity of C3 plastic explosives. They stuffed these into empty ration cans to make shaped charges that could break through ten or twelve inches of frozen ground, allowing them to dig decent fighting holes in a reasonable amount of time. The last thing the company did in preparing the perimeter was test-fire their weapons, part of the routine after the first attack on November 27th.

Sergeant Peters had ordered the platoon to spread their foxholes wider apart than usual because there were fewer resources available to cover the necessary distance. Hill 1276 anchored the Second Battalion's rear-guard defensive line that night, a line that ran along the ridges on either side of and over Hill 1276. Before it got dark, Chris could see that the soft tail of the withdrawing column hadn't moved for some time. The stalled column would depend on this thin line of defense to protect it if the enemy tried to roll it up from the rear. Adam had noticed a second defensive line being formed at the back side of the hill. Sergeant Hautman said the depleted Dog Company would be digging in there, the only reserve in the sector.

By late afternoon, Sergeant Hautman considered the First Squad's defense efforts as complete as possible given the resources available. Fires were allowed while daylight lasted, and the First Fire Team brewed a pot of coffee and heated up some canned fruit. Sergeant Hautman showed up with his mess cup.

The First Fire Team had begun to think being rear guard was not such bad duty. Nick Albano, the new First Fire Team leader guessed that from the rate the column had moved, there had been more fighting than moving up front. Adam had also deduced that of all the bad possibilities there were, being rear guard wasn't the worst. "Being in the column might be the worst," he said. "That's one big target."

Sergeant Hautman said that the advance out of Yudam-ni might be slow and miserable, but they were going in the right direction for the right reason. "Nobody knew where we were going and why before. Now everyone knows where we are going and is hell bent to get there. We're one big bunch of motivated motherfuckers."

Nick laughed, "Yeah, if them Chinese were smart, they'd get the fuck out of the way."

As the sun dropped behind the mountains to the west and the light began to fade, the First Squad could see Chinese foragers rummaging through the burned and blown up remains of the main marine encampment that had been north of Hill 1276. Chris figured they wouldn't find much. "We even policed the place for cigarette butts before we pulled out."

Sergeant Hautman ordered the fires doused, warning, "Them scavengers will be coming after us after they get done digging through the garbage."

At midnight, mortar rounds began falling on the Easy Company line at the summit of Hill 1276, waking up Chris and the other marines not on watch. Chris and Adam had their heads down. They had managed to dig deep and piled the foxhole spoils in front of their hole for additional protection. Machine guns couldn't touch them while they had their heads down, and it would take a direct hit for a mortar to do them real damage. They had stacked two cases of BAR magazines in the hole along with a box of hand grenades. The mortar barrage went on for longer than usual. Chris knew every one of those mortar rounds must have been humped into the mountains on the backs of the hapless Chinese. The Chinese solution to every problem seemed to be lots of Chinese. It seemed to be working out pretty well strategically but maybe not so well for the average Chinese grunt.

A mortar landed near them in the direction of the foxhole occupied by Nick Albano and Bert Holberg. No sounds were heard from their foxhole, but the mortar explosion must have caused some damage. Chris crawled over. Nick and Bert's hole had caved in. In the dim light, Chris could make out their torn and silent bodies. It helped that Chris had hardly gotten to know them.

Counter mortar fire had been initiated soon after the enemy mortar attack had begun. Adam said he didn't like the way the night seemed to be shaping up. Chris had to agree.

At 0130, flares revealed swarms of Chinese moving up the hill towards the Easy Company as green tracer trails of Chinese machine guns worked back and forth along the line. The steepness of the hill and the rugged terrain created a different situation than Easy Company had experienced in previous mass attacks. Many of the attackers were protected by the terrain as they advanced, but at the same time, they struggled with the steepness of the hill. Word came down to the platoons and squads to hold fire until the attackers hit the barbed wire where they would stack up and have to raise the trajectory of their machine gun fire. Chris questioned the wisdom of the order, but at first it seemed to work. However, the attack did not let up despite the enemy's horrendous losses. Eventually all of the trip wires had been tripped and the personnel mines set off yet the attackers kept coming. To the left of the First Platoon, the Second and Third platoons were overrun and fell back. The First Platoon found that Chinese were getting behind them, and Sergeant Peters ordered the platoon to fall back to the Dog Company line to avoid being surrounded. Chris and Adam still had about a dozen unused grenades. They threw them down the hill and backed out of their hole. Adam fired off a full magazine from his Browning in the direction of the oncoming Chinese before he and Chris took off for the Dog Company line. In their rush, they ran into a Chinese intruder and knocked him to the ground. Chris shot him without slowing down. They didn't know the Dog Company password, or even if they had one, and shouted, "MARINES, MARINES," when they got near where they thought Dog Company might be. They got through without being killed by friendly fire. The Chinese weren't too far behind Chris and Adam. The Dog Company line, reinforced by the Easy Company, stopped the Chinese advance for the moment, but to Chris it felt like they were trying to stop an ocean tide. Marine artillery had started pounding the crest of Hill 1276 after Easy Company pulled out, but it had not stopped the attack.

Then something unusual occurred. All the marine machine guns seemed to be directing their white tracers towards the same spot on the hill's crest. This strange behavior was followed by a burst of exploding bombs and flaring napalm on the top of Hill 1276. Air support in the middle of the night? The noise of the battle on the ground had drowned out the sound of anything else, such as low-flying aircraft, but there could be little doubt that a massive amount of ordnance had just been dumped on the hill by U.S. air support. Whatever the source, the air attack, the artillery, or a combination of both had a sobering effect on the efforts of the Chinese, and the resulting lull in the fighting brought relief to the beleaguered marines.

Sergeant Hautman rounded up the remains of his squad, and Sergeant Peters reassembled the First Platoon. The seemingly indestructible company commander, Captain Wilson, though wounded, started organizing Easy Company for a counterattack. Sergeant Hautman, who had been able to locate only six able-bodied First Squad members, wondered what in hell they would use to mount a counterattack.

Chris questioned Adam's comment about the rear guard being preferred duty. Adam said he had been rethinking that idea himself during the last couple of hours.

Orders came down the line that a counterattack to retake the crest of Hill 1276 would commence at 0400. The attack did move the line up the hill for a ways, but the Chinese were too strong for a single wounded company to move them off the hill. The marines would wait for daylight and full air support before going at the Chinese again.

At first light the next morning, the air over Hill 1276 filled with more marine Corsairs, navy ADs and Australian P51s than Chris had ever seen in one place before. The planes dumped tons of explosives and napalm on the summit. Chris wondered how they controlled all the air traffic over such a small site. When the planes finished their work, Easy Company advanced on the summit and found only remnants of the forces that had taken the hill during the night.

Sergeant Hautman figured when the Chinese weren't able to break through during the night they had no further use for the hill. "A bunch of them probably cleared out before the air attack. They'd hafta wait until tonight to do anything, and I'd hope the column would be out of their reach by then." Hautman looked south towards the MSR. "Hell, the column's out of sight now. We need to get the fuck off this hill."

"You saying all that ordnance was wasted?" Adam asked.

Hautman didn't seem to hear Adam. Chris thought about Adam's question and answered for Hautman. "War is one big waste. Wasted lives, wasted everything. It's all about waste. What's a few bombs one way or the other?"

Hautman must have picked up on the conversation and protested, "Hey, wait a minute, careful how you talk about war. My job depends on war. What would guys like me do without war?"

Adam laughed. "Maybe this is a case where nothing could be a good thing."

Hautman admitted he'd rather be somewhere else but when it comes to wars one can't be choosey. "You have to fight the war you're in."

At 1300, Sergeant Peters had the First Platoon pick up their gear and come off Hill 1276 to form up with the rest of Easy Company and move out. A large gap existed between the end of the main column and the Second Battalion when it began moving south on the MSR, and it moved as fast as marines on foot could move. The fast pace felt good to Chris, and they were going in the right direction. The Second Battalion continued the fast pace for almost an hour before closing the gap with the main column. As they approached some of the hills along the MSR, marines that had been occupying them dropped down to the road and joined in the march south. About midafternoon, the pace slowed and then came to a stop. But they were close enough to Toktong Pass to believe the front of the column must have reached and cleared the road's most imposing barrier between Yudam-ni and Hagaru-ri.

The men of Easy Company sprawled out in a ditch while waiting for things to pick up. The first squad built a small fire and made some coffee. The men who had survived below-zero temperatures for weeks had adapted. Temperatures in the twenty-below range hardly got their attention, colder than thirty below was a different matter.

Hautman and two regulars from the machine gun section joined Adam and Chris for coffee. Chris asked about all the machine gun fire that seemed aimed at the same target the previous night. Turns out they were marking the target for the night fighter planes that dumped on the hill. Hautman figured the night fighters turned things around. That and the rounds the 105-artillery battery put on the hill about the same time. He added, "Things were looking pretty grim for a while. The Chinese probably shit their pants when air support hit them in the middle of the night. They wouldn't be expecting that."

While they talked and drank coffee, they watched Corsairs attacking targets on some nearby hills on the west side of the MSR. They were close, less than a thousand yards away. Two of the Corsairs passed overhead and dropped napalm canisters. "Jeez!" Adam exclaimed. "Look at that, the Chinese that didn't get killed swarming around the napalm to get warm."

Chris watched the strange behavior. One had to respect the Chinese facing them. Poorly clothed, fed, and equipped, with no air support or artillery, they were threatening to destroy the UN forces in the Chosin Reservoir. Only the grit, sacrifice and suffering of the Chinese soldiers made them such a force. Yet the individual Chinese soldiers Chris had seen appeared more pathetic, needier than threatening. They seemed ready to sacrifice their lives for a moment of warmth or a bite to eat. Moments later strafing Corsairs chased the survivors away from the fleeting warmth.

"Just hope the Corsairs do a good job," Hautman said. "Else we'll be traipsing up there to clean them out."

Whether or not the Corsairs did a good job, Sergeant Peters showed up and led the platoon to check out the hill. Fortunately, the Chinese had withdrawn by the time the First Platoon got to the hill, and they returned to the MSR before dark. The column had begun moving again.

The Second Battalion cleared the Toktong Pass during the night, and it would be downhill the rest of the way into Hagaru-ri except that the tail of the column found itself stuck behind an artillery battalion. Its lead prime mover had run out of fuel and blocked traffic. Other artillery prime movers were running out of fuel and things were really stuck. To add insult to injury, the column started taking machine gun and mortar fire from Hill 1226, which dominated the skyline west of the MSR.

Easy Company got tapped to assault Hill 1226. The First Platoon would lead the charge, approaching on a ridge line.

"Damn," Adam muttered, "I can smell Hagaru-ri." Chris agreed. There were a lot of things he would rather be doing than assaulting a hill filled with Chinese. He had been anticipating getting to Hagaru-ri and didn't need another fire fight to spoil the day. As the platoon moved up the hill, the task at hand crowded out any thoughts Chris had about the rest of the day. They held up as friendly fire from weapons on the MSR—bazookas, recoilless rifles, mortars, and machine guns—worked on the hill. Two 105 artillery pieces were unlimbered and fired directly into the hill. A group of navy ADs circled overhead and took turns unleashing their heavy loads of napalm, high explosives, and rockets.

The First Platoon hunkered down on the ridge approaching the summit of Hill 1226 and watched the show. Sergeant Hautman guessed the poor bastards on the hill probably wished they were somewhere else.

After the long preparation, the First Platoon moved along the ridge towards the Chinese positions. A Chinese machine gun opened up, catching and dropping a First Squad rifleman just ahead of Chris. Chris flopped down beside the fallen marine who had been hit in the face and died without making a sound. Adam, just ahead of Chris, crawled forward to gain the protection of some large rocks. Chris joined him, dragging two BAR magazine containers. They could see the machine gun and its two-man crew in an exposed position. It had apparently been set up hastily to meet the threat coming up the ridge. That any Chinese had survived the bombardment or stayed on the hill amazed Chris, but he knew from experience that no matter the amount of munitions are delivered to a site by artillery, air support, or any other means, one soldier left standing with a rifle and a single bullet can spoil your day. No ground can be claimed until men on their feet are standing on that ground.

Adam fired a burst from his BAR and hit both machine gun crew members. The First Platoon moved forward, encountering more Chinese who popped up from fighting holes as they approached. Sergeant Peters warned the platoon to only shoot at known targets since a provisional platoon was moving towards them from the other side of the hill and the platoons of Dog Company were moving up the hill. The overwhelmed Chinese finally broke and ran for the back of the hill, taking fire from three directions. After clearing the hill, Easy Company was ordered to remain on the hill until the tail end of the column moved past the dangerous ambush site.

Easy Company finally entered the Hagaru-ri perimeter late in the afternoon of December 4. As Easy Company approached the perimeter, all of the men, without being commanded, formed up, straightened up, and without cadence fell into step, each boot hitting the ground simultaneously. Chris could feel the shared pride of the filthy, bone-tired, magnificent bastards as they marched into the perimeter.

A large tent served as a mess hall. Chris and Adam drank multiple cups of hot coffee and ate pancakes until they couldn't eat anymore. Their stomachs had been empty to near empty for so long that Chris started to feel woozy and worried he might get sick. The cold air that hit them when they left the mess tent straightened Chris out, and they found the Second Battalion bivouac area where tents had been set up for their use.

"A tent," Adam exclaimed. "I never thought I would be so happy to see a fucking tent." Chris had to agree. After sleeping under the stars for weeks, flat on the ground or snow or in a foxhole, the canvas looked like heaven on earth. An oil stove provided heat. There were no bunks or cots, but there was a wooden floor. All of the twenty-four remaining "effectives" (anyone not seriously wounded or killed) in the First Platoon crowded into the squad-sized tent, spread out their sleeping bags and fell into a deep sleep.

18.

A New Normal at Sangley Point

Pete did some reassessing about who he had been, who he had become, and who he wanted to be after his fallout with Alisa. He didn't want to be who he had been, someone with an unlikely future, unworldly, innocent to the point of being handicapped. He knew he had changed significantly during the past few months, but had it been for better or worse? His world had expanded, he had lost much of his innocence, he had become part of something he had no idea existed a few months previously, but again, had he become a better person or not? Was the new norm better than the old norm? He was different for sure and better in some ways, maybe. Chris's last letter had awakened him to the need to think about what he wanted to become. Chris, who faced the uncertainties of combat as a marine rifleman, had a plan for his future, a better future. Certainly Pete, whose main duty consisted of checking the passes of sailors and marines going on or coming off liberty, had fewer uncertainties and ample opportunities to do some planning for a better future.

Pete gave more thought to the idea of going to college. Other than because Chris planned to go to college, why would he go to college? Pete liked the idea of building things, things familiar to him like roads and bridges. Rather than driving a bulldozer, maybe he could design and plan things like that. Sangley Point had a small library located in a Quonset hut behind the chapel where he did some research and found that civil engineers did the kind of work he thought would be interesting. Pete talked to the young third-class yeoman in charge of the library about his plan and asked her what he needed to do to get into an engineering school. Carolyn White, the yeoman librarian, suggested he contact a school he would be interested in and find out. Pete thought South Dakota State College in Brookings had an engineering school, and Carolyn helped him prepare a letter requesting information about the entry requirements to the school.

Pete couldn't help but notice and appraise the librarian as she helped him. Her fair skin, freckled lightly where exposed to the sun, matched her strawberry blond hair. A little skinny and flat chested, Pete thought, but cute.

Pete received a response to his inquiry which informed him that if he were a resident of South Dakota and had graduated from high school or had passed the GED test, he could enroll as a student in South Dakota State College. However, he would need to meet prerequisites before taking any engineering classes, and the engineering curriculum included a heavy dose of math and math-rich courses. At a minimum, Pete would have to complete high school geometry, trigonometry, and algebra in order to take any college-level mathematics or engineering courses.

Pete had been exposed only to arithmetic in the one-room country elementary school. His teachers were young women who had completed high school with two years of normal school training. He had heard the words "trigonometry" and "algebra" but couldn't describe what the words meant. He knew geometry had something to do with shapes like circles, squares, and rectangles. Pete realized he couldn't go to engineering school as a math illiterate and talked to Carolyn about the problem.

"There's an Armed Forces Institute," Carolyn said. "You can earn credits for just about any high school-level course in a number of different ways, such as correspondence, testing out, and in some cases, taking classes with an instructor. In fact, we will be holding a geometry class here in the library in December. Want me to sign you up?"

Pete agreed to sign up for the geometry class and then went through the Armed Forces Institute catalog with Carolyn to see what else he could or should take. Carolyn suggested algebra after geometry.

"Why wait until after geometry?" Pete asked. "I can work on both at the same time."

Carolyn laughed. "What's the big hurry? I believe you said you had over two years left on your enlistment."

"I feel like I need at least two years to do some catching up. I figure the more courses I can take, the better, right?"

"You're different," Carolyn said. "Different than most men I meet around here."

"I'd guess you meet a lot of them." Pete surprised himself by engaging in the direction the conversation seemed to be going. A few months ago, he would have been awkward and tongue-tied.

"You'd think so," Carolyn replied. "There's about a dozen nurses and enlisted women and one-woman officer at Sangley, about a hundred-to-one ratio, but we're kinda like the condiments at a picnic. The natives are the main course. They provide everything most young men want without a lot of fuss or bother."

From what Pete had observed Carolyn had the situation pretty well figured out. Carolyn changed the subject. "You have two choices for getting algebra credit. One is a read-only course where you study a workbook and when you think you know the material, you take a test. If you pass, you get credit for the course. The other choice is a correspondence course where you study a section and then take a test that is graded by someone assigned to work with you. I suggest you do the correspondence course. You'll get more out of it."

Pete agreed. "Sounds like a good idea. I could use some feedback. Help me get signed up, and I'll take you to a nice Mexican restaurant in Manila this weekend."

The restaurant idea had popped into Pete's mind and mouth without any preliminary thought. Carolyn studied Pete before answering and then said she would like that, but added, "Don't feel you owe me anything. I would enjoy going out to lunch with you."

Saturday afternoon, Pete and Carolyn caught the Margaret to the Manila Hotel and hopped on a Jeepney for the short ride to the Más Grande. Pete and Tony had eaten enough at the Más Grande to be recognized by the owner. Tony rated the restaurant as good as any restaurant in Juarez. Pete didn't know if that should be considered a recommendation, but found the spicy food a good alternative to the bland Midwestern fare he had been accustomed to. Carolyn, who had grown up in Los Angeles and who knew something about Mexican food, rated it between good and very good.

At the restaurant, they talked and learned more about each other. Carolyn had attended college for one year but didn't know why. She joined the navy to see some other parts of the world and try to figure out where she fit in it. She seemed fascinated by Pete's description of his youth in what she considered to be Indian country.

They returned to Sangley Point early enough to watch the regular Saturday night movie shown outdoors beside the enlisted men's club. After the movie, Pete walked Carolyn to the Bachelor Officers Quarters where all of the nurses and navy women were billeted. Intending to part properly after their first date, they hugged lightly, but instead of separating, the hug became tighter, their lips touched and then pressed hard. Pete still felt the mingled wetness of their kiss on his lips as he walked back to his Quonset hut.

As Pete walked, his mind reran the evening's events. He couldn't remember when he had felt so good. He had had a real date with a woman, something he had never done before. He didn't consider his relationship with Alisa dating. That was an arrangement that failed because both of them began to think it was more than an arrangement. Alisa had been fantasyland, Carolyn was real world; a world he knew and could understand. Even his mother would approve.

Pete received the Algebra workbook before the geometry class started and got right to work on it. After previewing the algebra workbook, he wondered if he had tackled more that he could handle. Algebra dealt with abstract values that were represented by assigned letters or symbols, something unrelated to any of Pete's previous learning experiences. He decided there would be only one way to find out if he could handle it. He started on page one and then went to page two and so on. He kept doing that until he came to the first review and test. The review seemed easy enough and so did the test. The one-page-at-a-time process seemed to be working. Pete concluded that it was good that he only had to work on one subject for three weeks before the Geometry class started up in December, and he proceeded to work both math courses like a man possessed.

Tony found himself puzzled by the changed behavior of his friend. Pete hardly had time to go to the enlisted men's club for a beer and wasn't interested in attending one of Manila's biggest yearly mestizo parties. Tony had gone with Maria and had seen Alisa there with an older Chinese businessman. Pete seemed to have taken the breakup with Alisa pretty hard, but Tony didn't connect that with Pete's new obsession for studying some kind of courses. He asked Pete, "What's going on? You aren't tearing up the beach, chasing women and drinking. You're not upholding Marine traditions."

Pete told Tony about Chris, his boyhood friend now with the First Marine Division in Korea, a rifleman with a pretty low life expectancy who in his letters was writing about his plans for the future. "That got me to thinking. If Chris is thinking about the future, maybe I should be doing some planning beyond next weekend."

Tony appreciated the comparison. Recent news out of Korea hadn't been good. "For a while they were talking about the troops being home for Christmas and all of a sudden the Chinese were in the war. So, what has your future thinking come up with?" Tony asked.

"I'm going to go to college, South Dakota State, and get a degree in civil engineering."

"What?" Tony asked. "You told me you hadn't gone to high school.

Didn't anybody tell you? You have to go to high school before you go to college."

"That's why I'm studying my ass off," Pete replied. "I'll be ready."

Besides his obsession with his studies, Carolyn had become a high priority in Pete's life. Carolyn had played on her high school tennis team and introduced Pete to the sport. It didn't take long before Pete played well enough to make volleying with Carolyn interesting. They started playing games, which Carolyn always won. Pete didn't mind, his main goal being to make the game interesting for Carolyn. Pete and Carolyn's other on-base date activities included swimming in the pool near the officers' club and attending events at the enlisted men's club. Something else that Pete and Carolyn desired, but couldn't easily find on a military base, was privacy. Their hormone-driven desires to hug, kiss, touch, and fondle each other, or more, had to be suppressed.

One Saturday when both Pete and Carolyn were free, they decided to do some exploring in Manila. Pete wanted to visit the old walled city where the Japanese made their last big stand in Manila during World War II. Carolyn wanted to visit some shops on Escolta Street to pick up a gift for her mother's birthday. They left early in the morning and planned to spend most of the day in Manila.

Carolyn wore light-weight blue slacks with a white blouse and flat shoes. She said she hoped touring the ruins wouldn't be too difficult. Pete, who wore a flowery Hawaiian-style short sleeve shirt untucked over khaki pants, didn't think it would be. "We'll just walk around and look, not dig in the ruins."

They arrived midmorning and spent an hour and a half walking through what remained of the old fortified city that had been built when the Spanish ruled the country. Modern Manila spread out in all directions from the walled city, which covered only a few square blocks. Except that vegetation had overgrown the much of the area and a few roadways had been cut through the ruble, it appeared the site looked pretty much as it must have on the last day of the battle. Total ruins. Gaping holes remained in the fifteen-foot-thick fortified walls, as did the rubble of destroyed buildings inside the walls. The remains of substantial buildings still standing were riddled with holes made by cannons and smaller caliber shells. Well-worn paths and roadways made walking through the ruins relatively easy. Pete wondered if there were still bodies under the rubble. Many of the buildings appeared to have been impressive structures before all the destruction.

The tropical midday heat had started to settle in after about an hour and a half. Peter felt he had seen all that he wanted to see and asked Carolyn if she was ready to leave.

Carolyn was ready to leave. Said it had been helpful to understand how destructive wars are. "Now we are in another war in Korea"….her voice trailed off, not completing the thought.

The left and went to Escolta Street where Carolyn found a gift for her mother and then did some personal shopping before they hopped into a Jeepney and stopped for a late lunch at the Más Grande. Roberto, the owner, greeted Pete by name and showed them to a table.

Pete and Carolyn shared a bottle of wine with their tacos. The wine went quickly and they ordered a second bottle.

While lingering over the second bottle, they discussed what they should do with the rest of the day.

"Back to the base for a swim or tennis?" Pete asked.

Carolyn didn't feel up to it. "Feel lazy; just want to relax take it easy. The touring this morning, the shopping sort of did me in.

"Maybe the two bottles of wine," Pete suggested.

"That too," Carolyn admitted."

Without giving it much thought Pete suggested that they should get a hotel room and take a nap.

Carolyn laughed, "I've never heard that line before"

Pete felt the words came out wrong as soon as he said them, tried to explain." You said you wanted to relax, take it easy and I was trying to think of where one could relax in this sprawling city and the first thing that came to mind was a hotel."

Carolyn studied Pete for a moment and asked if he had a good hotel in mind.

Pete wasn't sure what Carolyn meant by her question but it sounded encouraging to him. "We are on Dewey Boulevard, some of best hotels Manila has are on the boulevard. There is one right next door. Not one of the big ones but it is on the boulevard."

"Is it expensive?"

"It has an impressive front, otherwise don't look too fancy. One way to find out."

They checked it out and found it cost a little more money than Pete was carrying but before Pete could give up on the deal Carolyn handed him enough money to cover the difference.

At that point Pete was sure Carolyn was with whatever the program was. Pete had never been in this kind of a situation with an American woman before. He wasn't sure what the protocol was but pretty sure it is different than he had experienced with the Philippine women that he had met.

They took the elevator up to the fifth and top floor of the hotel where they found that their room overlooked Manila Bay. Carolyn looked at the view and said it almost made it worth the price. The room was large and felt comfortable and was furnished with a settee, coffee table, desk and chair, and a large bed with an array of pillows. Its large connecting bathroom had a tub and shower.

"This is nice," Carolyn said. "Wish I'd brought an overnight bag."

Carolyn lay on the bed and stretched out on her back. "Ooh, this is what I needed," she said.

Pete sat down on the edge of the bed, not sure what to do. He started talking. "You are the first American women I ever dated. Never had any sisters, never went to high school, so didn't know much about girls but was attracted by them and thought about them a lot. I was a hick farm boy that didn't know how to act around women and still don't, But I want you to know I like you a lot.

Carolyn sat, put her arms around Pete, "Pete, I'm one woman that likes this hick farm boy very much, I like you so much I love you." Carolyn leaned forward and kissed Pete.

Sensations overwhelmed Pete consciousness as they embraced and he told Carolyn his feelings for her were beyond anything he had ever felt before. They kissed again and Pete worked at opening Carolyn's blouse without a lot of success. Carolyn helped remove the blouse and took off her other cloths while Pete undressed. They embraced, clung together as their emotions swept up and consumed them and they became one. They lay back blissfully exhausted, they fell asleep, woke up, took a shower and made love again.

Finally, they had to leave the hotel in order to catch the last boat back to Sangley Point before midnight.

Pete had not heard from Chris since the First Marine Division was preparing to leave Inchon, but he knew that the division landed at Wonsan a short time before the Chinese entered the war and that heavy fighting had occurred at a place called the Chosin Reservoir. Chris had seen almost constant combat as a rifleman since landing in Korea in August and had survived Pusan and Inchon. Pete said a silent prayer that Chris's good fortune would stay with him at the Chosin Reservoir.

Distances North to South Along the MSR

The map includes the identity of seven Chinese divisions attempting to stop the withdrawal

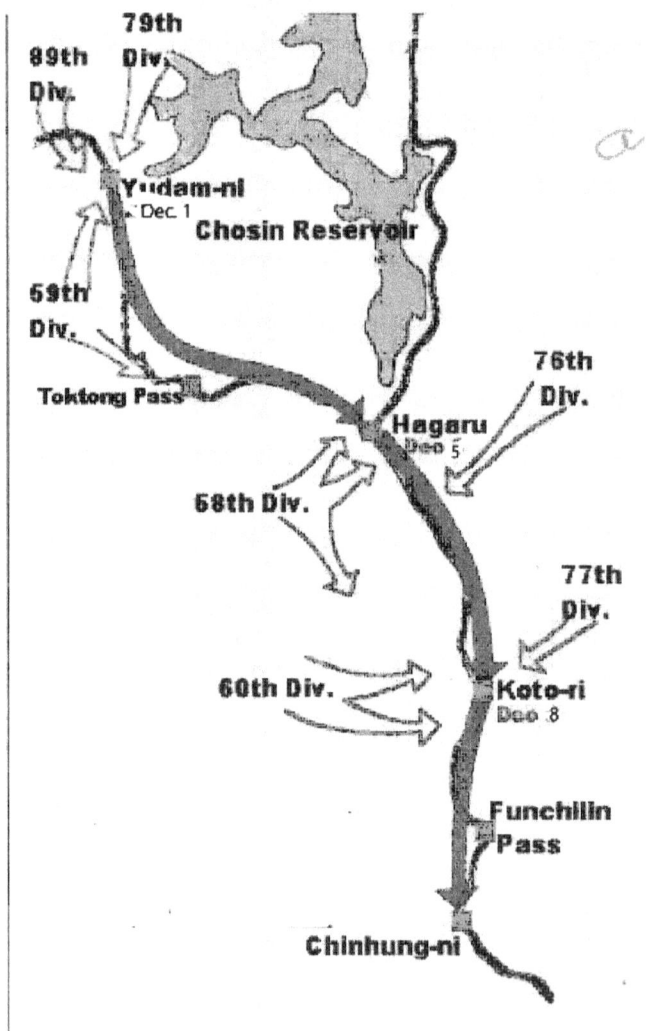

Distance between villages and cities:
Yudam-ni to Hagaru-ri—14, Hagaru-ri to Koto-ri—11,
Koto-ri to Chinhung-ni—10, Chinhung-ni to Sudong—6
Sudong to Hamhung—26, Hamhung to Hungnam—8
Total 78 Miles

19.

Attacking in a New Direction

The morning after Easy Company made it into the Hagaru-ri perimeter, Sergeant Peters, still acting as the leader of First Platoon, Easy Company, entered the heated tent where Chris, Adam, Sergeant Hautman and the rest of the First Platoon survivors had spent the night. Sergeant Peters rousted up any marines not awake. "Okay, you lucky bastards," he said. "Enjoy your vacation and be ready to move out at 1500 with your gear and all the ammunition and grenades you can carry. The people up on East Hill are about fought out, and we will be relieving them."

The announcement drew a chorus of groans from the men recovering from the first good night's sleep they had had in weeks. Chris, who was awake but still luxuriating in his warm sleeping bag, scrunched further down in the bag and pulled the end flap over his head. East Hill, Chris thought. We were on that hill the first time we got to Hagaru-ri. It seems like they should have it under control by now. A rifleman lying next to Chris got up on his elbows. "I think I'm having a freaking nightmare. Somebody wake me up."

Sergeant Peters wasn't done. "I've got more good news. The Second Battalion will get to enjoy this lovely place until everyone else leaves."

Somebody grumbled, "Fuck. Tail End Charlie again."

Sergeant Peters ordered the platoon to get some hot food while they could. "Be back at 1300. We will be doing some reorganizing before moving out at 1500."

Most of the platoon lay in their sleeping bags absorbing the information.

"Damn!" Chris exclaimed. "We better follow orders and get some hot food."

"Hot food, what's that?" Adam asked. They pulled on their boots and several layers of the outer clothes they had shed in the warm tent before heading out into the familiar cold. Sergeant Hautman joined them.

The transformation of Hagaru-ri since they had left it only two weeks earlier impressed Chris. What had been a small North Korean town overrun by an incoming Marine division had been transformed into a complex supply depot and divisional headquarters, its perimeter filled with thousands of men, artillery and their trains, heavy and medium tanks, engineering bulldozers, and innumerable "soft" vehicles of every description. The landing strip that had been under construction was now completed. Marine, navy, and air force C47 transport planes were hauling in supplies and replacements and hauling out the wounded and dead as fast as the single makeshift runway could handle them. Other transport planes were airdropping supplies into an open area in the perimeter.

Sergeant Hautman waved his arm as if encompassing the whole scene. "In a few days, this place will be ashes and a bunch of holes in the ground."

"Yeah," Adam replied. "And we'll get to see it happen. Second time in a week. We'll be expert scorched-earth watchers."

Chris wondered why the Second Battalion, Fifth Regiment always got the rear end job. "I'll bet the Seventh Regiment will be in Koto-ri while we are still sitting here watching them blow the place up."

"You got it right," Sergeant Hautman said. "Heard the Seventh is heading out in the morning and we'll be on East Hill waving as they go by."

As they made their way to the mess tent, they walked by some kind of a ragged formation of men near a helicopter that had recently landed. A second lieutenant moved from the formation and approached them. "You men come from Yudam-ni?" he asked. After confirming that was the case, the second lieutenant told them to follow him. "General Almond has a pocketful of medals to give out."

Hautman, Adam, and Chris joined two other similarly scruffy enlisted men and a group of scruffy-looking officers. General Almond dressed in spotless pressed wool dress pants, a starchy new-looking Mackinaw coat, and an army fur field cap with a bunch of stars on its front flap, moved down the line as an aid pinned silver stars on the officers and bronze stars on the enlisted men. After that had been accomplished, the second lieutenant dismissed the enlisted men and General Almond went into the Division Command Post tent.

While proceeding to the mess tent, Chris pulled off the bronze star and put it into a pocket filled with M1 30-caliber clips. "What the hell was that all about?" he asked.

"General Almond is known for carrying around a bunch of medals and passing them out," Sergeant Hautman replied as he took off his medal and put it into a pocket. "I wouldn't be caught dead wearing it in the mess tent."

Adam took the cue and pulled his off, too. "Maybe I can trade it for a bottle of that hooch I see floating around here."

They found Easy Company being reorganized when they returned to their tent. Captain Wilson had recovered from his minor wound and re-assumed command of Easy Company. The platoons had been fleshed out and a newly arrived lieutenant, Alvin Burkhart, took command of the First Platoon, Easy Company. The First Platoon reestablished its Third Squad by assigning Eleventh Artillery Regiment personnel as riflemen. A Sergeant Kolowski became the Third Squad leader, and Sergeant Peters reverted to being the leader of the Second Squad. Both Second Lieutenant Burkhart and Sergeant Kolowski had been rooted out of a security contingent at the Sangley Point Air Station in the Philippines when the Marines searched for replacements to be flown into Hagaru-ri.

The First Fire Team picked up two replacements dredged from the Marine security contingent at the Atsugi Naval Air station in Japan. They were PFC Rick Harkin and PFC Clayton Field. Rick, a big man with kinky blond hair, didn't have much to say. Clayton looked athletic, even when bundled up in layers of clothes, and was the only negro marine Chris had seen since arriving in Korea. They had both been in the Marine Corps less than a year.

Chris had considered continuing to act as Adam's BAR assistant, making both Rick and Clayton riflemen, but Rick informed Chris that he would not occupy the same foxhole as Clayton Field. Rick had grown up in Oklahoma and apparently had strong feelings with regards to Negroes. Chris recalled Sam and the ink bottle incident in boot camp, but he didn't have the time or the expertise to deal with the situation, so he made Rick the BAR assistant who would share a foxhole with Adam and Chris and Clayton would share a foxhole.

The newcomers felt the sting of the unrelenting cold soon after they arrived and piled on additional layers of clothing from the now abundant stocks at Hagaru-ri. Their clean clothes made the replacements easy to spot.

Easy Company, Second Battalion had a busy afternoon, reorganizing and preparing for the move to East Hill. Despite the confusion, Chris managed to get Sergeant Kolowski's attention long enough to ask if he had known a marine named Pete Houser at Sangley Point.

Sergeant Kolowski laughed. "Know Pete? I sat beside him when we flew from California to the Philippines and introduced him to the wonders of Cavite."

"He's from my home town," Chris replied. "We enlisted together."

"Small world. We need to talk when there's time," Kolowski replied before he went back to organizing the reconstituted Third Squad.

At 1500 the Second Battalion, Fifth Regiment formed up in open ranks and marched a mile to East Hill, the hill that dominated the entry to the MSR leading to Koto-ri. When they got to East Hill, the marines of the First Platoon, Easy Company learned they would be attached to Dog Company. Dog Company would relieve George Company, First Battalion which faced the Chinese on the summit.

In order to get to the positions they would occupy, the marines found they needed to use ropes previously rigged to get up the slippery hill. The handover went without a hitch and by 1700 the Easy Company's First Platoon had bedded down in prepared positions.

Chris noted that they had a bird's-eye view of Hagaru-ri from their position, and the Chinese above them would have an even better view. There would be no fires tonight. They were within range of the enemy and didn't need to provide lighted targets. He had some hard K-rations in his pocket and a half dozen Tootsie Rolls. That would be his dinner.

Clayton, Chris's new foxhole mate, seemed to be more concerned about the cold than the Chinese. "How in fuck do you guys survive?" he asked. "We heard about Chosin in Japan, thirty-below temperatures."

"You get used to it," Chris replied. "After a week or so you get so numb you don't feel anything. A big problem is getting a four-inch dick out of six inches of clothes."

Clayton laughed. "Niggers won't have that problem."

Clayton, despite being a minority, got on well with just about everyone and had a self-deprecating sense of humor. Chris found himself liking Clayton. He had nothing against Rick, but Rick didn't mix with anyone or have much to say. The only thing Chris knew for sure about Rick is that he didn't like Negroes.

At 0500 the next morning, Chris and Clayton were awake trying to figure out what if anything they would have for breakfast. Sergeant Hautman came by and said that Dog Company would be attacking the summit at 0700; First Platoon, Easy Company would be in reserve.

Chris became fully awake, remembering where they were and what they were doing. Obviously, the Chinese, who had a bird's-eye view of Hagaru-ri and the MSR running along the base of East Hill, would have to be dwelt with. They had a clear shot at anything moving on the MSR below the hill and their weapons could reach just about anything in the perimeter, including large stocks of munitions and fuel.

As Chris and Hautman talked, they could see the lead elements of the breakout, a tank followed by a bulldozer and infantry, moving on the MSR. Hautman commented that the Chinese must not be awake yet.

At 0630, the Chinese must have woken up because they started firing at a Seventh Regiment infantry company moving along the MSR at the bottom of the hill. Dog Company shot diversionary machine gun and rifle fire at the enemy positions, and mortars that had been scheduled to start prepping the hill for an attack at 0700 got an early start. At 0725, the air began to fill with the most planes Chris had ever seen at one time, even more than those that attacked Hill 1276. The planes roared low over the summit, delivering bombs that shook the ground, and fired rockets and machine guns into suspected enemy positions for ninety minutes.

Clayton seemed to be enjoying the show. "Them's the best fireworks I've ever seen."

Chris noted that the Chinese were no longer harassing the men streaming past the hill on the MSR.

Clayton laughed. "They's got their heads down as far as they can get them."

As soon as the air attack ended, the three platoons of Dog Company began to move forward. First Platoon, Easy Company stayed in reserve. Sounds of intense fighting were heard. Clayton guessed some of the Chinese must have survived. Soon Chris and his fire team saw stretcher bearers carrying seriously wounded men off the hill. Fortunately, even though marine and army engineers were busy burning and blowing up everything that wouldn't be carried out with the withdrawing forces, cargo planes were still landing and taking off. The wounded would have a fast ride back to Hungnam.

Two knobs on the summit of East Hill were the initial objectives of the marines' attack. After the lower knob had been taken, First Platoon, Easy Company moved in to occupy it while Dog Company moved on to attack the next knob which soon fell and things quieted down.

The First Fire Team built a fire to make some coffee, the first source of fluid they had had all day. Sergeant Hautman seemed to have a nose for coffee and stopped by. While drinking coffee and bullshitting, they observed a large group of men dressed in mustard grey quilted coats being led off the hill by a few marines.

"Prisoners?" Adam asked. "What in hell are they going to do with all those prisoners? There must be a couple hundred."

Sergeant Hautman wondered, too. "We been getting rid of anything we don't need. I heard they had turned a bunch of prisoners lose that were being held at Hagaru-ri."

Chris suggested giving them a hot meal and letting them go. "Bet most of them would be happy with that."

Adam agreed. "Put up a sign, 'Warm tent, hot meals,' and the Chinese would be lining up for miles to surrender."

Chris laughed. "They'd have to fight to keep the marines out of that line."

Clayton exclaimed, "What da fuck, my coffee turned to ice!"

Adam laughed. "You can tell these amateurs. Ya gotta catch it right between burning hot and ice. There's a little window where you slurp it down. How'd you like sleeping in a foxhole at twenty below?"

"No problem," Clayton replied. "'Cept Chris kept wakin' me up to go on watch."

Lieutenant Burkhart stopped by and informed the group that the First Platoon would be moving back to the Easy Company position on the perimeter at 1700.

Chris told Clayton and Rick they should heat up some C-rations. There wouldn't be any fires tonight to heat rations or water.

Easy Company's section of the perimeter straddled a narrow-gauge railroad track at the bottom of the west side of East Hill. The railroad bed, raised about five feet, ran at an angle from where the perimeter line was intended to go, but offered such a good defense structure that Easy Company took advantage of it by jogging the line, making it thinner and longer, but stronger. At the same time, the jog formed a salient, a prong of occupied ground that extended forward from the rest of the perimeter in that sector. Easy Company tied into Fox Company on its right on a lower slope of East Hill and with Charlie Company on its left. Marine engineers were planting mines and laying barbed wire in front of the Easy Company position when the First Platoon came up to the line.

Clayton wondered why the Chinese would attack. "They know we're leaving."

Chris answered, "The Chinese generals want to overrun Hagaru-ri and roll up the column from the rear and the grunts want to get at that supply depot before it gets blown up."

"You saying the grunts would die ta get at those clothes and food."

Chris nodded. "Put yourself in their shoes, near starving and your feet are freezing."

Using the railroad bed for defense relieved the First Fire Team of the need to make holes in the firmly frozen earth. A heavy machine gun team joined the First Fire Team at the point of the salient. The First Fire Team laid their weapons along the top of the railroad grade along with bandoliers of M1 clips, cases of BAR magazines, and grenades. They stockpiled additional cases of ammunition and grenades at their feet. Easy Company was as ready as they could be for whatever happened on what they hoped would be their last night at Hagaru-ri.

Chris still had a dozen Tootsie Rolls and shared them with the fire team members. It had started to snow and temperatures had risen to ten degrees below zero. Chinese began probing the line, their usual precursor to an attack, about the time the snow started.

Although tired, Chris knew he wouldn't sleep. He felt a tension in the air. Chris told Clayton to sleep if he could. Clayton answered that he had this spooky feeling and didn't think he could sleep either. At 1100, a Chinese probe bumped into the point of the salient and backed off after attracting a few Garand rifle rounds. After midnight, it got noisy on East Hill where Dog Company had dug in for the night. Soon after the action started on East Hill, Chinese bugles and whistles signaled that a massed attack force was forming ranks in front of the Easy Company position.

Soon mortar flares revealed waves of attackers moving towards the Easy Company lines. The First Squad marines leaned on the slope of the raised railroad track watching them approach. Chris glanced over to where Clayton lay on the rail embankment, visible in the eerie light of the mortar flares. Clayton leaned on his elbows, his head up and his rifle in his hands. He looked ready.

Marine mortars began dropping onto the columns of approaching Chinese. The small arms and machine guns were ordered to hold their fire until the Chinese hit the barbed wire where they became can't-miss targets.

When the first wave of Chinese hit the barbed wire, pandemonium erupted as the attackers in the front rows melted into heaps of dead and dying humanity. Chris had become more familiar than he cared to be with massed attacks. It seemed incomprehensible that so many human lives were being used in their attempts to break through Marine perimeters. Their losses had to be staggering. Yet they kept doing it. The columns did not waver or fall back, they simply no longer existed. Chris had often wondered at the discipline of the soldiers, both Chinese and North Korean, who carried out these attacks. Now he wondered if he was witnessing discipline or madness.

The attack finally faltered. The enemy stopped coming, perhaps an indication that the Chinese had run out of enough infantry to make up the columns.

Clayton asked, "Is it over?" It sounded like he was asking if the world had ended.

In answer to his question, mortars began falling on the Easy Company Line and the green tracers of Chinese machine guns lit up the night. If the attack had accomplished anything, it had mapped the marine defenses and identified machine gun locations. The First Platoon line along the railroad embankment started taking mortar rounds. The machine gun at the salient point took a direct hit and the mortar rounds marched down the line. Calls for corpsmen were heard. The First Platoon found itself on the other side of the devastation. Chris started to wonder about the wisdom of locating along the rail line. The mortar fire started to move back up the line. Things were falling apart. One mortar round fell near Adam and Rick. Adam had been lying flat on the railroad embankment and took a few shrapnel fragments while Rick, moving back for some reason, took the full impact of the blast. A corpsman already in the area pronounced him dead. Rick, the quiet one that hardly anyone had gotten acquainted with, had died before his uniform had become badly soiled. Chris had found war made dying impersonal, not a big deal if it wasn't you. Learning that Sergeant Hautman had been seriously wounded affected him more than Rick's death. Chris and Adam had been with Hautman since Camp Pendleton. Chris hoped transport planes would still be operating out of Hagaru-ri in the morning and Hautman would catch a ride out. A truck on the MSR didn't provide a good alternative to air evacuation.

Bugles and whistles were sounding. "Aw shit, not again," Clayton muttered. Chris took over Rick's role as Adam's BAR assistant and braced for the next attack. Serious losses made the First Squad more vulnerable than it had been during the first attack. Chris was relieved when he saw another heavy machine gun team settle in at the salient point where the previous machine gun had been taken out by mortar fire.

Chinese bodies were stacking up in the killing field, but the attack pressed ahead. The attackers again penetrated the First Platoon line and, this time, captured the machine gun at the salient point. The machine gun hijackers were in the process of turning the gun around to use it against the First Platoon when Clayton turned his rifle on them and killed them. Then he ran to the machine gun, turned it back around, and started firing at the incoming attackers. Chris tapped Adam on the back, handed him the BAR magazines he had in his hand, and ran to where Clayton had commandeered the machine gun. He fed ammunition into the gun until it jammed. By the time the gun jammed, the attack had petered out. The Chinese that had penetrated the line headed toward a huge dump that the departing marines had not yet destroyed, intent on finding food and or warm clothing.

Another attack followed, but by then the attackers had to negotiate such sizeable stacks of dead and dying comrades that they didn't seem to have the spirit or energy to press the attack home.

The sun finally rose, bringing an end to the senseless carnage. The First Platoon had lost half their number, dead or wounded. The platoon's men reorganized into two squads again. Sergeant Kolowski, the replacement from Sangley Point, became the First Squad leader.

Kolowski greeted Chris. "That was one hell of a night." He gazed over the piles of corpses in front of the perimeter. "I was on the Islands during the big one, never saw anything like this."

Chris said he had seen a few of these kinds of attacks since being in Korea, but also never anything like this one. "Why do they keep doing it? Chris asked of no one in particular.

Kolowski figured it was the only advantage the Chines had, numbers of fighters, enough to over whelm an opponent's advantages but it hadn't been working too well lately. Clayton guessed the reason the attack had been so furious was because the Chinese wanted to get to that supply depot before the engineers blew it up. As Clayton spoke, a series of explosions leveled the supply depot. "Bet that got the last of the scroungers," he added.

At sunrise, transport planes had started shuttling in. Chris felt confident that Sergeant Hautman would be on a flight out and soon be in a hospital in Hungnam or Japan.

By mid-morning, the remaining troops and vehicles in Hagaru-ri began to move out. Engineers were still blowing up things. The First and Third battalions took to the hills to control the skyline while How Company Third Battalion led the train of vehicles loaded with the last of material and supplies and bodies to be moved out of Hagaru-ri onto the MSR. Troops on foot were intermixed with the vehicles. As the last troops were departing, the Second Battalion moved off East Hill and out of the perimeter with a Sherman tank to bring up the rear of the train.

As the Second Battalion started down the MSR, a new phenomenon occurred. Thousands of civilians filled the road behind them.

Chris didn't know what to make of this development. Where did they come from? He had seen civilians but not in large numbers. Chris figured they must be North Koreans. There might be a few Chinese mixed in, but mostly it was a crowd of North Korean men, women, and children, young and old. They apparently wanted out, wanted to go wherever the marines were going.

During one of the column's many stops, Chris talked to Adam and Sergeant Kolowski about the civilians. Kolowski said it looked like a positive thing. "These folks think we're going to make it and they're going to go with us. They know better than the generals what the score is."

Adam felt sorry for whoever they were. "They only have what they are carrying and wearing. It's cold. Where do they sleep, what do they eat?"

Clayton agreed with Adam. "It kinda makes one know it could be worse," he said. "War's mean, that's one thing I'm learnin'."

Chris asked Sergeant Kolowski how he felt about being brought in as a replacement. "I get letters from Pete. Sounds like Sangley's a pretty sweet deal."

"Kinda like going from marine heaven to marine hell," Kolowski acknowledged. "But I re-upped, I know what marines do. You take what you get. In a way, the rush in battle is almost as good as sex, 'cept I never heard of anyone getting killed having sex."

"Not sure 'bout never," Clayton said. "Like with somebody else's wife, or a nigger with a white woman, dat can be life threatening."

Adam laughed. "Never say never."

The column started to move again. The Chinese continued to try to segment and destroy the column throughout the two days of the march, but Easy Company, Second Battalion never felt seriously threatened during the eleven-mile hike from Hagaru-ri to Koto-ri. At 2130 on December 7, Easy Company marched into Koto-ri at the end of the train.

As at Hagaru-ri, the mess tents at Koto-ri were open when the marines arrived. The men pigged out on pancakes, stew, and coffee. However, there were no heated tents to bed down in, and the marines spread out on the ground in a designated area for the night.

The next morning, December 8, Chris and the rest of Easy Company woke up to find themselves in the middle of a small perimeter now occupied by the bulk of the First Marine Division and parts of numerous army and Korean units that had bunched up at Koto-ri after the road to Hagaru-ri had been blocked. The arrival of the Hagaru-ri garrison on December 6 and 7 tripled the population inside the Koto-ri perimeter. In addition to the thousands of marines and army soldiers, there were tanks, artillery and their trailers, bulldozers, and armored and soft vehicles of every description parked everywhere. The small airstrip couldn't handle C47 transport planes, but small observation aircraft and single-engine navy torpedo bombers (TBFs) that had been converted to haul seven wounded at a time were shuttling in and out of the Koto-ri perimeter.

Lieutenant Burkhart held an informal muster after rousting the men out of their sleeping bags and found he had twenty-nine effectives—men still capable of fighting—in the First Platoon, Easy Company. After finishing the head count, Burkhart briefed the platoon on the plans for the next phase of the withdrawal. He said the Seventh Regiment had moved out earlier in the morning to occupy the skyline for five miles along the MSR from Koto-ri to a power plant where a bridge has to be repaired before the First Marine Division and attached units can continue to its final destination at Hungnam. At the same time, engineers with the Seventh Regiment would be pushing down the MSR to repair the road where necessary. A battalion of marines in the First Regiment on the other side of bridge that has to be repaired would move north from Chinhung-ni to occupy the skyline in that sector and meet the column moving south at the power station. "We expect the Chinese to be vigorously contesting these moves. The bridge at the power station, which has been blown, is the cork in the bottle. The power station sits on the edge of a two-thousand-foot drop off and the bridge is the only way the division can withdraw its fifteen hundred vehicles. We won't be going anywhere until that bridge is repaired."

Lieutenant Burkhart continued to tell who would be doing what that afternoon including that Easy Company would move out that afternoon to relieve Fox Company which is occupying Hill 1328. Lieutenant Burkhart finished by telling Easy Company to be ready to move out at 1400. "

For Chris, Lieutenant Burkhart's briefing was the most thorough description of what to expect over the next couple of days that he had experienced since arriving in Korea. He usually didn't know where they were going until they got there, or find out they would be attacking a hill until they arrived at the bottom of the hill they would be attacking. Chris mentioned to Sergeant Kolowski that this amount of information seemed a little strange. Sergeant Kolowski had the same feeling. "Maybe I don't need all that information. Now I'm worrying about the bridge. What good does that do?"

Later in the morning, the First Fire Team witnessed some strange activity. Eight C119 "flying boxcars" had lined up and were approaching the Koto-ri perimeter. Chris thought they would be dropping supplies by parachute and worried about boxes falling indiscriminately inside the crowded perimeter. It was not unusual for boxes to break loose from their parachutes and fall like bombs. Chris was surprised when each airplane pulled its nose up to about a forty-five-degree angle as it passed over the perimeter, a huge object rolled out the back, and then similarly huge parachutes opened and lowered each large object to the ground.

Sergeant Kolowski guessed that they were seeing Treadway Bridge beams that would be used to bridge the gap in the MSR at the power house. "Them things weigh tons," Kolowski said. Hope nobody gets crushed, Sergeant Kolowski's guess was confirmed when four huge army engineering Brockway trucks picked up the bridge sections like tooth picks and proceeded ahead of the vehicles lined up to move onto the MSR going south.

In a snowstorm at 1400, a depleted Easy Company headed for Hill 1328, south and west of the Koto-ri perimeter. They would join the Seventh Regiment in clearing and occupying the skyline above the MSR.

The First Squad, First Platoon had the lead as Easy Company moved single-file through waist deep drifts. Squad members took turns breaking the trail. Easy Company made contact with the Seventh Regiment's George Company as daylight faded. Chinese were still dug in on Hill 1328, and it had been decided that removing them would have to wait until morning. During the night the snowstorm subsided, but the temperature plunged past thirty below zero. The First Fire Team, down to three people, occupied a single good-sized hole someone else had conveniently dug. The fire team set a two-off, one-on watch for the night. The two-off, one-on watch schedule allowed for more sleeping bag time, the best place to be on that extremely cold night.

While Chris and Adam had become acclimated to twenty-below weather, when the temperature dropped below thirty, it became a different matter. That the First Fire Team hadn't lost anyone to frostbite seemed to be more the exception than the norm. To Chris, this night seemed the coldest they had experienced. While on watch, he stayed in his sleeping bag, keeping it pulled up to his armpits. He covered his face with a scarf so only his eyes were exposed to the cold.

In the morning, Easy Company began probing the Chinese position because the enemy's strength and location hadn't been accurately established. The First Platoon drew the assignment to probe a ledge on the south side of the hill where there appeared to be some well dug-in positions. The platoon approached the ledge carefully since the terrain offered little cover. After moving to within a hundred feet of an obvious fighting hole without drawing fire or seeing any activity, Sergeant Kolowski left cover, stood up, and walked over to inspect the hole. He waved the squad forward. In the hole were two Chinese, frozen to death. The squad found over fifty Chinese on the ledge, all dead or near death from freezing. A rifleman suggested they put those still living out of their misery. Kolowski disagreed. It might be merciful but it would be murder. "Besides," he said, "it's not easy to separate the living from the dead. We'd have to shoot all of them."

Chris didn't think he could have participated in a mercy execution. He had killed his share of North Koreans and Chinese during the past four months, hundreds he supposed, but this would be a different kind of killing. It was one thing to kill or be killed and another to kill someone who didn't threaten you.

While talking about the cold Chris said he remembered people talking about freezing in South Dakota, a place where freezing could be a real life-ending experience. "Something I remember hearing is that you don't feel the cold in the final phases."

"How'd they find that out?" Clayton asked. "I didn't hear any of those Chinamen telling how they's feelin'."

Adam had mixed feelings. He was glad the frozen Chinese weren't shooting at them, but couldn't help feeling sorry for the poor bastards. "We bitch about our gear, especially our shoe-pacs, but they're a world better than the canvas sneakers with cotton socks the Chinese wear. Marines bitch and get frostbite, the Chinese freeze to death." Chris had to agree with Adam. The marines were suffering from the cold, but the Chinese were suffering a great deal more.

After the First Squad rejoined Easy Company, other Chinese were found frozen or near death on other parts of the hill. A few were found still alive and coherent and were taken prisoner. Easy Company needed prisoners like a hole in the head but Captain Wilson ordered detaining able Chinese soldiers that wanted to surrender. Then Easy Company had to use scarce manpower to escort them down the hill to the MSR to turn them over to the regiment. One of the prisoners who spoke understandable English said his battalion had done a forced march to catch up with the retreating marines the previous day. The men's clothes were wet with perspiration by the end of the day. The thirty-below temperatures were devastating.

The next day, December 9, it was clear and the sun shining. From the Easy Company position high above the column strung out along the MSR they could see its head stopped at the power station and the tail still waiting to enter the MSR at Koto-ri.

Gap blown in Power House Bridge
This image is in the public domain.

At noon, Easy Company pushed to the south to another hill after a First Regiment Fox Company moved up to relieve them on Hill 1328. They moved to occupy another hill above and near the power house where the key bridge had to be repaired. While heading to their new position, Easy Company saw some Chinese moving away from them to the west. Marine Corsairs were notified, and they strafed and scattered the Chinese unit. Easy Company found the new position unoccupied but populated with numerous foxholes which they utilized to set up a defensive perimeter on the hilltop. From there, the First Fire Team could see down the valley to the power plant approximately two miles away. They could also see much of the MSR and the First Marine Division vehicles parked along its length. While taking in the view Adam noted that if the Chinese were up here, they could shoot up the whole column. Chris agreed, said "some of the sap seems to have gone out of them. You'd think they'd be wrestling us for this hill."

Some daylight remained after the perimeter had been set up, and Captain Wilson allowed Easy Company to build fires. In a short time, the First Fire Team had coffee going and warmed up some C-rations, the first hot anything they had had since leaving Koto-ri.

Clayton declared, "This is livin'. Hot coffee, C-rations, temps up to minus twenty. Life is good."

Sergeant Kolowski showed up. "Smelled the coffee, got any extra?"

"No, Sergeant," Adam replied, laughing, and added, "shit, you don't have to ask and usually don't. Gotta bring your own cup."

Kolowski said he had gotten a bunch of scuttlebutt from Lieutenant Burkhart. "He said there's been serious fighting on the other side of the power plant, but marines are in firm control of the skyline. All's needed is a bridge to get the vehicles going."

As it grew dark, they could still observe the bridge repair site lighted and a high level of activity where the repair was being made. Later that night the men of the First Fire Team noticed that the column on the MSR was inching forward. At 2200, Easy Company got orders to move back to the MSR and join the column. At 0200, Easy Company reached the power house bridge. Vehicles were slowly moving across the bridge, each carefully guided by engineers using hand signals. Men on foot moved single file hugging the power house wall, leaving room for vehicles to cross at the same time. As they crossed, the First Fire Team could see where a section of the bridge decking had been caved in and vehicles had to cross the gap with their wheels on separate girders that allowed only inches of purchase for each wheel.

Watching them made Chris's hair curl. There was nothing but rock and air below those girders for two thousand feet.

"Mother fucker!" Clayton exclaimed. "I'm glad I'm walkin'."

After they passed the power plant, the organizational structure of the column began to deteriorate. Companies and platoons got mixed up. The First Squad became separated from the Second Squad and the First Platoon from other Easy Company platoons. Sergeant Kolowski and the First Fire

Team became separated from the rest of the First Squad but were not concerned. They were less than five miles from Chinhung-ni, the place fixed in their minds as the end of their ordeal.

After Kolowski and the First Fire Team moved past the power station and started downhill from Funchilin Pass, the column encountered sniper fire from hills west of the MSR. The enemy had been reduced to harassing activities which didn't threaten the withdrawal but did create a nuisance. At 0400, a second lieutenant ran up to Sergeant Kolowski and said he was putting together a provisional squad to clear the hill where the sniper fire was coming from. He enlisted Kolowski, the First Fire Team, and six other men to do the job.

Chris had had enough experience to know that finding snipers in the daytime could be difficult. Finding them in the early morning darkness would be harder by quite a bit. But the clear night and bright moonlight reflected by snow cover added to the visibility, so seeing well enough to move around wouldn't be a problem.

The provisional squad moved off the MSR and headed towards a hill they thought the enemy fire had come from. The landscape featured a number of small hills covered with large boulders, small shrubs, and little else. As they moved towards the suspect hill, the firing increased.

"That's no sniper," Sergeant Kolowski pronounced. "There's probably at least a squad up there." The words had hardly left his mouth when a machine gun opened up, its green tracers placing it in a dip between two small hills. Without any hesitation, the second lieutenant no one knew signaled the provisional squad to follow him. He led them around one of the hills as fast as conditions permitted until they reached a position behind the Chinese who were shooting at the column on the MSR. He had the men spread out and then yelled for the men in his pickup squad to charge the hill and he began running up a small rise in back of where the Chinese were located. The squad followed. As they ran up the hill, Chris felt the adrenalin rush he had learned to associate with combat. The charging marines attracted the attention of the Chinese, who turned and started firing at them. Chris felt something hit his shoulder with great force. It threw him off balance and he fell.

It took a moment for Chris to realize he had been hit. His left arm did not work and pain began to seep in. Fuck, why now? He thought. Up until now, in all his combat experience, he had received only some nuisance shrapnel. But why not, it's a game of chance, of luck. It's about stray bullets hitting people who are in the wrong place at the wrong time. Up until a few minutes ago, he had been lucky.

The noise of the fire fight died down. Adam appeared and started checking Chris out. "Where's it hurt?" Adam had his gloves off and could feel blood soaking through the six layers of clothing Chris had on. "You're bleeding pretty bad. We've gotta get you to a corpsman."

They were not far from the MSR, and Chris was able to walk while leaning on Adam to support some of his weight. His shoulder had started hurting like hell. He knew he was losing a lot of blood but remained fully cognizant. When they got to the MSR a corpsman pulled off enough cloths to apply a compress to the wound. Then corpsman put the dirty cloths back in order and gave him a blanket to help keep warm and said he should be ok to make it to a place his could be treated as long as he wasn't bleeding. "The cold helps control the bleeding," the corpsman added "coagulates the blood."

The corpsman rigged up a sling to support Chris's useless arm. Then the corpsman put a morphine syringe in his mouth to thaw it out and gave Chris a shot. It helped the pain, but Chris felt lightheaded from loss of blood. The corpsman decided Chris shouldn't walk any further, got a litter and enlisted Adam, Clayton, and another marine to help him carry the litter to the closest aid tent a mile down the road. Chris felt like he had become the source of a lot trouble to a lot of people but couldn't deny he needed help. He doubted he could have walked much further.

The aid tent had heat and conditions that enabled a corpsman to clean and dress Chris's wound. After he finished dressing the wound, the corpsman apologized for not being able to provide clean clothes. "You'll be in a hospital soon," the corpsman added, "where they'll strip off your clothes and burn them."

Chris was told he would be transported to Chinhung-ni by the next available Jeep ambulance and by other transport from there to Hungnam. Adam and Clayton had been hanging around prepared to leave. Before they parted, Adam couldn't resist getting in one last dig. "Really a dumb thing you did, getting wounded the last chance you had."

"Yeah," Chris replied, "should have done that the first day I got to Korea and saved myself a hell of a lot of trouble."

After getting to Chinhung-ni, Chris was put into a truck headed for Hungnam filled with other wounded and frostbite cases. The truck moved into the traffic on the MSR which now traveled at a steady pace, its speed depending only on the capacity of the road to handle the traffic. When the truck reached Sudong, a village Chris had first passed through in early November, the mountains flattened out, the road widened and traffic moved at highway speeds. As the light of day faded, the truck arrived in Hungnam. In just a few hours, they had traveled more than half the entire distance the column had covered since the division left Yudam-ni eleven days before.

At Hungnam, the wounded were transferred to a landing craft that took them to the USS *Consolation*, a hospital ship. Once Chris and the other casualties were on board, the first order of business was to inspect their condition. If it wasn't critical, as in Chris's case, the men enjoyed a general clean-up. Most hadn't bathed, changed clothes, shaved, or had a haircut in weeks.

First, the filthy, sweat-in, bled-in, shit-in, and pissed-in clothes were removed. A corpsman cut Chris's boots off his feet since his feet had swollen so that he hadn't been able to take his boots off for several days.

"Got some frostbite there," the corpsman said. "Not bad compared to some of the stuff I've seen. Probably won't have to amputate anything."

"Amputate!" Chris said. "You think they might?"

"Feel that?" the corpsman asked, pinching one of Chris's middle toes.

"Yeah," Chris answered.

"Okay, they won't amputate. There's still life there. If it's dead, they have to amputate or it starts to smell after a while."

The corpsman checked Chris over as he pulled off the rest of his filthy clothes. "Looks like you had some shrapnel in your back. It's pretty well healed up. Some more on your arm, looks like there may be some infection there. Even a small wound can become gangrenous if not treated. The heavy clothes you guys were wearing probably protected you from worse damage from grenades. You have the usual frostbite scars on your face. Overall you are one pretty beat-up marine." The corpsman removed the old bandages, and helped Chris shower. Although the ship was at sea, the shower had fresh water and Chris could feel weeks of filth being washed away. Bandages were reapplied

A doctor took a look at the shoulder wound and the minor shrapnel wounds on his arm. The doctor instructed a nurse to clean and redress the shoulder wound and treat the shrapnel wounds with an antibiotic. Any necessary surgery would be done in Japan. Chris found he had lost twenty pounds while he was in the mountains.

The *Consolation* was already filled beyond its normal capacity with Chosin Reservoir wounded and frostbite cases by the time Chris came on board. Early the next morning, the ship set sail for Japan with its load of marine casualties. Two days later, the hospital ship unloaded its patients at the naval hospital in Yokosuka, Japan. Doctors looked at Chris's shoulder and decided he should be sent back to the states for corrective surgery and therapy as soon as transportation became available.

Chris's writing arm was still functional and he wrote his folks to let them know he had gotten out of the Chosin Reservoir wounded, but not seriously, and that he would be coming back to the United States soon. He also wrote a long letter to Pete and a note to Adam to let them know how things were with him.

While in the hospital, Chris followed any news he could find about the marines coming out of the Chosin Reservoir. He soon learned that all the marines, soldiers, and other United Nations troops that made it back to Hungnam were successfully evacuated along with their equipment. In addition, a hundred thousand civilians that wanted to leave North Korea were taken out.

Chinese casualties were estimated to have been nearly sixty thousand during the seventeen-day battle. Half of that total was due to weather; many froze to death. Marine casualties were near seven thousand. Approximately half were non-combat, due to frostbite in most cases. Total UN forces losses were approximately twelve thousand. The Chinese Ninth Army had twelve divisions in the area and had committed ten divisions to stopping and destroying the First Marine Division and other UN forces in the Chosin region. They failed and paid a heavy price for their effort. What could have been a debacle became what would be considered one of the proudest moments in the history of the United States Marine Corps.

While confined to the hospital in Yokosuka, Chris had time to think about everything that had happened in the Chosin Reservoir action. Even he, ranked only as a private first class, had wondered about the risk of stringing thirty thousand men and their associated equipment along seventy miles of a narrow, antiquated mountain road with no alternative routes on the advance to the Chosin Reservoir. It seemed as if General MacArthur, who thought himself godlike before Inchon, had become even more inflated with himself after the wildly successful Inchon maneuver and believed he could work his will on whatever he wanted.

That they had gotten out of the Chosin Reservoir successfully as an intact fighting unit seemed like more of a miracle to Chris now as he thought about it. When they were fighting their way out he was focused on the moment, fighting when necessary, keeping from freezing to death, putting one foot ahead of other when walking toward their destination than thinking about the big picture.

He believed the marine officers and NCOs on the ground had been crucial, making the decisions and leading the way they did. The enlisted marines, the grunts, made it happen because they never broke. They did whatever they were ordered to do under fire and in an extremely difficult environment.

Chris remembered boot camp, where they kept telling dumb farm kids like him and other scared green recruits that they were being trained to be the world's best fighting men. They were all the lowest scum that ever existed, but they would become the world's best fighters. Perception is reality. Recruiting literature proclaimed them "the few, the proud" and at Chosin, they were.

20.
The Holiday Season at Sangley Point

A week before Christmas, Pete finally heard from Chris. He had written a long letter from a hospital in Japan where he ended up after being wounded in one of the final skirmishes with the Chinese during the Chosin Reservoir withdrawal. He would be going back to the United States for further surgery and therapy. Chris's letter described the Chosin experience in detail. If Pete hadn't known Chris and that he didn't spread bullshit, some of it would seem unimaginable. Again, he felt guilty, comparing the base security duty he had in the Philippines with what the marines were experiencing in Korea.

Chris concluded his letter with: "The wound won't be disabling, long term, but repair and therapy will be complicated and lengthy so it will be back to the USA for me. It's my turn to do some tough duty. Won't be back for Christmas like MacArthur said, but it will be close. Also, it won't be home but to the Balboa Naval Hospital in San Diego.

"Hadn't had the time or inclination to think about the future while freezing my ass off at the Chosin Reservoir, but am thinking about it now. I will still have a couple of years in my enlistment, just the right amount of time to get myself ready for college. Good to hear you are going in the same direction. Your plans to get ready have been inspirational. We'll be the most prepared freshmen SDSC will ever see."

Pete had kept Tony apprised of what was happening to Chris. "Funny," Pete said, "Chris goes through all these battles, hardly a scratch, then gets hit in a little skirmish close to the end of the withdrawal. Guess that goes to show you, you're never home safe until you get there."

Tony still remembered Chris from their Tijuana adventure so could put a face with the name. He and all marines were keeping close track of the war in Korea with a portion of them wishing they were there and others glad that they were somewhere else.

Tony had also become aware of Pete and Carolyn's relationship, having had an occasional beer with them at the enlisted men's club. Tony thought Carolyn an improvement over Alisa, seeing her as a home town girl in a faraway place.

During one of their conversations, Tony revealed that he also had been edged out of the Mendez sisters' good graces. "You know, a number of things were working against me. I stopped driving my car to Manila at night, and most men that hang out at the Blue Note are business or professional types, not PFCs or Jeepney drivers. Some mestizo lawyer type is taking up Maria's time. More class than the fat old Chinese businessman who's been seeing Alisa. Hey, what can I say? Gotta go with the money."

Pete hadn't been bored. Taking two math courses through the Armed Forces Institute, developing his relationship with Carolyn, and his Marine duties kept him more than busy. It was the week before Christmas, and his geometry class was finishing up at the library. Normally it would run longer, but because of Christmas the last two classes were both scheduled for this week so the course could end before the holiday. There were only five in the class, and Pete felt confident that he would ace the course.

One day early in the week, Tony mentioned that the mestizo community in Manila would be having the annual Christmas party on Saturday, December 23. He wanted to know if Pete would care to go. "Bring Carolyn," he said. "They tell me it's the biggest party of the year."

Pete checked with Carolyn, and she wanted to go. Saturday evening, Tony, Pete, and Carolyn took the Margaret to Manila and then a Jeepney to the mestizo party. Tony had been right. The Christmas party attracted a large portion of the mestizo community plus a bunch of interlopers like Pete and Carolyn. At the last mestizo party Pete attended, he and Tony were with the Mendez sisters. He saw they were at this party, too, Alisa with an overweight, older Chinese man and Maria with a middle-aged mestizo that Tony had pegged as a lawyer. The sisters discreetly acknowledged Tony and Pete and gave Carolyn the once over.

Carolyn, who had lightened her already nearly strawberry blond hair, got plenty of attention from the mestizo men. Pete mentioned to Tony that, although he and Carolyn didn't fit in real well, Alisa's Chinese friend really broke the mold.

Tony laughed. "I don't know what the rules are exactly. Knowing Spanish helps. Who you know and having money helps, but after a few drinks, not much matters.

As luck would have it, Pete had perimeter guard duty from midnight to four a.m. on Christmas Day. His section of the perimeter started at the brig guard house on the east side of the peninsula, went past the Quonset armory and a ways past the enlisted Quonset huts on the west side of the peninsula. Pete liked walking this section of the perimeter because it offered a number of different views. On the west side of the peninsula, he could look out into the middle of the bay and see the lights of ships coming and going and also the bobbing lights of small fishing boats. At the point of the peninsula, he could look north and see the bright lights of Manila. After rounding the point, he could see the sea plane base, the lights of Cavite, and the Cavite army base.

At midnight, the start of Christmas Day, Pete was dropped off at the Quonset armory to relieve the marine who had been on duty from 2000 to midnight. He began walking the perimeter. When he passed one of the navy enlisted men's Quonset huts, a voice called out to him. "Hey, marine, merry Christmas! Come over here, have a drink."

Pete walked over to the hut. "Celebrating a little?" he asked.

He could make out two men sitting on the open porch of the hut. They were older men. Lifers, probably been in the service ten or fifteen years.

"Not exactly celebrating," one replied. "Commiserating is more like it. Second Christmas I've been away from my family, my wife and two boys in Texas."

The other man held out a bottle. "Good sipping whiskey," he said. "Have some."

"I'm on duty," Pete replied. "But thanks. Going back to Texas soon?"

"Nope, but the family will be coming here in two or three months. The holidays are hard."

Pete thought about his family. This was the first Christmas that he had not been with them. It seemed like he had been gone a long time, but really it had been less than a year. Much had changed for him during those few months. He had become a different person with a different future.

"Need to get back to my post," Pete said to the navy men, adding, "Good luck with your family," to the man from Texas.

He continued to walk his post, deep in thought on a subject that had recently become obsessive and made his whole-body ache. Carolyn. All of the things that Pete has rationalized as making the Aliza arrangement impossible didn't matter now. Pete and Carolyn were barely out of their teens; Pete was in no way ready to provide for a family but his thoughts weren't restrained by any obstacles. He wanted Carolyn and he wanted her now.

He wanted be one with that woman forever and nothing else mattered.

Bonga boats on a beach in Manila Bay

Photo by author

21.
In Another World

In a small fishing village on the shores of Manila Bay halfway between Manila and Cavite, a young man named Modesto tossed and turned in his blanket on the floor of a Nipa hut. Beside him, the frequent stirring of his wife betrayed her restlessness. Only their child in the near corner slept soundly. Finally, Modesto threw his blanket aside, picked his way to the doorway, and let his bare feet drop to the sand, still warm from the day's sun. From where he stood, he could see a large portion of Manila Bay. To his right and behind him the bright lights of Manila made the sky luminous, before him the bay lay dark except for the dim lights of fishing boats that flickered and bobbed. Over to the left, a cluster of lights marked Cavite and the United States Naval Air Station at Sangley Point. The lights of Cavite also backlit an array of ship superstructures protruding out of the water, the hulks of Japanese ships laying where they were sunk during the big war that ended five years ago.

Modesto, small in stature, lean and muscular, had been a fisherman since he was old enough to pull nets and row a bonga boat. His jet-black hair and bright brown eyes were complemented by chocolate-colored skin which still had the smoothness of youth.

Tonight, being Christmas Eve, he and Carlos and Chico were not fishing. Other than Christmas and Easter or during bad storms, they would normally be out in the bay fishing at this time of night. Their families depended on them to net fish nearly every night. No fish meant there would be nothing to barter for rice, no pesos, no centavos, and no fresh fish for the fishermen's families to eat. Modesto was a good fisherman. There were very few days when there was no fish or rice to cook in his hut. There usually were enough pesos for at least the necessities and even for some extras, like during the fiesta and at Christmas and Easter.

However, the three fishermen would be taking the bonga boat out onto Manila Bay this Christmas Eve, not to fish but on a special and unusual mission. Modesto left the hut and moved aimlessly along the beach. He recalled the events of the last three days that led to what he would be doing tonight.

Modesto and his two companions had been returning from an unsuccessful night of fishing in their bonga, a boat which was barely large enough for the three-man crew, their nets, and sometimes a good catch of fish. They were tired, wet, and aching from their night's labor. Intermittent rain, sometimes heavy, had combined with abnormally low temperatures to make it a bitter night. For their efforts and misery, a reward of only a half-dozen lapa-lapas lay on the bottom of the boat. They paddled towards shore in weary silence. As they rowed, they could make out the outlines of the hotels and casinos along Manila's Dewey Boulevard.

The crew sat in a row from front to back in the narrow boat. Chico, the youngest, held down the middle position. He looked small even huddled under a bulky poncho. Chico, the son of Carlos, the oldest member of the three men, had only recently joined the crew. Chico had been a hut boy for marines at Sangley Point, a good paying job. For reasons unknown to Modesto, Chico no longer worked at Sangley Point and Carlos had added Chico to the crew.

Chico stopped paddling and broke the silence.

"The casinos are still lit up. As they sow, so shall they reap. That's what the church tells us. Well, we have worked all night and are so tired we can hardly get back to the beach. What have we reaped? Six little fish, not enough to eat, none to sell or trade. Did we sow the wrong thing? What do those rich ones in the casinos sow? They sow money. They don't have to sweat or sit in the cold rain. Money does their work."

Carlos sat in the back, the commanding position in the bonga. Wrinkled skin that had seen many fishing seasons covered his gaunt face. He laughed softly. "That was quite a speech from someone that's cold and tired. Remember, fishermen live from God's hand, and sometimes the hand is empty. That's the way it is."

Chico replied, "You been doing this too long, don't know any better."

"Maybe," Carlos answered, "but I know complaining doesn't help anything."

Modesto listened in silence. There were times that he had felt the way Chico did, and still did, but he had a wife and child. He had to provide for them in the only way he knew how. Someday in the hereafter he would be on the same level as the good rich and above that of the not-so-good rich. Easier for a camel to pass through the eye of a needle than for rich men to get to heaven. That's what the good fathers say. Such thoughts made life a little more bearable at times.

Later that day, Modesto and Carlos were repairing one of the bonga boat's outriggers. Carlos owned the boat and therefore, when the catch was successful, received an extra share of fish. Carlos had inherited the bonga, his most valuable possession, from his father. Frequent repairs kept it usable.

"I wonder where Chico is," Carlos mused. "He should be helping us."

Modesto pointed down the beach. "Speak of the devil. People with him. Who are they?"

Carlos looked where Modesto pointed. "Don't know."

Two strangers accompanied Chico. One, a gaunt, small-framed young man, was unremarkable except for deep-set eyes which glowered under heavy, dark brows. His dress, typical for men his age consisted of loose-fitting grey pants, an un-tucked white shirt, and sandals. He could have been a Jeepney driver or a street vendor. The other man dressed in a similar way but was taller, heavier, and had a round face with Asian eyes.

Chico introduced them. He motioned first towards the smaller man. "Pepe from Bulacan, and Wan from up north in Baguio City."

The two men surveyed the boat. The one named Wan walked around it and kicked the outrigger Modesto and Carlos had been working on.

"Looks small," he remarked.

Chico gave him a worried look. "It can haul a lot of weight."

Modesto wondered what they were talking about. What did it matter if the boat was small or could haul a lot of weight? It worked for what they used it for.

Carlos also looked puzzled.

The two strangers and Chico moved some distance away and talked among themselves. After a short time, they came back to where Carlos and Modesto had started working on the outrigger again.

"Pepe and Wan would like to talk about a business deal," Chico announced.

Carlos looked skeptical. "A business deal. We are fishermen with no fish to barter or sell. What kind of business could you be talking about?"

Pepe asked, "Can you keep a secret?"

"Secret?" Carlos questioned.

"The business we are talking about depends on it."

Carlos answered, "You've been talking to Chico. He can tell you."

Pepe hesitated, studied Carlos, and then began to speak. "Chico has told us that every night you and your crew fish in Manila Bay, and that almost every night you go by Sangley Point. You may have noticed a Quonset hut that sits by itself right near the shore at the tip of the peninsula. Looks like an ordinary Quonset hut, but it's different. It's being used as an armory and it's full of 30-caliber ammunition."

Pepe again hesitated, allowing time for this information to be fully absorbed.

Modesto felt a tightening of his stomach.

Pepe continued, "We will pay you and your crew a good amount of money to go in and get some of that ammunition."

Beads of sweat were forming on Modesto's forehead. He thought, this man is loco, but he held his tongue and waited for Carlos to speak.

Carlos smiled slightly. "This some kind of joke you and Chico thought up?"

Pepe didn't respond to the question. "You will be able to make more money than you have ever seen before." As if to emphasize the point, he pulled up his shirt to reveal a money belt and a pistol stuck under his waistband. He pulled a packet of pesos in large denominations out of the money belt and fanned them slowly. "We will pay you one peso for every round that you bring out. Easy money, a lot of money."

The smile on Carlos's face had disappeared and the look of skepticism returned. "Easy, why pay so much if it is easy?"

Skeptical or wary, Pepe knew he had the fisherman's attention. "You will be surprised at how lightly guarded the armory is." Pepe picked up a stick from the beach and drew a sketch in the sand of the peninsula that projected into Manila Bay, the tip of which was occupied by the Sangley Naval Air Station. Pepe added detail at the very tip of the peninsula to show the location of the Quonset hut being used as an armory.

"There is only one marine guarding this stretch of beach that runs from the brig on the east side of the peninsula to a point on the west side of the peninsula approximately a kilometer away. The route the marine walks is on a beach five to ten meters wide from the water's edge to an embankment three to four meters high. The Quonset we are interested in sits on top of this embankment at the tip of the peninsula. The closest thing to the Quonset armory, about hundred meters away, are Quonset huts for hous-ing navy and marine enlisted men."

Pepe drew the guard route in the sand. "Besides the marine, there is a large searchlight mounted here on a water tower." He pointed to a spot near the center of the base. "This light sweeps the beach all around the base. You must have seen it when you were fishing. It makes a sweep about every fifteen minutes, then goes out until they are ready to make another sweep. Those are the things you worry about, the searchlight and the marine guard. Overpower the guard, avoid the light, and you can help yourself to as much ammunition as your boat can haul."

The fishermen were familiar with the navy base as seen from the bay and were able to follow Pepe's description easily. They were familiar with the searchlight and saw it sweep around the base's periphery many times when they fished at night.

Modesto did not want to hear any more, but Carlos asked, "You sure there is only one marine?"

"One marine, changes at midnight, next time at four."

"The armory is locked?"

"I would think so."

"We are supposed to figure out how to overpower the guard and get the ammunition out?"

"That's it."

"Why do you want that much ammunition?"

"Does it matter?"

"Are you a Huk?"

It didn't matter to Modesto if Pepe and Wan were Huks or not. He didn't want any part of this crazy idea, but he could see that Carlos was seriously considering Pepe's proposition. Of course, they had to be Hukbalahaps, the Huks, the Philippine communists. That was the only answer that made any sense to Modesto. They were the only ones that would have the need for that much ammunition and the means to pay that kind of money for it.

Modesto didn't know exactly what the Huks were trying to do, but he knew there was serious trouble between the Huks and the government in Manila. The Huks had been around for a long time. During the war they had fought the Japanese and were big heroes. Now they were fighting the government and weren't heroes anymore. It seemed like they wanted to fight whoever happened to be in power. Modesto didn't know if they were good or bad. Pepe looked like an ordinary Filipino, not like a revolutionary or communist, whatever they looked like. Not that it mattered much to

Modesto. Modesto considered himself a pretty good Catholic, while Carlos and Chico weren't and they would admit it and that's their business. If a person wanted to be a Huk, that's their business.

Apparently, Carlos had come to the same conclusion and answered his own question. "I don't suppose it matters as long as we get paid."

"If you decide to do it, a thousand pesos up front, the balance when you deliver."

A thousand pesos! That was more money than Modesto had ever seen at one time.

Carlos didn't reveal any emotion or surprise. "Sounds crazy. We will think about it."

"Someone will do it," Pepe said. "We know Chico, that's why you are getting first chance."

Carlos replied, "We need a day to think about it."

"We'll be back tomorrow."

Carlos had fished Manila Bay for a living since he was able to do it. He had no hopes or plans to do anything else, and he had no hope of ever having more than a bare living as a fisherman. When Carlos became too old to fish, he hoped he would sit in the Nipa hut of his son Chico until the day that they carried him out to the cemetery to lie beside the father that he had cared for so many years before and his wife who had died five years ago. It was not a great deal to anticipate, but realistic and predictable. The wild scheme they were considering now was something else.

After Pepe and Wan left, the three fishermen discussed the proposition that had been presented to them. Carlos had done the talking when Pepe made his proposal, but now he wanted to know what Modesto thought of the idea.

Modesto had known Carlos since he was able to remember. Carlos's life was a model for Modesto's life. Modesto respected Carlos's judgment in most matters, but had been surprised when Carlos seemed to be considering going forward with a raid on the armory on Sangley Point. Manila Bay fishermen considered Sangley Point off limits. Even fishing near it was questionable. To land on its beach and raid an armory seemed totally loco.

"It sounds crazy and dangerous," Modesto said in response to Carlos's question.

"Maybe," Carlos replied. He walked over to the outrigger he and Modesto had been repairing, studied it, then turned and spoke to Modesto and Chico. "We need more information before making a decision. Tonight, we will fish off Sangley Point near the armory and really study the layout. After that we will decide."

It was a little before midnight when they arrived at a position where they could observe the armory and the marine guard while they fished. The brightly lit up brig and lights from in the nearby enlisted men's hut area made the armory and guard path dimly visible.

At midnight they noted the changing of the guard and observed the marine on duty as he made his rounds. The marine moved back and forth along the beach between the brig and some point along the west side of the peninsula. As Pepe had said, it took the guard about fifteen minutes to walk from one end of the route to the other.

They had moderate success fishing and after a couple of hours had a large gunny sack half-filled with lapa-lapas.

At two a.m. Carlos suggested that they go onto the beach near the armory and check out the door lock.

"What! Why?" asked a surprised Modesto.

"We should know what kind of lock we have to break or open."

Chico agreed. "Let's see what it feels like to walk on the Sangley sand."

They decided that both Modesto and Chico would go to the armory to check the lock while Carlos stayed with the boat.

While they contemplated making the landing, they realized they would need to time their movements carefully. They wanted to go onto the beach once the guard passed the armory and was heading away from it at the same time the light on the tower had gone dark. This combination did not come up regularly. The first time they considered going in, the tower light had gone out but they weren't sure when the guard, who was out of sight on the west side of the peninsula, would reappear. The next time the light swept the beach, they could see that the guard was moving towards the armory from the east. They were concerned the light might come on again before he would be clear of the armory area on his way to the other side of the peninsula. Finally, the light finished a sweep just as the guard past the armory going towards the west end of his route. They pushed towards shore and were soon scraping the bottom of the boat on the sand.

Modesto and Chico jumped out of the boat and ran towards the armory. It took only a few minutes for the two fishermen to run to the armory and determine that a padlock secured the armory door and a pry bar could be used to break the lock. They ran back to the boat and rowed away from the shore towards relative safety.

The three stayed in their fishing location until the rising sun allowed them to observe the beach in more detail. It appeared that the path the guard walked was obscured from easy observation on the land side by the embankment that ran along the full length of the route. Their attention was drawn to two large tree trunks with roots attached that had washed up on the beach about a hundred meters to the west of the Quonset armory. Carlos suggested it would be a good place to hide while they waited for the right time to overpower the guard. They moved the bonga boat closer to shore and could see that the attached roots held the lower parts of the trunks off the ground far enough for a person to crawl beneath them. They all agreed that it looked like an ideal place to hide while waiting to overpower the guard.

Later that morning they returned to their home beach, tired from a full night of fishing and information gathering. They would get together that afternoon after they had rested to discuss the matter and decide what they would do.

Modesto tried to get some rest, but his mind continued to wrestle with the proposed raid. His first reaction had been to oppose the idea, even to the point of defecting from the crew if Carlos and Chico wanted to do it. But as he became more familiar with what the raid would involve, his mind grew more at ease. A big factor in his thinking had been their ability to get on and off the beach undetected the previous night. He contemplated the prize that would be theirs if they were successful. They could buy a large power bonga and have pesos to spare. They would be able to fish outside the bay and better their chances of success. When Modesto finally drifted off to sleep, the contemplated prize loomed larger and the risk seemed to be diminishing.

When the three fishermen met the next afternoon, Carlos again asked Modesto and Chico for their opinions.

Chico of course wanted to go.

Modesto had resolved his concerns. The prize seemed too large to pass up. He now supported going forward.

Carlos said he also favored proceeding.

They started to discuss the details. Anyone observing the three fishermen huddled on the sandy beach would have thought they were mending a net or visiting, certainly not planning a daring raid on a United States military installation.

They decided to stage the raid that night. The moon would be dark, everything could be ready, and the sooner they put the plan into operation the less likely the wrong people would become aware of it. Also, early Christmas morning might find the security forces less alert than normal. They intended to go in at about one o'clock in the morning, not too long after the midnight guard change. That would give them plenty of time before another guard change took place. Their only weapons would be machetes and iron pipes. The machetes were to be used only if absolutely necessary, although Chico had wanted the machetes to be the first option. He argued, "A live marine can be dangerous, a dead one isn't. Besides it takes more time to tie a man up than to cut his throat."

Modesto knew Chico had his own agenda with regards to Americans. That a former girlfriend now shared her place with a marine may have helped form his opinion. His abrupt departure from his Sangley Point job may have aggravated it.

"Taking some American ammunition is one thing, killing an American is a whole different thing," Carlos declared. "We'll use machetes only if we have to."

They continued planning. Modesto and Chico would be landed on the beach and take cover under the tree trunks. Carlos would move the bonga back out into the bay. When an opportunity presented itself, Modesto and Chico would overpower the guard and break into the Quonset hut armory. They would remove as much ammunition as the bonga could haul and stack it in the shadow of the armory to keep it out of sight of the tower. They would use a flashlight to signal Carlos to bring the boat back to the beach when they were ready to load the ammunition. To Modesto, the plan seemed simple and doable.

Later in the day, Pepe and his partner returned and learned that the decision had been made to proceed and the raid would take place that night. Pepe seemed surprised that they were moving so soon, but he had brought a thousand pesos in up-front money and they finalized the arrangements.

That night Modesto wandered along the beach, waiting for the time to pass so that he could join his companions and start on an adventure that would (pray to God, hail Mary) make them all rich. A few days ago, he wouldn't have dared hope for anything more than enough food to eat and bare necessities for himself and his family. Now heady dreams filled his mind. He would be part owner of a big power bonga, a big fisherman who went after the big catches outside the bay. He would have a Nipa hut with more than one room and furnished with a bed and a cooking stove. He curled his toes in the sand. He might even buy a pair of shoes.

It was early, but Modesto turned and walked slowly towards the place where the bonga rested on the beach. When he arrived, he found Carlos sitting on an outrigger silently contemplating the small waves splashing against the beach. Carlos looked up when Modesto approached. "Couldn't sleep? Me, either. That happens often at my age."

Modesto squatted beside Carlos. Carlos continued, "Sometimes being old isn't so bad. I have less to lose." He hesitated, then apparently feeling a need to reassure Modesto, added, "Don't worry, it's going to work."

Modesto wanted to agree with him. "I wouldn't be doing it if I didn't believe it would work. Where is Chico?"

Carlos noted it was still early. "Chico will be here. He wouldn't miss this."

Chico finally showed up, yawning, at the agreed-upon time.

Modesto asked, "You have trouble sleeping?"

"No, why?"

Modesto laughed. "The resurrection wouldn't disturb you."

Carlos stood up and started pulling on the boat. "Let's go," he said, and all hands joined in launching the bonga on its special mission.

Each person assumed his position, and soon their rhythmic paddle strokes were moving the boat smoothly through the water, the bow making a luminous splash as it broke the flat surface of the bay.

Modesto mechanically dipped his paddle. The closer they came to the base, the more uneasy he felt. Was he a coward? Modesto had never done anything like this before. He had known danger when they had been caught in storms while fishing, but that is a normal part of a fisherman's life. This would be something different.

Carlos started talking about how this raid reminded him of ventures more dangerous and not as carefully planned during the big war. There were other differences. Those raids had been mainly for food because he and his family were starving. Sometimes he had picked up other things, too, but food had been the main thing. This raid was for money, enough money to change their lives. Another difference was that he disliked the Japanese. He didn't particularly dislike the Americans. Americans were overbearing, over-paid, oversexed, and drank too much, but Carlos believed that overall, their intentions were good.

Modesto wanted to know if Carlos would feel guilty about stealing from the Americans.

"No," Carlos replied. "Americans have more wealth than the ocean has fish, and taking some ammunition out of that hut won't hurt America any more than I hurt Manila Bay when I pull lapa-lapas out of it."

Modesto had thought about the same thing. Was this really stealing, would he be breaking any of God's laws? He concluded that some of the laws of men might be challenged, but not God's laws. The commandments as interpreted by Modesto pertained to individuals, to neighbors. Who did that ammunition really belong to? Maybe Filipinos had as much right to it as Americans.

Chico's voice broke into his thoughts. "Are you afraid, Modesto?"

Modesto thought, Chico must have sensed my uneasiness. "Maybe, I guess I am, but I will be glad when we get on shore."

Maybe he would be. His mind would be fully occupied and he would not have time for imagined dangers. The thoughts of wealth and a new life he had had earlier in the evening were now crowded out by more urgent thoughts about the danger and what might go wrong. Sangley looked bigger and brighter than usual.

He turned to Chico and asked, "How about you?"

"Sure," Chico answered. "You can't be brave if you're not afraid, and I keep thinking the guard could be the one that's been screwing my girlfriend."

Modesto laughed. "Used to be your girlfriend."

"That's what I mean."

"Don't do anything dumb with the guard."

"I know."

They reached the position off the point where they would wait for a chance to go in. Again, they watched the changing of the guard. They waited for an hour and then began looking for the right opportunity to go onto the beach. They looked for the guard when the searchlight swept around the base perimeter. Twice they watched and did not see the guard when the searchlight swept the beach in front of them. Carlos leaned back against the stern of the boat. "No hurry, we will wait until we know where he is."

A while later the light flashed on again. This time it started at the far end of the base and moved towards the armory. As it swung around the peninsula, it caught the marine moving west away from the armory near the bend in the shoreline. As soon as the light went out, Carlos whispered, "Now!"

They rowed the bonga onto the beach. Modesto crossed himself, and he and Chico jumped out of the boat and found shelter under the large tree trunks. They carried iron pipes, machetes, and what they would need to bind and gag the guard.

Modesto knew that the marine would be armed with something better than an iron pipe. Successfully overpowering the guard had always been a concern, and the concern became magnified by the reality of their situation. Between the water and the tree trunks were over five meters of open beach, and the marine could be anywhere in that area when he passed them. What if the searchlight came on while they were overpowering him?

While Modesto contemplated these difficulties, he heard the guard approaching. He was walking slowly, quietly whistling some tune over and over. In the dim ambient light, Modesto could see that his carbine was slung over his shoulder and he had a soft-billed cap on his head. Good, he's not wearing a helmet, thought Modesto.

At that moment, the tower light snapped on and started sweeping the beach. The marine safely passed the hidden raiders as he moved towards the armory.

"Damn," Chico whispered.

Soon after the light went out after its next sweep of the base, the marine guard could be seen coming back from the direction of the armory, still whistling the same tune. He moved steadily towards the tree trunks where Modesto and Chico were crouching.

When Pete reached the vicinity of the tree trunks, he paused, stopped whistling, and turned to look at the bright lights of Manila. He sensed some unusual sound or movement behind him and had started to turn when he was hit hard in the back of his head by a heavy object. He felt himself falling and not able to respond to an urgent need to stop the fall.

As the marine fell, Chico swung his pipe at the back of his skull again. "That's for good measure, Joe!" he hissed.

They dragged the limp marine into the shadow of the tree trunks, rolled him on his stomach, and worked feverishly to bind and gag him. Chico put the gag in the guard's mouth while Modesto pulled his arms behind him and began wrapping the rope around his wrists.

Chico stood up. "You can finish this. I'll open the armory."

Chico disappeared into the darkness while Modesto began to knot the wrist binding. Suddenly, the marine gave a grunt, pulled his wrists loose and rolled over, throwing Modesto off his back. Modesto landed near his machete when he fell to the ground. He grasped the handle with both his hands, raised it over his head, and brought the blade down with all his might on the neck of the struggling marine. The blade cut through flesh and cartilage, stopping only when it hit the vertebrae.

Modesto, still grasping the machete, stood up. He started towards the armory and then paused to pick up the carbine the marine had dropped on the beach.

Modesto found an upset Chico attempting to break the lock.

"The bar doesn't go through the eye of the padlock. How in hell are we going to break the lock if we can't get the pry bar in there?"

Modesto took the bar from Chico's hand, took aim and brought it crashing down on the padlock. The padlock flew off, hitting Modesto in the leg on its way to the ground.

"Jesus Christ!" Chico exclaimed. "That should wake up the dead."

They groped their way into the dark armory. Inside, they could feel boxes that must be ammunition cases. They grabbed hold and started stacking the cases in the shadow of the Quonset. They had stacked four boxes when the light came on again.

While waiting for the light to go out, Chico asked if the guard was securely tied.

"He is secure," Modesto replied without going into any further detail.

The light went out and they finished moving two more boxes, as many as they felt they could haul in the boat, and then waited for the light to go on and off again.

When the light went out the next time, they signaled Carlos. He brought the bonga onto the beach near the Quonset, and they started loading the ammunition boxes. Then for some reason, the searchlight that had just gone out a short time before came on again and swept along the beach towards them. Carlos signaled urgently for them to push off, but Modesto ran back to get the last box lying in the sand. He gripped it firmly and had started running back towards the bonga when he was surrounded by the searchlight's blinding white light. He heard someone shout "Halt! Halt!" But he kept running until he was thrown down by something hitting him in the back. He tried to get up, but he didn't seem to have any strength in his arms and legs. Something under him felt warm. Blood, his blood.

He had the sensation that he was swimming underwater, swimming hard, but was not moving.

He could hear far-off voices. "Did we get all of them?"

"The old man looks like he has had it. The young one is alive but scared as hell."

Modesto felt something on his neck. A hand? He heard a voice again. "A very weak pulse. Amazing what these Huks will do for their cause."

A dim light shone under the water. Modesto tried to swim towards it, but it kept getting dimmer and finally went out.

22.
The Aftermath

With all the guard postings set for the long weekend and no other activities planned, there wasn't a formal muster for the marines at Sangley Point on Christmas Day. So, it wasn't until after breakfast that Tony learned from his squad leader why Pete had not returned to his bunk after his previous night's guard duty. The news that Pete had been killed by Huks who had broken into the armory shocked Tony. It seemed unbelievable, but there stood Sergeant Kemp, a man not given to messing around, telling him that Pete had been killed. This wasn't a joke or a bad dream. This had really happened.

Tony was given the task of cleaning out Pete's locker. While going through Pete's things, he found letters from Chris. Chris would likely hear about Pete's unfortunate death through his family, but Tony decided to write him directly with his thoughts and insights about what had happened. Tony needed to contact Carolyn, too, even though she was likely to have learned about the Huk raid already. Word about it had circulated quickly through the Sangley Point community. He wanted to contact her more as a mourner than as an informer, someone to talk to about this terrible unexpected event.

Tony and Carolyn met that evening on the patio of the enlisted men's club overlooking the seaplane base. A PBM flying boat being prepared for takeoff floated in the calm waters of Manila Bay.

Tony and Carolyn hugged took seats at a small table. Tony decided to have a San Miquel beer and Carolyn opted for coffee. Tony struggled to express his feelings. He had lost a friend, the best friend he had in the marines. He knew Pete and Carolyn were also friends but not to what extent that went beyond friendship. Should he extend his sympathies, was it that short of a relationship? Tony was certain Pete and Carolyn were at a minimum good friends as he was and he wanted Carolyn to know they had that common bond. Tony described how he and Pete were best friends and had spent most of their free time doing things together while at Sangley, really got to know each other. As Tony talked he noticed tears streaming down Carolyn's cheeks.

Carolyn sobbed, "Pete was more than a friend, I loved him."

Tony moved his chair next to Carolyn's, took her hand, put an arm around her shoulder. "I'm sorry," he said, "I suspected that was the case."

Tony wanted to say more words to comfort Carolyn but felt his eyes misting and as a man a marine he couldn't cry so paused while trying to get control of his own emotions

Carolyn broke the silence, "Sorry, I'm so emotional," she said as she used a napkin to wipe the tears. "Yes, we will miss Pete, you and I in our own way for our own reasons. It is so final, death at any age, and for the young so much life unlived. For me this is sad, the life unlived. I say this because Pete and I share something he will never know. I am pregnant with Pete's baby, a little of Pete lives in my womb. For that I can be thankful."

For some reason Carolyn's words made Tony feel good, but uncomfortable and concerned. How would Carolyn able to deal with this situation? "I am very happy for you," Tony said. "Will you need help? Is there anything I can do?"

"I'll be ok," Carolyn replied. She would be leaving the navy. "That's what happens to navy women that get pregnant; for the convenience of the government." I have very supportive parents, we have no secrets and I made a very expensive collect call to them this morning. I'm OK. I'm sorry

Pete didn't know. I was going to tell him but I wasn't sure, now I'm sure.

Before they parted Carolyn asked Tony if he knew the addresses of Pete's folks and his best friend Chris who was in Korea. Tony said he had the address information for Pete's family and Chris and would get information to Carolyn the next day. He also told Carolyn that Chris had been wounded and had sent back to San Diego to have work done on his wound.

Carolyn thanked Tony. She said she wanted to contact Pete's folks and Chris to find out as much about the father of their baby as she could.

In the middle of January in 1951, Chris arrived in Milbank to begin a well-deserved two-week leave and to attend Pete's funeral. Chris's mother had given him the date of the funeral in a letter, and the Balboa Navy Hospital pronounced him fit to travel, so things worked out.

On a cold and windy winter day, Chris, one of the pall bearers, stood at the Wilmot gravesite with a large group of friends and neighbors of the Houser family. Pete's coffin lay waiting to be lowered into the South Dakota earth near where he had lived most of his life. The wind whipped the dry snow as Reverend Rickman said a few words, keeping it short considering the weather. Earlier in the church service, the reverend had been more effusive. He had called Pete a hero, like all the men who served, like those in Korea. He died serving his country in the fight against Godless communism, a battle that is not only fought on battlefields in Korea, but around the world in many different ways. He said that these brave men are patriots, putting their lives on the line to preserve our way of life, our country.

As Chris listened, his mind questioned some of what Reverend Rickman said. That he had ended up in Korea in a war had been due more to circumstances than patriotism. He had joined the Marines not to serve his country but because he considered the Marine Corps his best alternative at the time in the quest to find his way in life. He couldn't recall anyone he knew in Korea putting their lives on the line for patriotic reasons. The forces driving these young men were more personal. There may have been men in Korea who were there for patriotic reasons, but he had never met them.

He did know men who put their lives on the line, but for each other, not for the country. They were the men in his squad, men he depended on to survive in combat and men who he would not let down regardless of the danger to himself. They were a band of brothers.

Chris offered his sympathies to Emil and Florence Houser after the funeral. Florence had tears that she did not attempt to hide, and Emil had aged visibly since the last time Chris had seen them. Florence hugged Chris. "We're so happy you made it back," she said. Then she broke down, sobbing. Florence the woman always in full command of any situation seemed broken. Emil put an arm around her to comfort her.

Chris's family had been happy to see him but seemed a little puzzled about who he had become. The Chris they had known had become a different person, and they weren't sure who that person was. In a similar way, for Chris, what had been his home no longer seemed like home. It remained the place where his family lived, where he had grown up but he no longer lived there. What had been his home had become a place to visit, not a place to go home to. In a similar way, he had become a stranger in his home town. People knew him and remembered him, but he was no longer one of them.

It took Chris a while to digest these changes and realize that this was a part of every life, the only difference being that it may have been accelerated in his case. Going from a farm boy to a combat veteran in a few months' time will cause rapid changes in how a person feels and acts and how one is seen by other people. In any case, these changes did not bother Chris. He had ideas and plans that did not include his home town and, for that matter, did not include his family. After a few days with his family, he felt anxious to get on with that other life he planned to live.

After Chris returned to San Diego, he collected his mail and found a letter from Carolyn White, a woman in the navy who had recently returned from Sangley Point in the Philippines. She wrote that she had known Pete and wanted to talk to Chris about him. They arranged to meet at a Denny's restaurant near the Balboa Navy Hospital on a Saturday morning.

Chris had a good first impression of Carolyn. She appeared alert, trim, seemingly a natural blond, and was overall an attractive young woman. He was a little puzzled about the Carolyn and Pete connection.

Carolyn explained that she and Pete met as a result of Chris letters talking about going to college after getting out of the marines. As a result, Pete had come to the base library where she worked looking for information about attending college. That is how they met and became friends and then lovers. Now Carolyn was interested in learning as much about Pete as she could.

Chris, who had known Pete as long as he could remember, had a wealth of the kind of information Carolyn was interested in.

Finally, Chris was able to steer the conversation away from Pete long enough to ask Carolyn some questions. How did she like duty in the Philippines, what would she be doing back in the United States?

"Duty in the Philippines had been interesting," Carolyn answered, "There is much to learn from a different culture," Then she asked, "What about you? How did service in Korea affect you?"

"In many ways," Chris replied. "I'm learning more all the time about how I've changed."

"What is it like, to be in combat?" Carolyn asked.

"I don't think I can put it into words so you would understand. In the infantry, war is a dirty, grubby, bloody business. You find you can survive conditions, do things you might have thought impossible. You discover who you are and who the men around you are in your first real fire fight. You learn who you can trust and depend upon and you form bonds stronger than you ever had before and ever will have again." A moment of silence followed Chris's reply. She then changed the subject. "Where are you going to go to college? What are you planning on majoring in?"

"I want to be a journalist," Chris replied. "I'm planning to go to South Dakota State, a school I'm sure I can get into. Like Pete, I never went to high school."

"I know about the high school thing," Carolyn replied. "I wonder if you might find a better school to study journalism."

"That I could get into?"

"I grew up in Los Angeles near USC. My parents still live there, I could check into it."

"Something to think about," Chris replied. "You never answered my last question. What are you going to be doing in San Diego?"

"I'm being discharged from the navy. I'm pregnant with Pete's child."

The answer stunned Chris, and he struggled to respond. Finally, he asked, "You going to be all right, do you need help?"

He asked the question fully intending to offer help if it were needed, as much for Pete's sake as for Carolyn.

Carolyn replied, "I have great parents. They don't want to hide me. They are looking forward to being grandparents."

Chris felt relief, and in a way, was happy for Carolyn and for Pete. Something good had been salvaged from this tragedy.

They parted, promising to stay in touch.

In March, Florence Houser walked to the mailbox a quarter of a mile from her house as she usually did after the noon meal every day except Sunday. She found the expected local weekly newspaper, the *Saturday Evening Post*, an auction sale flyer, the monthly bank statement, and a letter with a California postmark. The letter was addressed to her, Florence Houser, not to Mr. and Mrs. Houser or Emil Houser. She didn't recognize the name, Carolyn White, on the return address.

After Florence got back to the house, she sat down at the kitchen table and looked at the letter addressed to her. Who was Carolyn White? Finally she used a paring knife to cut open the letter. She read:

Dear Florence Houser,

My name is Carolyn White. I knew your son Peter when he was stationed at the Sangley Point Naval Air Station in the Philippines. I also served in the Navy at Sangley and worked in the library where I met your son. We fell in love and spent many wonderful times together. I want you to know I share your loss and also to let you know that I am now pregnant with

Peter's child.

As Florence read these lines, she stopped and caught her breath. Her first thought was what kind of woman is this Carolyn. They weren't married. She didn't say they were married. She just said she had become pregnant. What a sinful person. And her son, what had he been thinking? What does this Carolyn want?

Tears came to Florence's eyes. How could she think this way? About what is proper and not proper. She continued to read.

I am writing this letter to let you know I am happy to be carrying Peter's child and can hardly wait to hold and love this precious being now stirring in my womb.

I am fortunate that I have loving parents to help and who are looking forward to becoming grandparents. Someday I look forward to meeting you and your family and introducing you to your grandchild.

With love,

Carolyn White

Florence Houser sat at the kitchen table for half an hour, just sitting, thinking, and re-reading the letter several times.

Finally, she found some writing paper and a pen and started writing.

Dear Carolyn,

We have grieved and are grieving over the loss of our son Peter. We now know this grief is being shared by you and we embrace your presence. You sound like a wonderful person and mother to be. We are looking forward to someday meeting you and that grandchild that we will check to see whose eyes, nose, and hair it has inherited. If we can be of any help, please let us know.

Welcome to our family, welcome.

Love, Florence

About the Author

Alfred Wellnitz grew up in rural South Dakota, served in the United States Navy and worked in technology as an electrical engineer. After retiring from engineering, he worked as a real estate agent before deciding to become an author at age seventy-three. He has since published three novels and numerous short stories. Alfred's first novel *Finding the Way* was awarded an Honorable Mention in the 13th Writer's Digest International Self-Published Book Awards and *PushBack* was a finalist in the ForeWord Reviews' Book of the Year Awards. Alfred now lives in Bloomington Minnesota.

Also by Alfred Wellnitz

Novels:

Finding the Way
From Prussia to a Prairie Homestead

PushBack:
Deficit Triggers Hyperinflation, Terrorism

Short Stories:

For the Cause
Risk and Rewards

Auf Weiderssehen
Prussia 1871

U.S. Naval Air
Routine Patrol